NIGHT IN THE CITY

Other books by Michael McGarrity

The Long Ago

The Kevin Kerney Novels
Tularosa

Mexican Hat

Serpent Gate

Hermit's Peak

The Judas Judge

Under the Color of Law

The Big Gamble

Everyone Dies

Slow Kill

Nothing but Trouble

Death Song

Dead or Alive

Residue

Head Wounds

The American West Trilogy
Hard Country

Backlands

The Last Ranch

NIGHT IN THE CITY

A NOVEL

Michael McGarrity

W. W. NORTON & COMPANY

Independent Publishers Since 1923

Copyright © 2025 by Michael McGarrity

For information about permission to reproduce selections from this book, write to Permissions, W. W. Norton & Company, Inc., 500 Fifth Avenue, New York, NY 10110

For information about special discounts for bulk purchases, please contact W. W. Norton Special Sales at specialsales@wwnorton.com or 800-233-4830

Manufacturing by Lakeside Book Company
Book design by Lovedog Studio
Production manager: Delaney Adams

ISBN 978-1-324-06627-9

W. W. Norton & Company, Inc., 500 Fifth Avenue, New York, NY 10110
www.wwnorton.com

W. W. Norton & Company Ltd., 15 Carlisle Street, London W1D 3BS

10 9 8 7 6 5 4 3 2 1

NIGHT IN THE CITY

CHAPTER 1

IT WAS NIGHT IN THE CITY. MIDNIGHT IN MANHATTAN HAD come and gone. Sam Monroe sat at the back table of Stamm's Yorkville Bar and Grill nursing a scotch, watching Alfonso rinse beer glasses at the utility sink behind the bar. The only other customer in the place snoozed precariously on a stool close to the front door. For the umpteenth time, Sam glanced at the entrance.

Alfonso shook his head. "She's not going to show."

Three hours before, his ex-lover, Laura Neilson, had called Sam at home asking to meet him at Stamm's. She had something to talk to him about but wouldn't say what.

Sam agreed despite himself. He'd never loved a woman more. No one looked like her, talked like her, lived like her. She'd broken his heart. "I'll wait a little while longer," he said pessimistically.

Alfonso shrugged and returned to his chore.

The last time Sam had seen Laura was two years ago at Stamm's. The moment he'd walked in to see her sitting at *their* table snuggled close to a strange man, all his good memories about the place had evaporated. It had been their private haunt and rendezvous, a favorite place to top off an evening on the town or start a night of lovemaking.

She was there to dump him, and she'd do it quickly and make it hurt. Biting back his anger and disappointment, he'd approached, only to be met by Laura's icy stare and a sneer on her companion's face. She rose, blocked him from the man sitting at her side, and said, "Be a gentleman, Sam, and don't make a scene. It's over between us. I told you repeatedly this would happen, but you wouldn't listen."

"I didn't plan to fall in love with you."

For an instant, her expression softened, and a slight smile crossed her lips. "You really went and screwed it up, didn't you?"

He nodded in agreement as she brushed past him, her new lover in tow. With one mortal cut, she'd surgically slaughtered their love affair. He should have expected it. Even Alfonso, who often boasted that he'd witnessed everything possible to be seen inside a barroom, had been left speechless by her performance.

Alfonso joined him at the table with mugs of black coffee in hand. Dark-skinned, with a high forehead and long nose, he spoke flawless German thanks to his mother, who'd left the Fatherland and married a Cuban expatriate in Paris long before the start of the Second World War. He'd watched Sam's entire romance blossom, flower, and die.

"Drink your coffee and go home," he suggested.

"You're right, I should." Sam sipped his coffee, put some bills on the table, and stood.

Alfonso slid the greenbacks back to him. "It's on the house. A guy who's been treated badly twice by the same woman shouldn't have to pay for his coffee."

"Thanks. I'll be back."

"Did she say why she wanted to see you?"

"No, just that she needed to ask me something. It was like nothing bad had ever happened between us."

"Let it go," Alfonso advised. "She's dangerous. And don't be such a stranger."

Sam forced a smile. "I won't."

Outside, Sam turned and walked to the East River. He wasn't about to go home. He'd just sit in his railroad flat, brood about Laura, and wonder why in the hell she'd called him. What did she want, for chrissake? Why couldn't he get over her?

Late night in the city was his favorite time of day. Yorkville was quiet. The butcher shops, bakeries, corner markets, dry goods stores, and newsstands were closed, and the apartments in the row houses were dark and silent. The islands on the river were vague shapes barely visible in the light of a pencil-thin waning moon. The floating garbage, trash, and sewage on the water's surface were masked from view. An early fall breeze out of the west blew away the foul smells and gritty pollution that could turn the inside of a shirt collar charcoal-gray within an hour.

It had been a picture-perfect, mild late September day. At the end of the block, lights flickered at Gracie Mansion, the residence of the Honorable Robert Wagner, mayor of New York City. In the quiet of the night, he thought back to how he'd first met Laura.

After Korea, he'd moved to the city and enrolled in law school, using the GI Bill to pay for it. But New York was expensive, so to cover his living expenses he worked as a store detective at Best & Company, a Fifth Avenue department store, pulling evening and weekend shifts, which allowed him to carry a full class load during the day. Between his courses, the job, and constant studying, he'd had time for little else.

One Friday, working an evening shift, he watched an attractive, slender, dark-haired woman pocket a small box containing a bottle of expensive French perfume. He stopped her at the exit, escorted her to the small office used to interview suspects, and asked her to empty the pockets of her coat.

"I simply forgot to pay," she said apologetically, handing him the item. "Surely I can pay for it now and that will be the end of it."

Sam explained that he'd watched her conceal the perfume and head straight for the exit. "You'll need a better excuse than that," he counseled. "What's your name?"

"What's yours?" she countered. No more than five-three, she was beyond pretty, with large blue eyes, full lips, and an almost symmetrical face. He'd seen her on occasion before, making purchases, leaving with shopping bags filled with merchandise. Not your ordinary shoplifter by any means.

"Don't make this hard on yourself."

She nodded at the desk telephone. "Call Miriam Brewer, the jewelry department manager. Ask her if she knows Laura Neilson."

Sam picked up the handset. "Is that your name?"

"Ask her."

Sam could either complete the necessary time-consuming paperwork and report the misdemeanor shoplifting offense to the police or take the easier way out. He called Mrs. Brewer. The mention of the woman's name brought her to the interview room in a hurry.

"What is this all about?" she demanded, after warmly greeting the woman.

Sam picked up the perfume package. "Shoplifting."

"Nonsense," Mrs. Brewer snapped.

"I forgot to pay," Laura Neilson explained apologetically.

"Of course you did," Mrs. Brewer agreed.

"Can we just forget this?" Laura Neilson asked nicely. "Keep the perfume. I don't want it, after this misunderstanding. I would just like to leave."

"Certainly," Mrs. Brewer answered preemptively.

Sam wasn't about to argue. The item had been voluntarily returned. End of story.

"Thank you," Laura Neilson said. With her hand on the doorknob, she turned and gave Sam a once-over. "You didn't tell me your name."

"Sam Monroe," he replied.

She smiled. "Sam Monroe. I like it. Thank you for acting like a gentleman. I appreciate it."

After the door closed behind Neilson, Sam asked Mrs. Brewer what that had been all about.

"I have no idea," Miriam Brewer replied. "Laura Neilson is a member of an old and very wealthy family that settled here when this was New Amsterdam. She's a highly valued patron of the store. All I can imagine is that you may have used your position inappropriately to try and pick up what you thought was just another attractive young woman shopper."

"That's not who I am."

Brewer studied him carefully. "I certainly hope not, but don't let me hear of this kind of thing happening again."

The following evening, Neilson picked out a finely woven Italian scarf at a ladies' accessories counter, wrapped it loosely around her neck, admired it in the mirror, turned on her heel, and headed down the escalator to the Fifth Avenue exit.

Sam stopped her at the door.

"Hello, Sam Monroe," she said sweetly, glancing at his left hand. "Are you married?"

"What?"

She handed him the scarf. "Are you married?"

"No."

"Girlfriend?"

"Not presently."

She tucked a business card into the breast pocket of his suit jacket. "Call me soon. I'd like you to buy me a drink."

"Is this the way you usually meet men?"

"Call me."

"Are you serious?"

"Yes, I am. And don't wait too long to call. I can be very impatient."

"Are you always this dramatic?"

Laura Neilson nodded. "Isn't it fun?"

It turned out to be much more than fun, until it wasn't.

He shook off the memory, called Laura's number from a First Avenue booth, and let it ring repeatedly before disconnecting. It wasn't unusual for her not to answer, but her out-of-the-blue request to see him was not in character. Something was wrong. Or was he simply imagining it as an excuse to see her again?

It was hard to admit that he wasn't over her, especially now that she'd suddenly popped back into his life.

No solitary cabs cruised the neighborhood, and city buses ran infrequently late at night. If he set a fast pace, he'd arrive at her building within twenty minutes.

Sam checked his wristwatch. He'd find out what she wanted, see if there was anything to it, grab a cab back home, and have enough time to shower and shave before heading to the office. He could manage going without sleep, but as a junior lawyer in the district attorney's office, he couldn't risk being late. Although easy to work for, Marilyn Feinstein, his supervisor in the Criminal Prosecution Division, was a stickler when it came to punctuality at the office and in the courtroom.

*

LAURA'S PENTHOUSE WAS IN a twelve-story prewar building on the Upper East Side just off Fifth Avenue. They'd dated for almost three months before she invited him to come up. Starting out, it hadn't really been dating at all; just frequent, very satisfying sex at his apartment. She was wanton, uninhibited, imaginative, and playful, but had some carefully explained rules that she followed. She took only one lover at a time, but never an unhappily married man. She'd be faithful throughout the relationship, but when the relationship was over, it was over, and it was her call to make—no questions asked.

He never tried to control her, found her strong sexual appetites arousing, and her almost brutal honesty about herself unlike that of any other woman he'd known. The lack of pretense between them was liberating. As time passed, Sam conveniently forgot that the love affair had an end date. He was simply too head-over-heels to imagine it, and Laura seemed equally happy with the way they were.

The front entrance to the building was locked when Sam arrived. He had to lean on the doorbell several times before Carl DeAngelo, the night doorman, showed up to let him in.

"Nice to see you," Carl said with a grin. "It's been a long time." Overweight, with a bad cigarette habit, Carl wheezed when he talked. "Miss Neilson said you might show up tonight."

"She's expecting me?" Had she tricked him into waiting at Stamm's, only to stand him up in the hope he'd come to her apartment demanding an explanation? That made no sense. Her impulses were always spontaneous, never contrived.

"I guess so." Carl motioned at the two elevators at the back of the lobby. "Go on up."

"Is anyone with her?"

"Not as far as I know. Leastways, not since I came on."

The door to the penthouse was open. A table lamp next to the Swedish modern couch illuminated a twelve-inch maquette of a nude woman Laura had impulsively purchased at a gallery opening after dinner at an East Side restaurant to celebrate Sam's graduation from law school. It cost more than Sam had ever made in a year.

He called out, got no answer, and made a quick search of the apartment. She wasn't to be found, but her bedroom door to the outside balcony was open. She was lying on her back, naked, dead, with her eyes wide open. A silver chain with an old coin and an Army dog tag attached to it was wrapped around her neck.

He knelt at her side. She'd been strangled quickly, almost garroted, and her body was still warm. Sam clicked on the switch in his head, the one he'd used in Korea to deal with the gruesome deaths of men he'd led into battle. He ignored the dark red bruising around her neck, concentrating instead on her peaceful face. He closed her eyes and wished that she were simply sleeping, but he knew better. All emotion drained out of him.

The silver chain and circular coin with a square hole in the center were his, as was the dog tag with his name, rank, serial number, and religious preference stamped on it. The Korean writing on the obverse side of the coin proclaimed it to be a coin of the eastern kingdom. On the reverse, the engraved inscription read *Hill 180. Never Forget. C Co. 1st Platoon.*

It had been given to Sam by members of his platoon upon the regiment's return from Korea. After a fierce attack by Chinese infantry, he'd gotten every man off that hill, dead or alive.

How they'd come to possess a rare, thousand-year-old Korean coin, they didn't say, and Sam never asked, but he suspected it might have been discovered in the partially destroyed house where they'd taken shelter on that bitterly cold winter night.

He thought he'd misplaced it. Time and again he'd searched for it in his apartment. He was certain he hadn't left it at the penthouse. Why had she stolen it? As much as he cherished the coin, he would have given it to her for the asking. He'd loved her that much.

Once, toward the end of their relationship, on a summer's night with the bedsheets thrown back in the stifling heat of his apartment, she had questioned him about the coin. How did he come to receive it? Had he done something heroic? He'd explained it was simply a gift from the men he'd served with in Korea. Sometime later that night while he'd slept, she'd dressed and left. Had she taken it then? He couldn't recall when he'd first missed it.

Did she have mementos from all her past lovers? If so, he had no idea where to begin looking. He knew she kept a record of them, had even told him that he'd been Number 20. He'd once seen a diary with a locking clasp left out on top of the lamp table in her bedroom. Perhaps the names were in there.

As soon as the cops arrived, he'd become their prime suspect. His presence at the scene and the dog tag with the coin pendant were the kind of physical evidence that homicide detectives dream about.

He had to find the killer before the cops found him. Dawn was breaking. He didn't have time to make a thorough search of the apartment. He pocketed her diary from the bedroom nightstand, an address book from the top of the library desk, and a bound appointment calendar she kept next to a living room telephone.

In the lobby, he once again asked Carl if anyone else had gone up to her apartment.

"Like I said, nobody but you," he answered.

House rules were that the doormen and building superintendent couldn't smoke outside the entrance or in the lobby. "Did you take a smoke break in the basement stairwell and leave the front door unlocked before I got here?"

Carl gave him a fish-eye. "Yeah, once, about an hour before you arrived."

"Do you know who Laura's been seeing recently?"

"Yeah, a new guy. She's had him up three or four times that I know."

"When was the last time you saw him?"

"Last night. He left about six in the morning."

"Not night?" Sam asked.

"Nope."

"Does he have a name?"

"Kurt. Don't know his last name."

"Describe him."

"In his thirties, medium build, about your height. Dresses rich, if you know what I mean. Why all the questions?"

"Laura's dead. Call the cops and tell them she's been murdered."

Carl's eyes widened in shock. "Jesus, are you kidding?"

"No, I'm not."

"I'm gonna have to say that you were up there."

"Do that, and don't leave out the part about your smoke break, understand?"

Carl nodded and reached for the lobby telephone.

On the street, a taxi idled curbside at the end of the block waiting for a fare. Sam climbed in and told the cabbie there was an extra five spot for him if he could get him to his Yorkville address in a hurry. He needed to call in sick at the office, do a quick change of clothes, retrieve the stash of emergency cash he kept hidden in the apartment, and get started. It wouldn't take long for the cops to start looking for him.

*

AT HIS APARTMENT, Sam put the three hundred dollars of emergency cash he kept hidden in a law school textbook in his wallet. The equivalent of six months' rent, it was his buffer against going broke and should more than cover any expenses. If the money ran out, he could always pawn his wristwatch, a nice Swiss timepiece. He'd inherited it from his father, who'd died of a sudden heart attack during Sam's senior year in college.

He broke the clasp to Laura's diary and thumbed through the pages. She'd listed each of her lovers separately, starting with Number 1. Included were their names, addresses, and phone numbers, along with dates that indicated when the relationship started and when it ended. There were no personal comments or private thoughts about her lovers.

It read like a roster of sexual conquests, nothing more. Or a list of clients. But in Sam's experience, he'd never been asked to pay for his time with Laura. In fact, it was just the opposite; Laura was always treating. But what was the true cost to Sam? To be played for a sucker? Had it all been a ruse, some sick game that shrinks called role-playing?

Her last entry was for Kurt Bell, entered as Number 21, started two months prior. That pulled Sam up short. He'd been twentieth on Laura's list, dumped two years before Bell. Compared with the intervals between her other lovers, it was a huge gap. Why? What did it mean?

Kurt Bell's entry included two phone numbers and addresses. One was for an advertising agency on Madison Avenue. He'd start with Bell and work backward if necessary. But first he needed to explain to his boss, Marilyn Feinstein, what he was about to do. But not in person, for she would surely order him to voluntarily turn himself in for questioning. Or, worse, she'd call the cops while he sat there in her office.

He typed a quick note, sealed it in an envelope, caught a taxi to his office, paid the cabbie a couple of bucks to drop it off at the front desk, and took a bus to Times Square, where he found lodging away from the red-light district that catered to traveling salesmen.

At a small writing table, he cracked open the address book, hoping to find names he might remember of the people Laura had talked to him about. Nobody jumped out at him. What had she been up to between the time she'd dumped him and the arrival of Kurt Bell on the scene? There had to be someone out there who could fill in the blanks.

He picked up the phone to call Bell's office and changed his mind. Although he had a good reason to be hasty, rushing caused mistakes. He ran over the murder scene in his mind. It wouldn't take a seasoned homicide detective to deduce that Laura had been killed for a personal reason by someone she knew, even trusted. There was no evidence of forced entry or a struggle and there were no signs of a burglary gone bad.

That narrowed the focus to people like Sam, Kurt Bell, and who else? He forced himself to stop jumping ahead and concentrated on the list of Laura's lovers. Who could be eliminated as a suspect? How long would it take to cross a name off the list?

Sleepy and hungry, Sam closed the diary and went out for something to eat at a neighborhood delicatessen. A corner newsstand displayed a special edition of a tabloid newspaper trumpeting the shocking murder of a prominent heiress. The inside story explained that the victim, Laura Neilson, had been found in her penthouse apartment nude and strangled to death. Police were seeking to question Sam Monroe, an Army veteran and assistant district attorney. Authorities were also attempting to contact the victim's parents, who were traveling in Europe.

He ordered a take-out sandwich at the deli, returned to the room, locked the door, and considered his next move. Technically, taking the diary, the address book, and the appointment calendar from Laura's apartment was a felony. He couldn't risk the cops finding him in possession of incriminating evidence. He needed a place to stash it. But first he decided to look closely through everything again, page by page.

In the back of the address book, he found a business card lodged between two pages. It read: *DJ Ryan. Discreet Inquiries. Licensed. Bonded. Insured.* The address for the business was on Broadway, close to Herald Square. Sam called the number. There was no answer.

Why did Laura need a private investigator? He tucked the card into his wallet behind his driver's license, shook off his drowsiness, and made one more pass through everything. What was he missing?

Suddenly it hit him. If he was Number 20 and Kurt Bell was 21, who was the man with Laura at Stamm's Bar the night she'd dumped him? Was he the missing piece?

He took a cab to Penn Station, stowed the "stolen" items in a rental locker, and hoofed it to the address for DJ Ryan. It was on the second floor of a four-story building anchored by a variety store and a haberdashery on the ground floor. The office was locked and no one in the storefront shops knew Ryan or when he'd return.

Afternoon traffic had turned heavy. Cabbies were leaning on their horns and busting through traffic lights. Curbsides had filled up with the trash, garbage, and discarded household items left for Department of Sanitation trucks to pick up on their weekly runs. Pedestrians crowded the sidewalks in sufficient numbers for Sam to feel inconspicuous enough to walk back to his hotel room. He was halfway there when a voice from behind called his name. He looked back just as Officer Johnnie Turner clubbed him with his nightstick.

*

SAM REGAINED CONSCIOUSNESS IN a precinct interview room with a thunderous headache. His face was swollen and bloody and he was handcuffed to a table. Johnnie Turner stood over him with a malicious, gleeful smile on his face. The duty sergeant, Patrick Hanrahan, a pint-sized troglodyte of a man, was at his side.

Turner had been a plainclothes vice cop in line for a detective's shield when Sam caught one of his cases to prosecute. Turner had busted a working girl for marijuana possession under the Boggs Act, which carried a mandatory two-year prison sentence. It appeared straightforward enough until Sam found out that Johnnie had planted the marijuana on the defendant with drugs stolen from an evidence room. The case got dismissed along with six other identical busts made by Turner. Instead of getting kicked to the gutter, he'd been slapped on the wrist and returned to patrol duty. An uncle who worked at police headquarters, which was colloquially known as the Great White Castle, had reached out and saved Turner's ass.

"We've got you on resisting arrest and assaulting a police officer," Sergeant Hanrahan said.

Sam shook his head. "I want to speak to Deputy District Attorney Marilyn Feinstein right now."

"That will happen after our homicide detectives are done with you," Hanrahan replied cheerily.

"Don't fuck this up, Sergeant," Sam counseled. "I'm an officer of the court. Call Feinstein and tell her I'm here. Otherwise, it's your shitstorm."

Hanrahan hesitated. If he'd done his homework, he might know that Sam was a decorated Korean War veteran, and considered by some to be an up-and-comer in the DA's office. It might make him wonder if Sam had a rabbi in the department or was related to someone high up on the DA's staff.

Hanrahan glanced at Turner. "Stay with him. I'll make some calls."

As soon as the door closed, Turner's smile widened. He had a head the shape of an orange, a drinker's ruddy complexion, and a widow's peak. He leaned close, pulled Sam's chair out from under the desk, and hammered him twice in the ribs with his beefy fist.

"I've dreamt about doing that for a long time, asshole," he said with satisfaction.

Sam gasped in pain. "You don't dream very big, do you, Turner?"

Turner hit him again. Sam felt a rib crack.

Sergeant Hanrahan came back with a detective in tow and ordered Turner to do his paperwork. For the next hour, Sam answered every question by refusing to incriminate himself. Until he knew what the cops had on him, other than his presence at the murder scene and evidence that could be linked to him, Sam was determined to say nothing.

Marilyn Feinstein arrived, ordered Sam uncuffed, and shooed the detective away. She glared at him, eased into a chair, and said, "Well?"

"You got my note?" Sam countered.

No more than five-two and a hundred pounds soaking wet, Marilyn Feinstein, a forty-five-year-old widow, could terrorize most people with a piercing look. "So, you didn't kill her?"

"Correct."

"And you want me to believe you?" she added.

"Correct."

"I do believe you, but the district attorney isn't convinced. However, he wants to avoid nailing your hide to the wall until you're formally charged with murder. Then he'll crucify you."

"He said that?"

"No, I'm putting it nicely. It was the Distinguished Service Cross you received in Korea that swayed him. Until then, you're suspended without pay, ordered to cooperate fully with the police, and are to cease interfering in the investigation."

Sam raised an eyebrow. "Until then?"

Marylin sighed. "The police want to search your apartment," she added.

"By all means. My landlord, Abe Silverstein, owns the appliance repair shop on the first floor of the building. He'll let the cops in."

She handed him the phone. "Call him."

Sam made the call, hung up, and smiled at his boss. "I resign effective immediately. I suppose you want it in writing."

"Don't be foolish."

He wrote it out on a yellow tablet and left it on the desk. "I'm not going to become low-hanging fruit plucked by some eager-beaver detective hoping to move up through the ranks. I just quit. Have the cops either book or release me."

Marilyn's expression hardened. "I have been ordered to fire you if you decided to quit."

"Fair enough."

"I thought you'd like to know that Neilson's maid has been questioned. She swears several items are missing from the penthouse."

"Really?"

"Aren't you interested in what was taken?"

"I thought you were going to tell me."

"You're hopeless. I doubt you have more than twenty-four hours before they pick you up again."

"Are there any other charges pending against me?"

"Not yet, and I'll keep it that way for now." Marilyn knocked on the door and an officer stepped inside. "Good luck, Sam Monroe."

"I know you can't stand sentimentality, but you really are the best."

"Don't get schmaltzy on me." She smiled and left.

Sergeant Hanrahan released Sam and handed him his wallet, which had been seized at the booking desk. Outside, Sam checked the contents. DJ Ryan's business card was still in place behind his driver's license. But except for ten dollars, all his cash was gone.

He started out for Times Square, where the pawnshops never close. Hopefully, he could get a few bucks for his father's watch. When he was a block from the precinct house, a radio patrol car stopped in the middle of the street and Officer Johnnie Turner got out of the passenger side.

"Don't try to coldcock me again, you son of a bitch," Sam growled.

Johnnie smiled happily. "Once the arrest warrant is signed and we pick you up, I'll get another crack at you, asshole."

Sam bit his lip to keep from telling Turner what a turd he was.

"Nothing to say, big war hero?"

"Don't tempt me." Sam stood his ground until Johnnie drove away in the radio car. It had been a hell of a day. Would it only get worse? His side throbbed painfully as he hobbled down the street.

CHAPTER 2

AT A PAWNSHOP, SAM GOT LESS THAN HE'D HOPED FOR THE watch. He put the receipt in his wallet along with the cash. If he wasn't locked up awaiting trial for murder one, he'd retrieve it before the loan fell due.

He slept fitfully, his aching ribs complaining every time he turned on his side. Although he didn't think the cops knew where he was holed up, he half expected them to kick in his hotel room door at any moment.

In the morning, on the off chance Sergeant Hanrahan had discovered Ryan's business card in his wallet, he staked out the address. His uneasiness had continued unchecked, fueled by the early edition of the daily newspapers. One front-page headline read: "Fired ADA Possible Suspect in Laura Neilson Murder."

The DA hadn't wasted any time covering his ass. Sam owed Marilyn a huge debt. By forestalling any additional charges against him, she'd bought him time he otherwise would not have had.

He kept an eye out for cruising squad cars, patrolmen on foot passing by the building, and plainclothes officers on surveillance. Everything looked okay. As early morning lengthened, employees of the storefront businesses arrived, followed shortly after by a nicely dressed younger woman who entered the doorway to the upper floors. Still uneasy, he continued to wait. Soon, an older woman hurried into the building. Presently, a portly man in a business suit carrying a briefcase followed. Several more men wandered in.

Sam joined them. The businesses on the upper floors were listed on a glass-enclosed sign by the entrance. DJ Ryan's offices were on the second floor. Wincing in pain, he climbed the stairs. Lights were on behind the frosted window of the door bearing Ryan's name. He opened the door to a reception room, where the older, slightly buxom woman he'd seen arriving earlier sat at a small desk typing.

She looked up and smiled. "May I help you?"

"I'd like to speak to Mr. Ryan."

"Mr. Ryan," she repeated, looking vaguely amused. "Do you have an appointment?"

"No, but it's important."

She reached for the telephone. "Your name?"

"Sam Monroe."

She spoke into the phone, hung up, and nodded at the door to the inner office. "You may go in."

"Thank you," Sam said as he stepped inside.

Mr. Ryan turned out to be the well-dressed younger woman he'd seen entering the building. In her thirties, she had green eyes, a small birthmark on the corner of her right cheek, and red hair that was cut to accentuate the curve of her neck. She bordered on striking.

There were framed certificates on the wall behind the desk where she sat, including a baccalaureate degree from a prestigious women's college, a U.S. Naval Justice School graduation certificate, and an honorable discharge from the United States Navy. A smaller, framed document proclaimed Ryan to be licensed as a private investigator by the state of New York.

"Mr. Monroe," she said as she rose and extended her hand. "Debora Jean Ryan. Call me DJ. Have a seat."

Sam did as told. At five-eight, Debora Jean was a tall girl, and she wasn't wearing a wedding ring.

She settled back in her chair. "From what I've read in the newspapers, you're a murder suspect. Personally, I have my doubts about what the tabloids have published regarding the case."

"Any particular reasons why?"

"Healthy skepticism and a dislike for sensationalism." Ryan leaned forward in her chair. "How did you find your way to me?"

"Is that important?"

"Very. My professional reputation is vital to my continued success in this business. I do not offer my services to the general public. Potential clients must be personally recommended by a trusted source and then carefully screened by me."

"A select clientele. I'm impressed, but I didn't come here to hire you."

"You haven't answered my question."

Sam placed DJ's business card on the desk. "Laura Neilson."

Ryan didn't bother to look at it. "Did you kill her?"

"No."

"If you have no interest in retaining my services, why are you here?"

"She had your card in her possession. I'm assuming she may have hired you. If so, what you know might help me find her killer."

"I can't help you, Mr. Monroe."

Sam pushed back. "Did you know Laura personally? Was she a client of yours?"

DJ Ryan rose. "Goodbye, Mr. Monroe."

Sam turned the business card over and scribbled the name, address, and phone number of his hotel. "I'm in Room 317. I'm there for two more nights. If you change your mind, leave a message for me at the front desk and I'll get back to you."

DJ held Sam's gaze and said nothing.

Sam stood. "I don't see how you can possibly tarnish your professional reputation by helping me find Laura's killer."

"I have no reason to doubt your innocence, Mr. Monroe. I simply can't be of service. Good day."

Sam pushed the card closer to DJ. "Several years ago, Laura and I were lovers, until she decided to move on to someone new. The night of her murder, she called me out of the blue, asked to meet me, but she never showed. I found her strangled in her apartment, and it wasn't pretty. I want the person who killed her."

"Do you know why she called you?"

"She didn't say."

"Was she upset when you spoke to her?"

"At the time, I didn't think so. In fact, she sounded cheerful. Why the sudden interest?"

DJ smiled. "No reason. I'm sorry if you've wasted your time."

"No, you've been very helpful. Good day, Miss Ryan."

She smiled warmly. "Good luck, Mr. Monroe. Be careful out there."

Sam looked around cautiously before venturing onto the sidewalk. Had DJ Ryan just given him a friendly warning, or made a veiled threat? She obviously knew more than she'd let on. If she took him up on his invitation to call him, he might find out.

No cops—including Johnnie Turner—were in sight. The noise was deafening. Broadway was one big traffic jam with vehicles blocking the intersection. Clouds that looked the color of soot hung low over the city.

Sam decided to pay a visit to Kurt Bell at his Madison Avenue office. But first he had to pick up a few things at his apartment.

*

YORKVILLE APPLIANCE REPAIR SHOP, the store on the ground floor below Sam's apartment was operated by Abe Silverstein, who also owned the building. Abe repaired lamps, toasters, radios, clocks—whatever customers carried in the door. If it was mechanical or electric—no matter—Abe would fix it. A bachelor, he lived alone in a fourth-floor apartment. Quiet by nature, unassuming by disposition, Abe was a true mensch—a rarity among Manhattan landlords. Sam found him in the back of the store bent over a worktable studying the innards of a large tabletop shortwave radio.

Abe looked up and shook his head in dismay. "I'm gonna have to special-order replacement vacuum tubes for this radio, and they aren't easy to find. By the way, the cops ransacked your apartment. It's a mess."

"Did they break anything?"

"Your radio and a table lamp, but I can fix them. The lamp will need a new shade."

"What about my footlocker in the basement?"

Abe smiled. "They didn't ask, so I didn't tell."

In the dim light of the solitary basement ceiling lamp, Sam opened the footlocker and reclaimed the badge case that contained his private investigator's license ID card and the permit for his Smith & Wesson .38 Special. Both were still valid.

He grabbed the pistol and shoulder holster and went upstairs to his apartment. The cops had dumped his clothes in a pile on the floor. He pawed through, plucked out some fresh but wrinkled clothing, and changed on the spot. A sports coat that he'd had specially altered hid the strapped-on shoulder holster nicely. He reshaped a fedora that hadn't been badly crushed and stuck it on his head. All in all, he'd pass easily for an ordinary Joe on the street.

At Abe's shop he stopped by to thank him. "I might be a little late on the rent," he added.

"Not to worry. Don't do anything foolish," Abe admonished.

"That's not my style. Thanks again."

Abe waved off the thanks. On the seat of his worktable chair was a special edition of the *Herald Tribune* that in bold type named Sam as the possible murder suspect. A true mensch, Abe hadn't said a word about it.

*

THE ADVERTISING AGENCY WHERE Kurt Bell worked embraced the top three floors of an unimposing prewar office building. At the executive suite reception desk, Sam identified himself, flashed his credentials, and asked to speak to Bell. "It's about Laura Neilson," he added.

The young woman barely glanced at his ID as she dialed the phone. No more than a minute passed before a man in his late thirties, trim-looking in an expensive business suit, came through the double oak doors.

"I'm Kurt Bell," he said, stepping out of the receptionist's earshot. "Come with me."

Bell's office consisted of a desk, a swivel chair, two visitors' chairs, a bookcase, and a couch. A tall window looked out over the avenue. A mock-up of a poster on an easel targeted a breakfast cereal for kids. Apparently it was yummy. Pure genius, Sam thought.

He figured Bell still had a long climb up the corporate ladder before he could claim a corner office and a personal private secretary to guard his inner sanctum. But what did he know?

Bell eased onto his swivel chair. "I knew the police would want to speak to me about Laura."

"I'm not the police." Sam pulled an armless chair close to the desk and joined him. "I'm the guy they think murdered her."

Bell's eyes widened.

"Before you reach for the phone, I found her body, but I didn't do it."

"Why should I believe you?"

"Because I came here hoping you did it, which would get me off the hook. Did you kill her?"

"No. How did you find me?" Bell asked suspiciously.

"The doorman at her apartment," Sam answered. "You were dating her, correct?"

Bell nodded.

"Where did you meet?"

"At a party of some friends of mine."

"When was that?"

"Three months ago, almost to the day."

"How did she pick you up?"

The question seemed to puzzle Bell. "She didn't. We were introduced at the party. We wound up chatting and enjoying each other's company. Before the evening ended, I asked if I could call her, and she gave me her number."

Sam didn't buy it. Laura could be very sneaky. "Was the person who introduced you to Laura your friend or hers?"

"Mine, an old college classmate, Julia Anderson. She brought Laura to the party."

Sam asked Kurt to tell him more about Anderson. An archaeologist, she'd recently divorced and moved to the city to take a faculty position at Barnard, one of New York's nationally renowned universities. She'd met Laura after renting an apartment in her Upper East Side building.

Until the night of the party, Bell hadn't known about Julia's divorce and relocation from Chicago. She'd parted amicably from her ex-husband, an older man and prominent economist at the University of Chicago. They'd had no children.

"You're absolutely sure Laura and Julia didn't know each other prior to that time?" Sam inquired.

"I can't say for sure. Julia and I have only casually remained in touch over the years. If she'd known Laura previously, I imagine I would have heard about it. Laura makes a huge impact on everyone she meets."

Enough of an impact to get her killed, Sam thought. "Did she ever ask if you were married?"

Confused, Bell shook his head. "No."

"How long did it take for her to seduce you?"

"Are we talking about the same woman? We dated for a good two months before anything happened. Occasionally, after a night out, we'd have drinks in her penthouse, but she always sent me packing, until one night she didn't." He smiled at the memory.

"Where were you on the night she was murdered?"

He nodded at his office couch. "Here, all night. I was working on a presentation for a major client. About four, I caught a couple of hours' sleep."

"Were you alone in the building?"

Kurt chuckled. "There were six of us pulling an all-nighter. We had to be ready to pitch a new concept to the client at ten a.m."

"They can vouch for you?"

"You bet."

"You didn't go out for coffee during the night?"

Bell frowned. "I've been polite, but now you're treating me like a suspect. That's you, not me. I want you to leave."

Sam stood. "Of course. Thanks for your time. You'll have to go through this again with the police."

"When will that be?"

"Right after you call them. Or I can do it for you, if you like."

"Exactly who were you to Laura?" Kurt Bell asked.

"I thought I knew, but now I'm not sure. Call me Number Twenty."

Bell was reaching for the phone as Sam left.

Outside, he missed not having a watch. It didn't matter, he was running out of time anyway. But if Bell was calling the cops, it might derail their one-track minds and give them another suspect to consider.

He wasn't about to wait to see if they showed up. He'd initially planned to recover Laura's diary from the Penn Station locker and start working on the list of her old lovers. He set that idea aside in favor of learning more about Julia Anderson and headed uptown to Laura's apartment building.

*

SAM SLIPPED INTO THE building through the service entrance and found Dennis Finch, the building superintendent, in the small cubbyhole he called his office. It contained a desk, a secretarial chair, a file cabinet, a telephone, and a wall-mounted pegboard with rows of tagged keys.

A retired city firefighter in his forties, Finch was good-looking in a rough-hewn way and had a compact build, a thick chest, and muscular arms. He still looked capable of carrying a two-hundred-pound man out of a burning building or running up ten flights of stairs dragging a high-pressure fire hose.

Sam had spent a lot of time with Laura in her penthouse but had only met Finch occasionally in passing. He'd seemed rock-solid and sensible. Hopefully, he wouldn't put Sam in a chokehold and call the police.

Dennis looked him up and down suspiciously. "Mr. Monroe, what are you doing here? Should I call the cops?"

Sam tried not to twitch. "Do you know any cops that you like?" he countered. "Like maybe one who isn't corrupt or tied to the mob?"

Dennis smiled. "That's a good one, I grant you. Still, you shouldn't be here. The penthouse is sealed off and a patrolman is at the door."

"I'm not here for that. What can you tell me about Julia Anderson?"

"I don't know that much about her. She's been here six months. Ex-husband is a professor in Chicago at some university. He had to cosign the lease. No children that I know about. She teaches college. Archaeology."

"I've heard she was friendly with Laura."

"That could be. I saw them leave the building together frequently. They looked, you know, comfortable with each other."

"How would you describe her?"

"Nice-looking without being pretty, if you know what I mean. Brown hair, wears eyeglasses, kind of stocky. A big-boned girl, my mother would have said."

Sam asked if he had Anderson's work address. Dennis checked his card file. She had a faculty office in a building on the Morningside Heights campus.

Sam changed the subject back to Laura and learned she'd gone away for more than a year and had been back for about six months. Dennis didn't know where she had gone, but in her absence Adella Diaz, the housekeeper, had stayed on at the penthouse as caretaker. Perhaps she would know.

He asked for Adella's home address.

Finch's expression turned serious. "Maybe I shouldn't do this."

"I understand your concern. Let me ask you this: If you were me, would you trust the cops to do the right thing?"

Dennis shook his head but didn't say anything. Sam pushed his argument. Every week there was another story in the papers about cops on the take, shaking down small business owners, or in bed with the mob. As a criminal prosecutor in the DA's office, he'd seen first-hand how ineptitude and cronyism in the police department meant innocent people were sent to prison while criminals went free.

"I can't leave it to them to get this right," he concluded, hoping his rant had worked. "It's my butt on the line."

"That may be so, but I don't want any trouble."

"And I don't want that for you either. After I leave, call the police, and tell them I showed up, tried to ask you some questions, but you sent me away."

"Are you serious?"

"I am. Do you have Adella's home address?"

Dennis wrote it down and handed it to Sam. "So, if you didn't kill Miss Neilson, who did?"

"I'll have to get back to you on that."

"I sure hope you know what you're doing."

"So do I."

He got Finch's telephone number in case he needed to talk to him

again, then left. On a crowded subway car traveling uptown, Sam
hung on to a pole, trying not to bump into the elderly woman holding
a heavy shopping bag standing next to him. Not one man sitting rose
to offer her his seat.

He wondered if it had been smart to tell Dennis to call the police.
Maybe not, but it felt better to have the cops one step behind him
rather than one step ahead.

He'd forgotten to ask Finch if Dr. Erica Birkenfield still had her
psychiatric practice in the front office of her ground-floor apartment.
Laura had been in therapy with Birkenfield for a time, but she'd never
told him why.

If he ran out of leads, he'd circle back and see Birkenfield, if she was
still there. But what would he do if his efforts went nowhere? If there
were no creditable suspects other than himself?

He wasn't Nero Wolfe, Sam Spade, or Mike Hammer. Maybe it
wasn't smart to play private eye. This was his life, not a dime novel.
He shook off the self-doubt. He knew the law, how to gather evidence,
and how to question hostile witnesses. Just get on with it, he decided.

*

COLUMBIA AND SISTER SCHOOL Barnard sprawled across the high
plateau of Morningside Heights. Classic in its original design, with
welcoming spaces, it seemed easy to navigate but wasn't. It took Sam
several failed attempts to find his way to the right building. In an infor-
mational brochure for prospective students there was a brief résumé
of Anderson's academic credentials. Her three degrees were from mid-
western universities, and her research concentration was the Anasazi
and Pueblo cultures of the Southwest.

The door to her office was locked. He asked for her at the depart-
mental office and was told Professor Anderson was attending a one-
day symposium off-campus and was not due back until tomorrow for
her regularly scheduled office hours, from ten until noon.

Breaking into the professor's office to snoop around wasn't an
option. He'd come back in the morning.

He grabbed a cab to Adella Diaz's address in Spanish Harlem. She lived on a block of run-down row houses that had been turned into tenements and were, according to a city of New York sign, scheduled for demolition. It was a tough neighborhood of working-class, immigrant families. Parts of it were in serious decline. Empty lots filled with rubble served as playgrounds. On some blocks, boarded-up stores and vandalized vacant buildings dominated. Cannibalized cars sat curbside, waiting to be hauled away once the city got around to it.

Sam asked the cabbie to wait and knocked on Adella's door. In her forties, Adella hadn't lost her figure, and she matched it with a proud bearing and polite manner. Divorced, with two children in high school, there was nothing common about her. Laura had always treated Adella as a friend, not an employee.

"Sam," she said quietly.

"Adella, I am so sorry. You know why I'm here."

She nodded gravely. "But I cannot talk to you."

"Why not?"

"I signed contract not to. Laura required it when I was first hired."

"But you've talked to the police."

"Yes, but that was different. I had to, and the lawyer said it was allowed."

"Did you tell them anything helpful?"

"Please stop."

"I'm a lawyer , Adella. What you tell me will be privileged and confidential. Promise."

"I cannot."

"Where was she all the time she was gone?"

Adella shook her head. "No more questions."

"Who was she sleeping with? Give me a name. Help me find her killer."

"I don't know who did it. Please go." She started to close the door, and paused. "The police asked me about you, Sam. I said you were always good to her. That you would never hurt her. Go now."

The nervous cabbie leaned on his horn. Sam didn't want to hoof it to the nearest bus stop or subway station. Even when packing heat, Spanish Harlem wasn't a safe place for a gringo to be alone on the streets. He thanked Adella and hurried down to the taxi.

*

THE CABBIE DROVE CROSSTOWN and let Sam off at a West Side subway station, where he rode the train to Penn Station. He took everything out of the locker and went to a nearby Automat. The workday had ended, and office workers were pouring out of buildings and heading home. It was one of those between-meal periods when a few pensioners and some vagrants sat alone in the big, uninviting dining room, eating whatever they could afford. There wasn't a smile on anyone's face.

He bought franks and beans, some black coffee, and thumbed through Laura's address book and diary. What was he missing? He didn't have a clue. Frustrated, he returned everything to the locker and walked to his hotel. Parked at the front entrance, an all-black two-door Ford sedan, like the radio patrol cars the department used, screamed cops. He walked on. How had they found him so quickly? Had a judge already signed an arrest warrant? Was Johnnie Turner in the room upstairs waiting to beat him to a pulp? Did DJ Ryan turn him in?

He ditched Times Square. In the Bowery, he got a room in a hotel that was a cut or two above skid row accommodations. Across the street, there was a cheap men's clothing store. It was time for a costume change. In the morning, he'd go shopping.

Sam paid for the room and pocketed the key. Too restless to stay inside, he walked the neighborhood. The night couldn't erase its seamy side. The men looked either down-and-out or just plain mean. The few working girls on the street looked desperate and worn out. Stores that specialized in selling used commercial appliances, tools, and restaurant equipment were sprinkled between the flophouses, saloons, and inexpensive diners. An occasional large warehouse loomed over the street, further darkening the night.

Not a beat cop was in sight. The Bowery was a place where you could go to die alone and forgotten, never to be missed or heard from again.

Sam bought a miniature bottle of scotch at a liquor store, sat on the rickety chair in his room, and drank it neat. He decided to sleep in his clothes in case the cops came calling in the middle of the night.

CHAPTER 3

THE BLUE JEANS, WORK SHIRT, AND LIGHTWEIGHT BOMBER-style jacket that concealed Sam's shoulder holster and pistol gave him a whole new look. He topped it off with a flat cap. To a casual observer, he'd easily pass for just another working stiff. He left his old duds in the room for the next lodger and at a pay phone dialed Marilyn Feinstein's direct office number. She picked up after the first ring.

"Should I go into hiding?" he asked.

"Aren't you already?"

"Not completely."

"No warrant has been requested, so you're okay for now. Of course, the police still want to talk to you again. Is this why you called me?"

"Not completely," he repeated. "Have you reviewed my caseload yet?"

"It's next on my list."

"Look for the Susan Cogan case file. You assigned it to me last week."

"It's a straightforward solicitation case I expected you to plead out," she replied without hesitation. "What about it?"

"The arresting officer was Johnnie Turner. He doesn't like me. Wants to beat me to a pulp for ruining his career. Promised me that he'd do it. I need Cogan's address. If I'm not mistaken, Turner busted her on a trumped-up charge when she refused to pay protection money. I doubt she's the only one."

"I shouldn't do this."

"He's a dirty cop, and you know it. Without any leverage to use against him, I may have to shoot him the next time he comes after me."

After a silence, Marilyn gave him the address. "Don't shoot him," she cautioned.

"No promises," Sam replied. "And thanks, at the risk of sounding schmaltzy—"

The line went dead.

*

ON HIS WAY UPTOWN to see Professor Anderson at the college, Sam stopped at Ryan's office to ask if she'd ratted him out to the police.

"You're the only one who knew where I was staying," he noted.

DJ came to the front of her desk and examined his outfit closely before responding. "I like your new look. It suits you."

"Don't be cute," Sam replied. "Did you call the cops on me?"

She gestured at a chair for him to sit. "No, but late yesterday evening I did leave a message at your hotel to call me."

"To talk about what?"

She picked up a file from the desk, sat across from him, and adjusted her skirt. "I've been retained to assist in your investigation."

"By whom?"

"I can't tell you that."

"Who would even know that we had met? Or that you are in any way involved?"

"I can't tell you that either. But I will tell you that my client knows Laura Neilson hired me to find out what you'd been doing for the last two years, and who you'd been doing it with." She handed him the file. "My report."

Sam thumbed through the narrative and glanced at the photos. It included all the basic up-to-date information about his job and his personal life, right down to the women he'd sporadically dated, his current financial situation, and his military service record. He clearly wasn't on his way to getting rich or about to walk down the aisle with the girl of his dreams.

The photos, all recent, showed him on the sidewalk outside his office, entering his apartment building, having lunch and dinner with some colleagues, and on a date at a jazz club in the Village with a woman he quickly realized he couldn't stand. That one had been taken three weeks ago.

Sam held up the photos. "You took these?"

DJ nodded.

Sam was impressed. She'd shadowed him without ever once raising his suspicion. "Why did Laura hire you to do this?"

"She didn't say. In fact, she never saw my written report. I called her two days before she was murdered and told her it was ready. But all she wanted to know was where you were living, working, and if you were married or seriously seeing someone."

Sam almost laughed. Instead, he shook his head. "She had a rule to never get involved with an unhappily married man."

DJ raised an eyebrow. "Now, that's interesting. What can you tell me about her? I never met her in person. We only spoke over the phone."

Sam stood and handed DJ the report. "You've been very helpful. Thanks."

"Don't walk away from this, Sam," DJ chided. "I have resources you can use."

"Who's your client?"

DJ shook her head.

"Sorry, but no thanks. Right now I'm not in a trusting frame of mind," he added.

"How can I contact you?"

"I've booked a suite at the Waldorf. Leave a message."

She wrote down an address and gave it to him. "You can sleep on my couch. Apartment 3C. Ring the buzzer twice."

"I'll think about it."

On his way out, he grabbed several of DJ's business cards. On the subway, he thought about her tempting offer. Sure, he'd stopped by to find out if she'd squealed on him. But he could have just as easily done it by phone, not in person. He had to admit he was taken with her. She was smart, good-looking, with an independent spirit that he admired. One of a kind, just like Laura.

But why was she suddenly so forthcoming? And who in the hell was the anonymous benefactor that had hired her to help him?

*

ON CAMPUS, SAM LOITERED in the hallway until Julia Anderson arrived ten minutes late for her office hours. Dressed in slacks, sensible shoes, and a lightweight turtleneck sweater, she was in her mid-thirties, hefty but not fat, and pleasant-looking. There was a softness about her face. It was pliable and needy-looking in a seductive sort of way.

He gave Anderson one of DJ's business cards and flashed his PI identification, hoping she wouldn't ask his name. It worked. "I know you're busy, and I won't take much of your time. We're working on behalf of Miss Neilson's family to assist the police in any way we can. I understand you became friendly with her soon after you moved into your apartment."

She removed her glasses and wiped away a tear. "This is so very terrible and unsettling. To have someone you know be murdered. Yes, we were friendly, but I can't say we'd reached the point of being the best of friends. I like to think that would have happened. Now I'll never know."

"When did you last see her?"

"We briefly exchanged greetings in the lobby three or four days ago. I was on my way to work. I don't know where Laura was going."

"How did she seem to you?"

"Happy, in a good mood. Her usual self."

"Did she ever talk to you about her personal life? About men she was seeing or sleeping with?"

"We really weren't that close."

"What about your old college friend, Kurt Bell?" Sam probed.

Anderson nodded. "Oh, yes, I introduced Kurt to Laura at a friend's party. I know they dated for a time, but how do you know about Kurt?"

Sam sidestepped the question. "Tell me about him."

According to Anderson, Kurt Bell was a levelheaded, dependable good guy. The thought that he might have killed Laura never entered her mind. In fact, she couldn't think why anyone would want to kill her.

"She was so vibrant and alive," she added. "You couldn't help but enjoy her company."

Anderson said she'd given a statement to police detectives that she'd been in her apartment and asleep on the night of the murder. She didn't know of any conflicts or disagreements Laura might have had with other residents. "She wasn't small-minded about others," she concluded.

The top shelf of a low bookcase held several framed photographs taken at archaeological fieldwork sites. One showed a team of about ten people dressed in safari hats, shorts, and hiking boots clustered around Anderson in front of a surplus World War II jeep. The second photo was of Anderson leaning against the front fender of a sports car with sunset-tinted low desert hills in the background.

"One of your graduate student summer digs?" Sam inquired.

"Yes, in New Mexico, at a little-known site south of Santa Fe. It has exciting research possibilities." She glanced at the closed office door. "I have students waiting to see me."

Sam smiled apologetically. "Of course. I may want to talk with you again."

Julia Anderson looked at the business card. "DJ Ryan, right?"

"That's right." A knock came at the door. "Call me if you think of anything that might be helpful. Thank you for your time."

At a pay phone on campus, he dialed Dennis Finch's number.

"I told the cops everything we talked about," he said after Sam identified himself. "And I'll do the same again."

"That's perfectly okay, Dennis. Does Dr. Birkenfield still live in the building?"

"No, she closed her practice, retired, and moved out about a year ago."

"Where to?"

"Someplace in Westchester, where her niece lives."

"Gotta name for me?"

"It's the same last name. Don't recall her first name or the town."

"Thanks, Dennis."

"Yeah," Finch said unenthusiastically. "Don't call me again, okay?"

"I'll try not to."

At the university library, Sam paged through Westchester County phone books, and found Anna Birkenfield listed as living in a small town along the commuter rail line corridor. There were no other phone subscribers with the same surname in the local directories.

The most recent American Medical Association directory showed Erica Birkenfield still in practice at her New York City address. She was a visiting lecturer at a university medical school and specialized in the treatment of children and adolescents.

That surprised Sam. Laura had gone to see Birkenfield several times during their affair. Why would an adult seek therapy with a child psychoanalyst? From an outside pay phone, Sam called Anna Birkenfield's number and got no answer. She lived about an hour away by train, so it was worth a shot. He headed for Grand Central Station.

ANNA BIRKENFIELD LIVED ON a lovely country lane just outside of a charming small town that looked like a Norman Rockwell painting. At the top of the hill, the house overlooked an open field where a dozen or so cows loitered. Poets would call it bucolic. Sam always thought the word ill-suited to describe something so pleasing to the eye.

No matter, he was happy to be away from the city. The change in scenery temporarily lifted his spirits and he didn't mind waiting for a car that arrived soon with two occupants and pulled into the attached garage. He gave it a full five minutes before ringing the doorbell.

The woman who opened the front door agreed that she was Anna Birkenfield. She'd just returned from taking her aunt to a doctor's appointment. Sam said he was DJ Ryan, gave her one of the purloined business cards, and explained that he'd been retained by an attorney to find someone that Dr. Birkenfield may have treated in her private practice.

Anna told him that her aunt was in her bedroom, resting. "Sometimes she has trouble remembering things, and she tires easily," she advised before she stepped away to fetch her. She returned with her aunt, got her settled in an easy chair, and left for chores that waited in the kitchen.

Rail-thin, tall, and elderly, Dr. Birkenfield's narrow face and slightly weak chin reminded him of Eleanor Roosevelt. She appeared alert and chipper. He asked if she remembered Laura Neilson.

She smiled and nodded. "Oh, yes, I've known her since she was a teenager."

"You were her psychiatrist then?"

"Yes, and a family friend."

"But you saw her in your practice after she grew up."

"Sometimes she'd ask for my advice."

"About what?"

"How to escape."

"From?"

"Everything," Birkenfield replied. "Is she missing? Anna said you're searching for someone."

"Miss Neilson has gone out of town and is needed back in the city for a pressing legal matter," Sam said, straight-faced. "Do you know where she might be?"

"No, I'm afraid we've lost touch since I've moved here."

"How did you come to live in the same apartment building with Laura?"

"Laura's trust owns the building. When the first-floor apartment became available, she asked her broker to offer it to me."

"You must have been very helpful to her during her teenage years, for her to do that."

"It's often not easy being a young person burdened with excessive parental expectations."

"Did she ever talk to you about Sam Monroe?"

Erica nodded in recognition of the name. "Oh, yes, Laura liked him very much. Are you looking for him also?"

"We think he might be with her, but there's nothing to worry about. What did she say to you about her relationship with Sam Monroe?"

Dr. Birkenfield smiled. "I can't discuss confidential matters with you. Ask Laura to call me once you find her."

Sam promised to do so. He thanked Birkenfield and left. The afternoon sky was clear, the air was fresh and clean, and the countryside was quiet. He thought about spending the night away from the city, but instead headed to the train station.

What had happened to Laura as a kid? Did she have a mental break-down? He'd never thought of her as crazy, but according to Birken-field, she'd needed to escape from everything. That could only mean something major had happened to her, but what?

And the last bit about Laura owning the apartment building was another surprise. He knew she was an heiress, but they had never talked about money. Was her murder somehow connected to her wealth?

On the platform, the train to the city rattled to a stop. It was all interesting, fresh information, but was it getting him anywhere?

FOR MANY YEARS, the Tenderloin district below Times Square had been the low-rent neighborhood for vice. Parts of it were slowly returning to earlier residential roots, but on the avenues, working girls still promoted their talents curbside within a block or two of the hotels that catered to their trade.

Those very few ladies who were the cream of the crop entertained in their apartments and had a regular clientele of businessmen and professionals in need of discreet relief from the pressures of a busy life. Susan Cogan was one of them. Her apartment was in a well-kept building on a quiet side street.

She was about five-six with honey-blond hair, a full bosom, and a tiny waist. Sam had to look closely to see the age wrinkles at the corners of her blue eyes. He asked if she had a moment to spare and explained that until very recently he'd been assigned to prosecute her for soliciting.

"You're that Sam Monroe guy," she replied. Her outstretched arm barred his entry into the apartment.

"I am, and I need your help."

Susan Cogan sized him up. "What kind of help?"

"Getting Officer Johnnie Turner permanently kicked off the force."

She lowered her arm. "Come in."

The front room was comfortably furnished, especially the uphol-

stered couch, which looked inviting for a man in need of a nap. Sam
sat on it and asked Cogan to tell him what had happened with Turner
to get her busted.

She explained it all. For some time, he'd been shaking down the
girls on the street for protection money. Then he decided to move up
to the independents with the higher-class clients. When Susan balked,
Turner arrested her. That brought the others into line. When she continued to refuse to pay up, he filed the charges.

She made a sour face. "He's a pig and he's hurting my business.
What were you going to do with my case?"

"I was expected to plead you out, but I know Turner is dirty. If I
could point your attorney in the right direction, and if he was smart
enough to get my drift, that would give him enough to impeach
Turner on the stand."

"Could you do that?"

"Only in a roundabout way."

"How are you going to catch him?"

"I'm not; you are." Sam sketched out his plan. Susan would entice
Turner to her apartment with the promise to pay up. Sam would be
there within earshot to witness the transaction. After that, he'd take
care of the rest.

"You give him the money, let him walk away, and I get an arrest
warrant," he concluded.

"And if he wants a little bonus on the side?"

"I'll have a little heart-to-heart with him right then and there," Sam
replied, relishing the thought of busting Johnnie Turner in the chops.

"Why are you doing this?"

"I cost Turner his chance to make detective. To pay me back, he
coldcocked me and cracked a few of my ribs. He's promised to do it
again, only worse. I'm not going to give him that chance."

Susan nodded. "Okay, I'm game. When do you want to do this?"

"As soon as possible."

Through the window of Susan's apartment, dusk had settled in. He
asked if she was busy all night. It earned him a hard frown.

"I don't do quickies," she said.

"I wasn't asking for one. But if your next hour is open, I'd love to borrow your couch for a nap. I've run out of steam."

Susan Cogan nodded in the direction of a narrow hallway. "There's a second bedroom in the back you can use. Sleep as long as you like, but just don't make a racket when you wake up."

"You're an angel."

She almost smiled. "I've never been called that before."

CHAPTER 4

SAM WOKE UP TO A STIFF BACK, A BOTHERSOME ACHY RIB, and the smell of coffee. Unsure of where he was, he sat upright, fumbled for the table lamp light switch, and glanced around the room. Aside from the small single bed and the lamp on the side table, the room overflowed with costumes on racks. There were nurses' uniforms, military outfits, glitzy showgirl ensembles, schoolgirl uniforms, expensive women's tailored suits, even a wedding dress and a priest's black suit with a clerical collar. Susan Cogan was obviously well prepared for whatever sexual fantasy a client might have. It was an impressive collection.

In the bathroom, on the top of the toilet tank, she'd put out a razor, a shaving brush, shaving cream, and a new cellophane-wrapped toothbrush. This was a woman who anticipated her clients' needs. A fresh towel and washcloth hung on the rack. Taped on the mirror above the sink was a one-word note in capital letters: "SHOWER!"

Sam didn't need a second invitation. He stood under the spray until he had washed off every trace of the Bowery hotel. On top of the toilet seat was a new set of underwear in his size. He dressed and found Susan in the small dining area adjacent to the kitchen with a cup of coffee in hand that she gave him. He could smell bacon. His stomach rumbled in anticipation.

She looked as fresh as a daisy. "How do you like your eggs?"

"Over easy. What time is it?"

"Seven. You slept like a log."

"You searched my things," he challenged.

She nodded and handed his ID case to him. "Along with your gun and holster. What are you; a lawyer or private investigator?"

Sam said he was both and briefly explained. "Where's my revolver?"

"Do you need it right now?"

Despite himself, he laughed. "No, give it back to me when I leave."

"Deal." She nodded and served breakfast. It was the best he'd had in days.

They talked about setting up Johnnie Turner. Sam said he needed at least a day. To make it stick, a cop had to be present when the trap was sprung, which meant finding someone trustworthy. He had a DA investigator in mind he would approach.

Susan asked him about Laura, and he was deliberately vague talking about her. "Something may have happened to her when she was young," he speculated. "But I don't know what."

"Didn't Freud say everything was about sex?" she replied.

Remembering Laura, Sam said, "Why didn't I think of that?"

At the apartment door, Susan handed him his pistol and holster. He strapped it on under his jacket. "I'll call you this evening. You've been very kind."

"And you've been a true gentleman."

"I haven't been called that in a while." He kissed her on the cheek. Her smile was electric.

"Don't get hurt," she said.

"Yes, dear."

She laughed, stuck her tongue out, and closed the door.

Walking to Penn Station, he marveled about how much Susan Cogan reminded him of Laura. Was he a sucker for a certain type of woman? The uninhibited and unconventional?

With a coffee, a pocketful of change, and Laura's diary from the luggage locker, Sam settled into a phone booth, closed the privacy door, and started calling Laura's old lovers. To start, all he wanted to do was find out how to reach them. He learned one had died in an auto accident, three had moved away, and several others were now married with families and living in the suburbs. Two hung up on him, and the phone number for the last one on the list was no longer in service.

Except for the dead lover, Sam couldn't completely discount any of the others. He decided to put the out-of-state ones and the married men aside temporarily and concentrate on the rest. One was a ranking staff member at the consulate general of Mexico's New York office. Another was a supervisor for a high-rise construction company. A third, who had been a minor league utility infielder, was a scout for the Brooklyn Dodgers. Left were the playboy son of a Wall Street stockbroker, and a woodworker in the Village who made one-of-a-kind custom furniture. The task was daunting. Maybe he should have taken up DJ's offer of help.

Sam gumshoed around the city all day and only managed two face-to-face meetings with men on his list. He caught up to the construction supervisor at a huge hole in the ground on Park Avenue, where site work had started on what was to become a thirty-eight-floor office building. The man knew about Laura's murder. He wasn't shaken up or surprised about it.

"She lived on the edge," he commented. "And she was way smarter than me. Wanted to discuss things I didn't know anything about. I finally bored her to death, but why anyone would kill her is insane."

Laura had cut him off with a handwritten note delivered to him at a job site by a courier. In retrospect, he was glad she'd dumped him. Sam didn't bother to ask for an alibi.

The playboy, Richard Carlin, had a Central Park West penthouse apartment twice the size of Laura's. He said he had just returned from a week of fun and frolic in Havana and hadn't heard about her murder.

"She was about as hot as they come, and the sex was unbelievable," he reminisced. "She wore me out. But she was too emotionally unstable. She'd go from the heights to the pits just like that." Carlin snapped his fingers for emphasis.

Laura had sent a private investigator to give him the bad news. An older guy, beefy, with a fat nose and bad breath. He didn't remember his name. "She was unforgettable," Carlin added, as he walked Sam to the elevator.

"So I hear," Sam replied. Carlin's week in Havana should have resulted in a spectacular tan, but obviously he hadn't spent much time poolside. What had he been doing there? Sam shrugged it off. He had no time for distractions.

*

QUITTING TIME HAD FLOODED the sidewalks, packed the buses, and filled the taxicabs with people in a rush to get home. Sam joined the multitudes on a crosstown bus and hoofed it to Duffy's Pub & Restaurant, where he was sure to find DA Investigator Mike Dalton parked in his favorite booth nursing an Irish whiskey.

Mike had been a city detective before joining the DA's office. Smart and resourceful, he had an Irishman's broad face, a hearty laugh, and possessed a tenacious temperament when bird-dogging a suspect. He left the soul-saving to Francis, his Catholic priest brother.

A World War II veteran, Mike had seen some of the heaviest fighting in Europe. Their shared experience of combat had made for an immediate connection. Sam hoped he would jump at a chance to get a dirty cop off the streets.

Duffy's was smoke-filled and loud with the after-work, pre-dinner crowd. Sam circled around the jampacked bar to Mike's booth and stopped short. Sitting with him was Dalton's old cop buddy, Lieutenant Jack Osborne, a Central Robbery Unit supervisor who liked the limelight and had a reputation as a ladies' man. A bachelor, Osborne dressed way above the average lieutenant's pay grade, but he wasn't flashy about it.

Mike looked up, spotted Sam, and shook his head to warn him off. But it was too late. Jack Osborne piled out of the booth as Sam wheeled to leave, but the crush of the crowd kept him from escaping. Osborne yanked him back.

"You're under arrest, Monroe, for the murder of Laura Neilson," Osborne announced without enthusiasm. He didn't appear pleased with himself. "Sorry, Sam," he added in a whisper.

No one in the bar seemed to notice or care. Mike downed his drink and stood. "Your timing sucks, pal," he said glumly. "The DA caved to pressure and got a warrant. He's got no choice but to book you, right?"

Sam nodded. "It's okay. Keep me out of Rikers if you can."

"I'll head back to the office and see what I can do," Mike replied.

Sam walked outside, sandwiched between the two cops. From a

police call box on the corner, Osborne asked for a radio car to rendez-vous with him.

"Can you book me downtown, instead of at a precinct?" Sam asked. At any precinct in the city, the word of his arrest would spread like wildfire throughout the ranks. He didn't want Johnnie Turner turning up to beat on his bruised body some more.

Jack cuffed him. "Sure, I can do that."

The radio car arrived. Osborne stuffed Sam in the backseat, climbed in the passenger seat, and ordered the driver to head to the Great White Castle. Through the rear window, Sam watched Mike hail a taxi to go back to the office.

He took a deep breath and let it out slowly. Okay, this was bad, but he'd been through worse. He'd survive.

AFTER FOUR HOURS OF interrogation and no sign of Mike, Sam got loaded into a paddy wagon with a bunch of low-level miscreants and was taken to Rikers Island. It was a place he thoroughly disliked. His story about waiting for Laura at Stamm's and then finding her dead body when she didn't show had failed to impress the detectives. He was just another smart-ass, cagey lawyer trying to pull the wool over their eyes. Sure, they'd talk to Alfonso, but they were more interested in Sam's motive for killing Laura. They favored jealousy. He couldn't dissuade them. At least they didn't try any rough stuff.

As always, Rikers smelled of urine, tobacco, sweat, mold, and despair. The metallic clank of the steel gate that closed behind him rang like a death knell. It was the city's twentieth-century version of a medieval dungeon. Some of the guards resembled troglodytes like Sergeant Hanrahan. Maybe they were related. There were no friendly faces to greet him—no Mike, no Marilyn, nobody.

Two guards locked him in a dark, uncomfortable holding cell by himself, which was not a good omen. He was hungry, tired, and not enjoying life to the fullest, when late in the night the ceiling light came on and Johnnie Turner, grinning from ear to ear, stepped into the cell.

Turner went to work on him. Sam passed out twice. This second

time he woke up in the infirmary with more bruised ribs, a busted
nose that got roughly put back into place, and a hell of a headache. The
night duty nurse, a woman with a thick Eastern European accent and a
tough bedside manner, informed Sam that officially he'd been jumped
and attacked by other inmates. Sam saw no reason to disagree. He fell
asleep when the pain medicine kicked in.

In the morning, patched up and given a breakfast that approached
gruel, Sam was transported to court and charged. The pain meds had
worn off, his face was still swollen, one eye remained partially closed,
and it was hard to breathe through his broken nose, which had been
strapped with a bandage to keep it stationary.

He pled not guilty. Bail was set at five thousand dollars cash or bond.
He couldn't think of anyone he knew to stand his bail and get him out
of jail. The possibility of another late-night beating at the hands of
Johnnie Turner depressed him. As he mulled the bleak reality of his
immediate future, a bondsman appeared, posted his bail, and said that
his mystery benefactor was waiting for him outside. It happened to be
Debora Jean Ryan.

"Why did you come here and save me?" he asked.

"I'll explain later." She gave him the once-over. "What happened
to you?"

"An unfortunate incident. I'll explain later. Thanks for springing me."

"You're welcome. Once the swelling goes down, I think you'll
look better."

"That's cheerful news. Better than what?"

"Before." She guided him to a waiting taxi. "Do you have a doctor?"

Sam shook his head. "Haven't needed one until now."

"We'll stop at my gynecologist's office."

Sam slumped against the seat. "Right now, anyone with painkillers
will do."

*

AFTER A QUICK EXAMINATION, the gynecologist predicted that the
swelling would go down and Sam would heal nicely if he followed her
prescription of bedrest and aspirin as needed.

DJ lived in a brownstone off Lexington Avenue. Her third-floor, two-bedroom apartment had a view of the tree-lined street and was nicely appointed without being fussy. After consigning him to the couch, DJ left to make a quick run for some groceries at the corner market. Sam fell asleep.

He woke up with a start, suddenly realizing his revolver and shoulder holster had been confiscated at Rikers and never returned. In the darkened room, he sat up, fumbled for his wallet, and switched on a table lamp. His cash hadn't been touched, but the pawn ticket for his father's wristwatch was missing. Also gone were his PI license and gun permit. Both could be replaced. The Smith & Wesson, maybe not. He didn't really like guns all that much anyway.

Out the front window, night had fallen. The kitchen wall clock read eleven o'clock. Sam had slept for twelve hours. On the counter, DJ had left a note to wake her when he got up. Instead, Sam quietly left the apartment and hailed a cab on Lexington to take him home to Yorkville.

He wasn't in a trusting mood. Until he knew more about DJ and her allegedly anonymous client, he wasn't going to fully embrace her generosity. Yes, she'd posted his bail. And yes, she'd somehow learned of his arraignment. And, finally, her couch was his to use until further notice. An explanation of the reason for her motives was necessary, but not yet.

He had the cabbie drop him off two blocks from his apartment. Jolts of pain in his rib cage slowed him down as he slumped his way home. The avenue was awash in an undertone of noise that wouldn't completely vanish into silence until the deepest hours before dawn. Even then, some human catastrophe could cut right through it. Night could be very unforgiving, and in the city it often was.

He spotted no surveillance outside his building. In his apartment, he searched through the mess until he found his checkbook. The account balance was enough to last a week or more, and he'd have one final paycheck to deposit. Whatever happened after that would be a new beginning, whether he liked it or not.

He stripped down to the waist, washed up over the kitchen sink, shaved, and put on a clean shirt. His ribs were taped—as was his nose—the swelling around his mouth had gone down, and his eye was less angry-looking.

He got to work putting his apartment back together, and the routine of restoring order out of the cop-created mess calmed his nerves. If he couldn't make things right with his life, he could at least make them seem so.

He finished, achy and tired, with a new morning lighting up the front room windows. A can of tomato soup and a cheese sandwich eased his hunger. The beating he'd taken at Rikers put Johnnie Turner at number one on his list of things to do. He called Mike Dalton.

Mike answered and immediately asked what had happened to him at Rikers. He'd been told by an observer at Sam's arraignment that he'd appeared to have been worked over hard.

"Johnnie Turner paid me a visit," Sam summarized. "What happened with you? I thought you were going to try to keep me out of jail."

"I tried, but the DA is acting chickenshit about your case," Mike explained. "No one in the office is to have any contact with you, period. Let's forget about that for a moment. What do you need?"

"Preferably, I want Johnnie Turner drawn and quartered. Barring that, I need someone outside the department with a badge, muscle, and enough hutzpah to help me bring him down."

"Eddie Snyder's your man. We were patrolmen assigned to the same precinct before the war. He is with the U.S. Marshals Service now. He's known on the streets as Tough Eddie. Where are you?"

"At home."

"I'll have him call. Marilyn sends her love."

Sam scoffed. "You're kidding, right?"

"She didn't put it that way, but she's pulling for you. We all are."

"Thanks."

"Stand by." Mike disconnected.

Eddie Snyder called within the hour. Sam explained his plan to wrap up Turner using Susan Cogan as bait. They agreed to meet at a bar in Cogan's neighborhood that evening to go over specifics. If it all sounded copacetic, Snyder would meet with Cogan and inspect the layout of her apartment before agreeing to the caper.

Sam smiled as he hung up. For the first time in days, he felt upbeat. He called Susan Cogan, apologized for waking her up, and asked if he could stop in that evening with a cop friend.

"If this is about Turner, you bet," she said. "He was here late last night for a little extra on the side. The man's a pig."

"Don't I know it," Sam replied agreeably.

*

SAM DRAINED HIS CHECKING account at the bank, got Laura's address book from the Penn Station locker, and spent several hours at the Forty-Second Street public library paging through reverse telephone directories. Many of Laura's address book telephone entries were by first name or initials only. Others were just numbers hurriedly or haphazardly scribbled on otherwise blank pages. He wound up with twenty-seven names and addresses of individuals and businesses.

In a public phone booth, he broke open a roll of nickels and started making calls to the businesses. First up was the Oliver Chanute Travel Agency, located on Madison Avenue. He introduced himself as an accountant for the Neilson family making inquiries into the late Laura Neilson's personal debts and financial obligations. He was put through immediately to Quentin Chanute, the current owner. Chanute, who spoke with a clipped, private-school accent, said the company had been doing business with the Neilson family since the day his father had opened the agency in the twenties and that they were among their most valued clients. The murder of Laura had come as quite a shock to all of them at Oliver Chanute. He went on to say that the Neilson account was current, with no outstanding balances.

Sam politely questioned if indeed that was the case, noting the discovery of unpaid lodging and travel bills among her personal papers. "When was the last time Miss Neilson used your services?" he probed.

Sam waited on hold while Chanute took a few minutes to retrieve Laura's file and review it.

"She had my staff research a rather extensive road trip for her," he said. "She planned to start by exploring the Great Smoky Mountains and then travel west. Our notes say she was particularly interested in touring the Rocky Mountains and seeing the more remote coastline regions of the Pacific Northwest."

"Do you have a record of the bookings you made for lodgings or other services?"

Chanute said that there were none for lodging. Laura had not wanted to be bound by a set schedule. What the agency had provided to her were detailed maps, exhaustive lists of highly rated accommodations, and brochures of regional and local points of interest. The company had made only one booking on her behalf. Several weeks in advance of visiting the Grand Canyon, Laura had called long-distance to ask them to reserve a pilot and private plane for her use in Flagstaff, Arizona. She planned to take a day-long aerial tour of the canyon. The booking was for two passengers. The invoice from the air service company itemized the flight. It had occurred as scheduled.

Sam hung up feeling a little let down. Months after she'd kissed him off, Laura had gone soaring, free as a bird, above the Grand Canyon, but with whom? The latest version of a lover? The mystery man at Stamm's? An inconsequential intermezzo dalliance?

No matter, Sam thought. There was no reason to think he'd meant anything more to her than a number on her list of lovers. He dialed the next business. The operator reported it was no longer in service and there was no new listing for the firm of Everett Scott Baldwin, private investigator.

He had hours before the local state licensing office closed for the day. While there, he'd find out what he could about Everett Scott Baldwin, replace his PI identification card, and get a copy of his police-authorized gun permit.

*

LICENSING RECORDS HAD EVERETT SCOTT BALDWIN'S last known address listed as a Staten Island residence. Before boarding the ferry, Sam used his police firearm permit and bought a snub-nosed .38 Special from a licensed dealer. The weight of it in his windbreaker pocket made him feel a bit more confident about going up against Johnnie

Turner. Plus, he'd yet to find out how tough U.S. Deputy Marshal
Eddie Snyder really was.

The neighborhood was one of the growing number of subdivisions in the outskirts of the city that was favored by cops, firemen,
and blue-collar workers who kept the city off life support. Lined up in
neat rows, the houses were small on tiny, nicely landscaped lots. The
man who answered Sam's knock at the door was Baldwin's nephew,
Timothy. About forty, he had a high forehead and carried a few extra
pounds around his belly. He told Sam that Uncle Everett was on his
boat somewhere between Martha's Vineyard and Puerto Rico.

"He's a lifelong bachelor," Timothy added. "Served in the Coast
Guard during the war. He closed his office last year, gave up his Manhattan apartment, retired, bought a boat, and started sailing. He calls
me when he's on dry land for a spell, which isn't often."

Sam explained he was investigating one of Everett's former clients,
and wondered if Tim knew where his uncle might have stored his old
records. The information could be useful.

Tim took him to the basement, where floor-to-ceiling shelves
held dozens of business-sized file boxes, each with the contents carefully recorded on the outside. Laura Neilson's file was in a box of its
own. Sam asked if he could review it and make notes. With permission granted, Sam sat at a small table and read each investigative
report Baldwin had prepared on Laura's prospective lovers, including
his own.

He was impressed with the thoroughness and amount of background detail in Baldwin's reports. He made quick notes on each but
saw nothing in the files that suggested any one of them were likely
murderers. The big surprise was Laura's request that Baldwin find her
a good-looking male she needed for one night to impersonate her lover.

He'd located Jeremy Lancaster, an aspiring actor and occasional
model, who worked as a bartender at a Greenwich Village tourist
hangout. The photographs of Lancaster included in the report showed
that he'd been the same man with Laura at Stamm's on the night she'd
ripped Sam's heart out. What crazy game had Laura played on him?
Was she simply cuckoo, and he'd completely missed it? Did Jeremy

Lancaster kill Laura? Yes or no, Sam had to find him. He thanked the nephew and made tracks for the ferry.

Daylight faded into an angry sky as the ferry pushed through choppy harbor water toward the tip of Manhattan. If he didn't hurry, he'd be late, and Eddie Snyder might not want to wait around to meet him at the tavern in Susan Cogan's neighborhood.

CHAPTER 5

A FAST-MOVING RAINSTORM CAUGHT SAM A BLOCK AWAY FROM the tavern. Inside, he looked around for Eddie Snyder and didn't see anyone who matched Mike Dalton's description of his old NYPD buddy. According to Mike, Tough Eddie stood five-eight, weighed a hundred and fifty pounds, and had brown hair and brown eyes.

With some paper towels, he dried off as best he could in a stale-smelling bathroom, found an empty corner table, ordered a beer, and kept his eye on the entrance. Snyder slipped inside out of the rain and flashed a friendly smile as he approached.

"Sam Monroe," he said, extending a hand. "Mike says you're one of the good guys."

"High praise, indeed." Sam didn't see anything tough about Eddie. He had a handsome, open face and the slender build of a dancer. Supposedly he was a jujitsu master who had studied in Japan after the war.

"So, did you kill your ex-girlfriend? Mike says no."

"Can't you take Mike's word for it?"

"Not when it comes to murder. Nobody is immune."

Sam laughed. "Well, since you put it that way, when I think about Johnnie Turner, the thought of killing him is appealing."

"Tell me about him," Eddie urged.

Sam summarized his history with Turner, including that he was on the take, extorting money from working girls like Susan Cogan.

"Now that he's lost his shot at making detective, he's moved on from planting evidence on streetwalkers to extorting a higher class of prostitutes," Sam concluded.

"Looks like he planted some serious evidence on your face," Eddie noted.

"Believe it or not, I'm getting better."

"Bad pennies like Turner don't usually work alone," Eddie said.

"I've considered that," Sam replied. "Maybe we should cast a wider net."

"As long as it doesn't take us too long to do it," Eddie said.

"Then let's make it a one-shot deal," Sam suggested.

Eddie nodded. "Agreed."

From the bar pay phone, Sam called Cogan and asked if he could bring Eddie Snyder over to meet her right away. She gave him the green light. At the apartment, Eddie eased Susan's worries. He had no desire to see her hurt or hassled in any way. He probed her for more information about Turner. She told him when Turner came to visit her, he always arrived in a radio police car that idled curbside at the corner. She'd never seen the driver.

"Beat officers don't drive," Sam said. "It has to be Turner's supervisor, probably a Sergeant Patrick Hanrahan."

Eddie turned his attention back to Susan. "What if we could nail Turner and his sergeant?"

Cogan asked how, and Eddie outlined a plan. Susan would offer to collect the protection payments from the other girls on Turner's behalf. But she'd only do it if he gave her a cut of the action. Plus, she knew some other working girls who might be interested in having police protection. Reducing Turner's risk and increasing his profits would be an irresistible carrot.

"You'll do it, but only if he introduces you to the officer waiting in the police car," Eddie emphasized. "You insist upon knowing everyone you're dealing with."

"What if he doesn't buy it?" Susan asked.

"If he says no, we'll take him down anyway," Sam answered. "When do you see him next?"

"Tomorrow night, late. I had to change my appointments to accommodate him."

Eddie asked where her meeting with Turner would take place. Susan rolled her eyes in the direction of her bedroom. To record the conversation, they'd put a reel-to-reel tape recorder in the spare bedroom where Sam and Eddie would be stationed and run a concealed cable with a microphone into her bedroom. Susan's offer to fix Turner a drink would be the cue for them to make the arrest. If Hanrahan was in the living room waiting for sloppy seconds, they'd pounce on them both simultaneously.

"You'd better make this work," Susan cautioned.

"We will," Sam promised.

On the rain-wet sidewalk, Eddie shook his head in wonder. "That's one classy gal. Makes you question what makes some people do what they do."

"People get wounded in lots of odd ways," Sam suggested, thinking of Laura. "How they survive can be just as inexplicable."

"Mike said you were a smart guy. Which reminds me, you're bowing out of this tomorrow night. Dalton will help me take Turner down."

Sam pulled up short. "What?"

"It's not open for discussion. Any mouthpiece Turner hires would blow this case out of court if you're involved in the bust. You should know that. Mike and I will take it from here. You get to be on stakeout. Understood?"

"Cogan won't like being misled."

"She won't have time to be upset." Eddie looked Sam in the eyes. "Are we clear?"

Sam nodded.

They parted company at the corner. The remnants of the earlier rain had coated the streets with a glistening sheen. The sparkling streetlights and flashing neon signs made the city look jewel-like in the night. It was all a mirage. Year after year, amid the growing noise, congestion, and pollution, New York sucked in thousands of hopeful, starry-eyed newcomers and spewed out in vast numbers almost as many of them, disillusioned and defeated.

He grabbed a bus down to the Village, where Jeremy Lancaster had once lived and worked. It would be nice to find that in this case, someone had stayed put.

*

AT THE TAVERN WHERE Lancaster had worked, Sam learned that he'd quit his job over a year ago and moved out of the neighborhood after getting a gig as a stage manager in an off-Broadway Village production. The play had opened to bad reviews and closed quickly, but the theater manager remembered Lancaster, who'd recently been cast in a revival of a 1930s Jazz Age musical. It was currently in rehearsal at a small theater inside the West Side YMCA near Columbus Circle. Sam turned around and traveled uptown.

Fourteen stories high, the YMCA had been built to echo the architecture of a medieval castle. The theater had its own separate entrance on Sixty-Fourth Street, within steps of Central Park. Sam slipped into a back-row seat in the darkened auditorium and watched as the director blocked out the stage movements of a love song for an actor and actress. Cast as the romantic lead, Lancaster had good stage presence and a clear, strong voice. His love interest was a young, petite, all-American-looking woman with a big voice perfect for musical comedy.

Although Sam was eager to speak to Lancaster, he enjoyed watching how the mechanics of a play were put together. When the director called for a break, Sam stood at the stage apron, showed Lancaster his PI credentials, and asked for a minute of his time.

"What's this about?" Lancaster asked.

"Several years ago, you were hired by a private detective named Baldwin to pose as Laura Neilson's lover."

Lancaster nodded. "That was one strange gig. I didn't even meet the client until an hour before we went to that Yorkville bar. One of those depressing neighborhood joints. Besides being paid more than I made in a month for a few hours' work, I got two hundred dollars to buy a new suit. I had to look upper crust and successful. I read she got murdered."

"That's true. Did she say why you were to pose as her lover?"

"Man, she barely spoke to me at all. I sat with her in the dark in the back of a limo two blocks from the bar before we went in and tried to make small talk. She wouldn't even look at me. Kept staring out the window."

"What did she say?"

"She just gave me instructions. I was to act like her lover. Be cuddly and lovey-dovey in the bar. Make sure the bartender saw us. Look cool when the old boyfriend arrived. When I told her I needed some motivation for the role, she almost started crying, but she had turned away and I couldn't see her face."

"She said nothing else?" Sam probed.

"Just that she had to break up with some guy, and this was the best way she could do it."

"No other explanation?"

Lancaster shook his head. "The old boyfriend came in, the scene played out, and we left. That was you, wasn't it?"

"Yes. What happened after you left the bar?"

"Nothing. She didn't say a word. She dropped me at a taxi stand and drove off in the chauffeured limo. End of story."

"Thanks, you've been very helpful." Sam asked for Lancaster's phone number in case he had more questions. It was a Butterfield number downtown on the East Side.

"That was one crazy, sexy lady," Lancaster noted. "She almost made me want to be her best girlfriend. What a time that would have been."

"I bet."

The rehearsal resumed. Sam walked home through Central Park, followed part of the way by a policeman on horseback who clip-clopped behind him before veering off in the direction of the Great Lawn. It was nice to see the sky, unencumbered by towering buildings, scoured ink-black by the passing storm, stars brilliantly aglow above a sliver of the city that was lit only by an occasional lamppost.

Under any other circumstance, it would have been magical, but not tonight. According to Lancaster, Laura said she'd *had* to break it off. Why? If there wasn't another lover in her life, what was it? And was it connected to her murder?

Sam crossed Fifth Avenue, his thoughts churning, the city inconsequential around him. When he got to his building, lights from the front room of his apartment brought him to a full stop. Through the partially open apartment door, a pot simmered on the stove and smelled wonderful. His small café table was set for two. Flickering candles, an open bottle of wine, and two stemmed wineglasses completed the arrangement.

Sam got the pistol from his windbreaker pocket anyway. DJ was snoozing in his easy chair, eyeglasses perched on her forehead, an open paperback book in her lap. He stuffed the pistol back in his pocket and tapped her on the shoulder.

"How did you get in?"

She smothered a yawn and smiled. "I thought you'd never show up."

"How?" Sam repeated. There was no sign of a forced entry or a broken lock.

DJ rose and smoothed her skirt. "Out of boredom, I took a correspondence locksmith course while I was in the Navy. Yours was a piece of cake. Let's eat. I'm starved. Do you like beef bourguignon?"

"I do. Why are you here?"

"I needed someone to fix dinner for. Your name popped up."

"Funny, but you'll have to do better than that."

DJ took him by the hand. "I will after dinner. Promise."

OVER DINNER, SAM LEARNED a few things about DJ. A native of the city, she was the only child of a renowned physician and former ballet dancer. She'd been born late in her parents' marriage. Now retired, they lived in Connecticut. She'd attended an all-women's college in New England and had joined the Navy after graduating with a degree in history.

"It was either marry a boy I truly didn't love, apply to law school, become a beatnik, or join the Navy. I decided I needed some adventure. My father had been a naval surgeon during the war, so he didn't protest too terribly much. My free-spirited mother thought I was being charmingly idiosyncratic. Besides, I look great in uniform."

Figuring it would give her an advantage if she decided to apply to law school afterward, she'd enlisted to train as a paralegal in the Judge Advocate General's Corps. After her basic and advanced training, she had been assigned to the Office of Naval Intelligence. And although she'd loved the work of digging into cases to collect raw intelligence, anything other than desk jobs were closed to her. With her discharge in hand, and a small inheritance from a great-aunt, she'd opened her PI firm and never looked back.

Sam put his plate aside and leaned back in his chair. "You can cook," he praised her.

"Only about six different recipes decently," DJ replied. "I know my limits."

"Why do you think Laura hired you to investigate me?"

DJ sipped her wine. "Haven't we been over that? You read my report. She wanted an update about your personal life."

"But why you? You offer discreet inquiries to select clients. When Laura contacted you, didn't you ask who had referred her?"

"Of course I did." She refilled Sam's wineglass.

"So, who gave Laura your number?"

"Sam, that's not playing fair. I'm not going to breech confidentiality."

"Then tell this so-called mystery client who retained you I don't want their help and refund their money. I'll make good on the bail."

"You're being obstinate."

Sam rose and cleared the table. "And you're being evasive. I think you'd better go."

DJ stopped him at the sink. "You loved her a great deal, didn't you?"

"That's not your concern."

"Didn't you?"

Sam turned and faced her. "I tried hard not to, but yes, I did. It wasn't part of our deal. I never once let on to her about my feelings."

"Don't you think she knew?"

Sam turned back to the dirty dishes in the sink. "Yeah, probably."

"Maybe she loved you too. Otherwise, why check up on you? Why would she want to know if you were still available?"

"I've found out that she hired an actor to impersonate her new lover in order to break up with me."

"Because she needed a crutch to do it," DJ proposed.

"That bothers me. Toward the end, she constantly encouraged me to find another lover."

"Because she wanted *you* to call it off, not her."

Sam rinsed dishes under the faucet. "Whatever. It's old history now, not your concern."

"But I am concerned." DJ got her coat and purse from the hook next to the door. "The fact that you're an innocent man who could go to prison for her murder concerns me a lot. I can help you, Sam, and you need my help. Don't let your pride stand in the way."

"I'll think about it. Thanks for the meal, the wine, and the advice."

"You're welcome. Good night."

DJ had left her paperback book and eyeglasses behind on the lamp table in the front room. Sam looked for her out the window, but she was gone. She'd given him a lot of sympathy and little else. He believed what she'd told him about herself was true. But what else was there to her story that she wasn't telling?

He put DJ's book and eyeglasses on the stand next to the door. He'd return them, but not until he'd done a little digging into Debra Jean Ryan's past.

CHAPTER 6

IN THE MORNING SAM THOUGHT BACK OVER HIS CONVERSA-
tion with Jeremy Lancaster. The part about Lancaster sitting with
Laura in the limo before the orchestrated charade at Stamm's had
stuck in his mind. She never drove in the city, and always rented cars
when she made short trips out of town. Had she rented a vehicle for
her road trip out West? Her address book had included a phone number for a parking garage three blocks from her penthouse. Had she
purchased an automobile?

He looked up the business in the telephone directory, called, identified himself as an insurance adjuster, and asked if Laura Neilson kept a
vehicle at the garage. According to the attendant, her Porsche 356 Continental could be found in space 117. Sam finished his coffee and took
the bus uptown. The sports car was a brilliant red two-seat convertible
with a rear-mounted engine and New Jersey license plates. The top
was down and the vehicle registration, in a steering wheel holder on
the column, was in Laura's name with a Stillwater RFD address. Sam
had no idea where Stillwater, New Jersey, might be. He'd look it up.

The glove box was unlocked, and in it were gasoline company road
maps, and brochures from the travel agency that Laura had used to
plot her trip, along with receipts for various items purchased at highway travel stops. In the tiny front luggage compartment, Sam found a
pair of prescription eyeglasses with a broken frame and a missing lens.
As far as he knew, Laura didn't wear eyeglasses.

The glove box also contained the driver's handbook with a business card from the Porsche dealership on Park Avenue. A photograph
at the back of the handbook showed Laura at sunset standing alone
at the edge of the Grand Canyon. Taken, perhaps, by her companion

on the chartered airplane tour. Someone who wore eyeglasses? Was it way off base for him to know who had traveled with her? Could it have something to do with her murder? Sam knew to never dismiss a potential lead.

The Porsche was covered with a thick coat of dust. The parking attendant said the car hadn't left the garage in months. "It's a shame nobody drives that car," he added.

Sam agreed. He gave the man a five-spot and his phone number. "If you call me the next time the Porsche leaves the garage, I've got another five with your name on it."

The attendant grinned and pocketed the greenback. "Easy money."

In a booth at a deli on Madison Avenue, he ordered coffee and went through the glove box items one by one. All the receipts were dated right around the time of the chartered flight over the Grand Canyon. The travel maps had circles around key tourist sites, national parks, and towns and small cities off the beaten path. Sam figured they denoted stops Laura had made along the way. On her travels, she had zigzagged across a wide swath of the Rocky Mountains and Far West. He didn't see any rhyme or reason to it.

He used the phone book to locate a nearby optician, stopped in, and asked the owner, a balding older man, to examine the lens and broken frame. The concave shape of the lens was used to correct myopia, or nearsightedness. It had been produced by an optical shop in the Midwest. He gave Sam the information, but cautioned it was such an ordinary prescription identifying the customer would be exceedingly difficult. That said, the frames were a lady's size.

"You're sure?"

"Anything smaller would be for a child," the man answered.

Sam thanked him and left, wondering if the glasses were Laura's. Or had they belonged to her traveling companion? It could be of no consequence, but he'd hang on to them anyway.

A sidewalk newspaper box in front of a drugstore contained a late-breaking edition of the *Daily Mirror* announcing the impending return of Laura's parents from their European holiday. Sam dropped a coin in the slot and scanned a copy. Dirk and Elizabeth Neilson would arrive

at Idlewild late, and be immediately driven by police escort to meet
with Mayor Robert Wagner at Gracie Mansion. The grieving parents
were demanding answers about the release of their daughter's suspected murderer. A subordinate headline blared the question: "Why
Was Sam Monroe Given Bail?" In the court of public opinion, he was
already guilty.

The East Ninety-Sixth Street branch of the public library was a short
walk from the optical shop. Using an atlas in the reference section,
he looked up Stillwater, New Jersey. It was a small farming township
of about nine hundred people in Sussex County, the northernmost
county in the state. Within easy driving distance from the city, it was
an area of rolling hills, low valley floors, dense western mountains,
and numerous lakes and streams. Dairy farms predominated.

He flipped through various Sussex County phone books, searching for Laura's name. There was no listing for anyone named Neilson. At a library microfilm station, Sam scrolled old newspaper society
pages until he found an announcement of the engagement of Elizabeth Shafer to Dirk Neilson. The daughter of a prominent German
American family that had settled in Sussex County during the 1820s,
Elizabeth's family operated the Kittatinny Valley Farms, a combination dairy and cattle operation. Further research revealed that it was
a family-owned conglomerate under a company label that distributed
high-quality meats and foodstuffs to grocers and restaurants throughout the Northeast.

The phone book showed a business listing for the company and the
Yellow Pages displayed a prominent advertisement for it. But was it
even relevant? He reread the Shafer-Neilson engagement article in
the *Times*. Among the women Elizabeth Shafer had chosen to be her
maids of honor was Jacquelyn Cullen.

DJ had told him her parents' names were Daniel and Jackie. Short
for Jacquelyn? Yes, indeed. Jacquelyn Cullen, a ballerina with a professional New York City dance company, had married Daniel Ryan, MD,
an Annapolis graduate, in a private ceremony at the home of her ballet
teacher, a retired Russian prima ballerina. Where that might lead was
anyone's guess. He'd have to ask DJ.

All morning, Sam had carried her book and eyeglasses in a jacket pocket with the intent of returning them. Now was as good a time as any. He'd checked the frames; the glasses were non-prescription. And the book was a Nero Wolfe mystery.

He stepped outside and was greeted by Marilyn Feinstein, standing next to the open passenger door of a brand-new government Cadillac limo.

"Get in, Sam," she said.

"How did you find me?"

"Easily. Right now you're one of the most recognizable New Yorkers in the city. Get in."

In the backseat of the limo, Sam sat sandwiched between Marilyn and Stephen Watts Key, the new police commissioner. A career cop, Steve Key had just been appointed to his position by the mayor. He'd been in Sam's law school class and had a reputation as one of the good guys on the force.

Approaching fifty, Key was gangly and still boyish-looking. He smiled warmly. "How are you, Sam?"

"Just peachy, Steve. Congratulations on your new job."

"I appreciate that. I hear you've made plans to take down the dirty cop who worked you over at Rikers."

Sam groaned and turned to Marilyn. "Has Mike Dalton been telling tales out of school again?"

Marilyn gave him a motherly pat on the shoulder. "Unlike you, Mike plays by the rules. He wants Johnnie Turner as much as you do—but done the right way. And I agree."

"Don't torpedo this on me," Sam cautioned.

"That's not the intention," Steve Key replied. "But I want more than one dirty cop and a scumbag sergeant. That whole precinct is corrupt, and I intend to chop its head off."

"Admirable," Sam said. "Do I get a stay-out-of-jail card for helping?"

"In a way," Marilyn answered. "Commissioner Key will make sure the mayor doesn't demand that your bail be rescinded. And the district attorney will issue a statement saying new evidence in the Laura Neilson case points to additional persons of interest."

"What new evidence?" Sam asked.

"Everything you've learned since the night you found her dead," Marilyn replied.

"You're kidding, right?"

"No, she's not," Key answered. "I've talked to my chief of detectives, and he admits the case against you is weak. Especially because of the bartender who can vouch for you for several hours before you found Neilson's body. There have been no other breaks, just dead ends. Give us what you know, and we'll peel it back layer by layer."

"You can do it this way, or flounder out there on your own," Marilyn suggested pointedly.

The limo pulled up in front of a precinct in the south Bronx. The building looked weary and neglected, just like the neighborhood. "And Turner?" Sam asked.

"First, finish up with Marilyn and my people," Key said. "You're out of the way up here, so nobody will be snooping around. Give us everything you've got on the case so far. And I mean everything. We'll meet again at the U.S. Marshals office when you're finished and take it from there. Deputy Marshal Snyder has agreed to work with us."

"And if I refuse to cooperate?"

"I can keep Turner off your ass, but I can't promise you won't get gangbanged in Rikers when your bail is revoked," Key replied.

"Fair enough," Sam said.

The limo pulled away. Sam followed Marilyn into the precinct wondering if he'd been suckered or saved.

THE INTERROGATORS KEPT SAM busy for several hours. The questions they asked gave him good insight into the scope of their investigation. They'd followed up on Julia Anderson by questioning Laura's building superintendent. Kurt Bell had been questioned after he'd called the police because of Sam's surprise visit. Carl, the night doorman, had confirmed Bell's frequent penthouse visits, which meant the boyfriend remained a suspect. Questioned again, Laura's housekeeper, Adella, had only told them about Sam's surprise visit to her apartment, and nothing more.

They'd pushed hard about how he'd learned of Laura's previous lovers. Unwilling to admit to the crime of theft, he avoided direct answers by intimating that Laura had kept no secrets from him. It did not go down well, but it beat shooting himself in the foot.

When the session ended, the cops had learned about Laura's car, her road trip, and the mysterious fellow traveler who had toured the Grand Canyon with her by airplane. Sam had also summarized his conversation with Jeremy Lancaster, the actor who had impersonated Laura's lover the night she broke Sam's heart. He gave them Alfonso, Stamm's bartender, as a corroborating witness, which was not news to them, and threw in Dr. Erica Birkenfield as an expert with professional insight into Laura's troubled past.

He wasn't sure if any of it would help or hurt him, but the fresh leads made the cops eager to follow up, at least for the moment. They especially liked how DJ Ryan had helped getting him sprung from Rikers.

Sam wondered how DJ would hold up when questioned about the allegedly anonymous client who'd paid his bail. She wouldn't cave easily, if she caved at all. He'd sidestepped any mention of her connection to Laura's family. Until he knew more, it was interesting, but extraneous information.

On the drive with Marilyn to the U.S. Marshals, Sam wondered aloud what exactly Commissioner Key had in mind as a plan and why was the meeting being held outside the department. Marilyn replied that Key was going after high-ranking corrupt commanders and secrecy was paramount to ensure there would be no internal leaks. She didn't offer any additional information about the operation, just that everyone involved had been fully vetted, including the team of officers who would conduct the arrests. Her role would be to expedite the warrants. Sam's function would be to hand-hold and reassure a nervous Susan Cogan.

"Seems you're the only one she trusts," Marilyn noted.

"That's it?"

"As far as I know." Marilyn reached for the door handle as the car eased to a stop. "I haven't spoken to her yet. She had to be coaxed to cooperate. Last night, when she refused to pay up, Johnnie Turner took his fists to her."

"Dammit," Sam muttered, his blood pressure rising.

*

SUSAN COGAN HAD BEEN sequestered in an office away from the meeting room where the commissioner and his team were strategizing task force logistics. Johnnie Turner had bruised her lips, given her a black eye, and raised an angry welt on her cheek. She was scared, silent, and agitated. When Sam asked if Turner had hurt her in other ways, she shook her head and averted her eyes. He didn't believe her.

"Take me home," she said.

"They won't let me do that."

"What do they want?"

"What we talked about doing before. You call Turner, he goes to your apartment to collect the protection money, and we arrest him along with his accomplice."

Susan shook her head. "I'm not going to do it. I already told them that. Why can't they just arrest that pig for beating me up?"

"It's not that simple," Sam answered. "The bigwigs want to shut the entire protection racket down. That means arresting the police commanders and supervisors behind the scheme."

Susan fidgeted with the sleeve of her blouse. "What do I get out of it?"

"What do you want?"

"If I do this, I can't live here anymore. How many cops are there in the city? Thousands. How many are corrupt? Or brutal? Or just crooked? Do you think they'd let me go unpunished for helping with this? Can the commissioner promise to arrest all the bad ones?"

"Even if he did promise, you know that's not possible. What do you want?"

Susan took a deep breath. "First, I want you to be with me tonight."

"I can do that," Sam said.

"And I want ten thousand dollars cash and an airplane ticket to Tulsa."

"Is that where you're from?"

Susan's glare turned frosty. "Or I'll go to Denver. What does it matter to you?"

"You're right, it doesn't. How about ten thousand with enough
extra to buy you a plane ticket to anywhere in the country?"

She nodded. "Do you think I'm just a greedy little whore?"

"No, I think you're smart." He reached for the phone. "If they don't
agree to your terms, then what?"

Susan smiled. "As my lawyer, you'll sue them for unlawfully detain-
ing me. I told them I wanted to leave, and they wouldn't let me."

"I'm your lawyer?"

Susan nodded. "And I'll pay your fee."

Sam smiled. "That won't be necessary. You are something else."

"Thank you."

Sam used the phone to let Stephen Key know Susan had some concerns but was ready to talk.

*

COMMISSIONER KEY PAUSED HIS meeting and met with Susan, who
refused to budge on what her cooperation would cost. He reluctantly agreed to her terms but wasn't happy with the non-negotiable
demand that Sam had to be present throughout the operation. With
the agreement typed out and signed, they joined the meeting in the
conference room.

An outline on a chalkboard diagrammed the sequence of events.
Once probable cause was established, Mike Dalton and Eddie Snyder
would arrest Turner. Two detectives on stakeout would detain the officer waiting in the radio car. Turner and his accomplice would then be
taken to a secure location, interrogated, and offered leniency if they
rolled over on their superiors. No mention was made of the interrogation methods to be used. It was assumed it would be sufficient to cause
them to crack.

All targeted personnel would be under surveillance, with officers
on standby poised to make arrests. Apprehensions would occur simultaneously. A total of twelve ranking precinct officers, including cap-
tains, lieutenants, sergeants, and detectives, would be swept up in the

first wave. Others would be detained for questioning after the initial arrests. Marilyn and her team would expedite warrants.

Given the complexity and reach of the operation, it would last all night. When it wrapped up, the commissioner and the district attorney would make a joint statement to the press.

Sam was both impressed and troubled by what he learned. Obviously, the commissioner's plan had been in the works long before Susan Cogan had surfaced as bait. Key knew who he was fishing for, and a lot of good intelligence-gathering had been done. But was he rushing it? Was he too eager for early, quick success?

Sam saw no need to erode any of Key's goodwill, so he held his counsel. His job would be to stay with Susan but remain out of sight once the operation commenced. Snyder and Dalton would tell them exactly what to do. End of story.

Key adjourned the meeting, cautioning everyone to avoid arousing suspicion and to proceed normally throughout the remainder of the day. Susan departed in a taxi, with the signed payment agreement in her purse, and a promise from Sam to arrive at her apartment early in the evening.

He had hours to kill, so he hotfooted it in the direction of DJ Ryan's office to return her book and eyeglasses, hoping for a good old-fashioned heart-to-heart talk. This time, she might tell him the truth.

Traffic was loud and noisy, the sidewalks were jammed with hordes of rushing New Yorkers, and a stiff breeze off the harbor kicked newspaper litter into the air. Underneath was the ever-present hiss and rumble of the city; a living machine that was populated by seven million people. Some would not survive the night.

CHAPTER 7

FINDING DJ'S OFFICE CLOSED, SAM WASTED AN HOUR OUTSIDE her apartment hoping she'd return home. He finally gave up, left her paperback and eyeglasses with a neighbor, and hightailed it to Stamm's Bar and Grill. Alfonso was in the back storeroom, stacking cases of Knickerbocker beer against the far wall.

"The cops are going to want to talk to you again," Sam said.

"They already have." Alfonoso dried his hands on a bar towel. "They said you believe Laura hired some actor to pretend to be her lover so she could dump you. Do you really think she did that?"

"I know so. The guy told me himself. Think back to that night. How long were they waiting before I arrived?"

"Maybe ten, fifteen minutes."

"And how did they act with one another?"

"Casual would best describe it. No billing and cooing."

"Not like lovebirds," Sam restated. "And Laura?"

"She seemed okay. Gave me a smile and a big hello when they came in. Ordered her usual, a shot of tequila with a lime twist, no salt."

Sam followed Alfonso into the bar. The waitress who'd been covering returned to the separate dining room. "That night, was there anyone in the place you didn't know? Hadn't seen before?"

"I can't be sure."

"No strange faces at all?"

"I'm thinking there was this woman who came in alone before they arrived and had a drink at the bar. She left soon after you. Never saw her before or after."

Sam had a vague memory of a woman at the bar. Turned away, head lowered. Was he making it up in his mind? "Can you describe her?"

Alfonso shook his head. "Come on, Sam, I'd like to help you, but I can't pull something out of thin air."

"That's okay."

"Why did Laura set you up like that?"

"That's the sixty-four-thousand-dollar question."

Alfonso got busy with some customers. Sam had a draft beer at the bar, hoping it would make him feel that his life someday might return to normal. It didn't work. At his apartment, Abe had tacked a note on the door. The cops had come by for another search, and his repaired lamp and table radio were on the kitchen table. No charge.

Expecting a mess, Sam was happily surprised to find everything shipshape and tidy. It was impossible to tell what had been searched, or what they were looking for. The missing items from Laura's penthouse? That made sense.

He cleaned up at the sink. All in all, he didn't look too bad. The swelling was mostly gone, the black eye had faded from an angry red, and he had some color back in his face. Slowly he peeled off bandage from across his nose. If he could avoid getting punched out again anytime soon, it would heal nicely.

His ribs were sore, but they weren't overly painful when he struggled into a fresh shirt. He switched from the windbreaker to his car coat, found a gray fedora to match it, stuck the pistol in a handy pocket, and hit the street. He had time to run down a few more names on Laura's list of lovers before he was due at Susan Cogan's apartment.

MIKE DALTON ANSWERED SAM'S knock at Susan's apartment. She was on the couch smoking a cigarette and looking unhappy. "What have you gotten me into?" she demanded.

"What's the problem?" Sam asked.

"She doesn't like it that we won't make the pinch if we don't get the self-incriminating statements on tape that we'll need to make the charges stick," Mike replied. "The commissioner wants an airtight case."

"That makes sense," Sam said.

"He wants me to ask Turner and his sergeant questions," Susan said. "I'm no police detective."

"Simple stuff, like asking them when they expect their protection payments," Mike amended. "Or what happens if she can't collect the full pad for the week from the other girls?"

Sam turned to Susan. "You can handle those two questions, right?" She crushed out her smoke and nodded.

"Great," Mike said. "Let's review the plan."

The tape machine would be started when there was a knock at the door. Mike and Eddie Snyder would be in the spare bedroom ready to make the arrest as soon as Turner and Hanrahan took the bribe. Only because Cogan had demanded it, Sam could remain in the apartment, but in the kitchen out of sight.

"It's not your play, Sam," Mike reminded him. "Don't interfere."

"Gladly."

"Okay, now we wait," Dalton said.

There were hours left to kill. A deli delivery of cold cuts, potato salad, and some bakery cookies kept everyone fed, although Susan picked at her food. Eddie Snyder's arrival prompted a game of gin rummy at the coffee table with Mike. They acted like old friends, casual and at ease with each other.

Susan fidgeted and watched TV with the sound turned down low. Sam sat next to a slightly open window wondering which was worse: the stink of cigarette smoke in the apartment or the foul-smelling smog that hung over the city.

The late local news was on when the call came that the radio car had arrived. Mike and Eddie hurried to their post in the second bedroom. Sam fled to the back of the kitchen, pressed up against the noisy refrigerator, hoping to remain invisible. He heard Johnnie Turner's voice when Susan opened the door.

"I brought my sergeant this time. He wants a quickie."

"No, that's not our deal."

"A blow job will do," Hanrahan said.

"I said no," Susan said. "Take the money and go."

"You'll do what we say, bitch," Turner snapped. "On your knees."

The sound of Turner's hard slap against Susan's face made Sam wince. When Turner slapped her again, he expected Mike and Eddie to appear and make the arrest.

Nothing. Jesus, even the good guys could get it wrong. Susan didn't matter; the money had to change hands.

Sam couldn't take it. He came out of the kitchen, pistol in hand. Susan was on her knees, her face red from Turner's slaps. Turner stood behind her, hands pressing down on her shoulders. Hanrahan stood in front, unzipping his trousers, a mean grin on his face.

"Back off, assholes," Sam ordered. "Or I'll drop you both where you stand."

Turner started to laugh but was cut off by Mike and Eddie's arrival. Hanrahan looked peeved as he zipped up, which was apparently somehow more important than the pistol in his face.

"Dammit, Sam," Mike groused as he dug his service revolver into Turner's kidney and disarmed him.

"You blew it," Eddie sourly noted as he put Hanrahan face down on the floor, his handgun in the sergeant's ear.

"I don't think so," Sam retorted as he got Susan on her feet and led her to the front door. "You've got enough for two or three felonies. That should do nicely."

"Where are you two going?" Mike demanded.

"Someplace safe," Sam replied. "I'll be in touch."

Susan grabbed her purse. On the stairwell she asked where he was taking her.

"There's a woman who owes me an explanation. We'll try there first."

"And if that doesn't work?"

"We'll get a room."

Susan laughed. "I thought you'd never ask."

Her laugh was irresistible. He hurried her down the stairs. "Don't try to be cute."

"I wasn't."

"You're one ballsy lady."

"Thank you, kind sir."

At DJ's apartment, she invited them in without hesitation. Although

Susan Cogan was thick-skinned, the night had brought on a heavy shock. After one stiff drink, she was fast asleep on DJ's bed.

Dressed in her pajamas and house slippers, DJ settled into a wing-back chair and asked for a full rundown on the day's events. Sam gave her an abridged version. By the time he finished, he couldn't quite remember what he'd planned to ask her. He fell asleep on the couch.

*

SAM WOKE UP IN the morning wrapped in a blanket, the smell of coffee and bacon in the air. DJ was in the kitchen, whisking up some scrambled eggs, wearing a striped housedress that accented her small waist and showed a fair amount of shapely leg. She told him Susan Cogan had left at dawn to return to her apartment.

"You let her go?" Sam complained.

"Don't worry, she'll have police protection. I spoke to Commissioner Key, and he promised."

"How do you know Key?"

"Years ago, he was critically wounded while arresting a felon. My father performed the surgery that saved his life. He's been a friend of the family ever since."

"Interesting. Speaking of family, your mother was a maid of honor at the wedding of Laura's parents."

DJ stopped whisking. "My, my, you've done your homework."

"Only partially. Why the big lie?"

Scrambled eggs temporarily forgotten, DJ turned the heat off under the frying pan and joined him at the kitchen table. "Excuse me?"

"Tell me again how you never met Laura. Only spoke to her on the phone."

"I told you that to protect your feelings. Laura wouldn't tell me why she wanted me to find out about your current personal circumstances. When I asked for an explanation, she said it scared her to contact you on her own. She was afraid of what she'd learn."

"It *what?*" Sam asked. "Scared her?"

DJ stood, poured two coffees, and returned to the table. "I know, it's crazy. Laura, scared?"

"That makes no sense."

DJ's expression softened. "You loved her, didn't you?"

Sam nodded. "How well did you know her?"

DJ leaned back in her chair. "We were childhood friends, went to private school together. She was two years ahead of me, popular with everybody, especially the boys. In the ninth grade, something happened that made her change. I don't know what, but she turned into a big tease overnight. With her looks and brains, she'd twist boys into a knot and then drop them without the slightest care. It was like a game to her, and she could be vicious about it."

"What's your point?"

"I don't think she wanted to be that way with you, and that's what frightened her."

"But she did it anyway."

"Not as completely as she would have liked. Otherwise, why bother wanting to get back in touch?"

"I don't buy it. She cut me to the quick. It was a surgical masterpiece."

"Maybe you'll never know why she wanted to see you again." DJ settled back. "You know, after ninth grade, she attended a private school in New England until she graduated. I'd only see her when she came home during the long Christmas holidays and summer vacations."

"Why the sudden switch in schools?"

"Ask her parents. Or someone at the school she went to knows, if they're not all retired or dead. But I doubt they'd tell you anything. Your parents send you to that kind of school to hide family secrets."

"What is yours?"

DJ smiled. "I'm not telling."

"You bailed me out of Rikers, didn't you?"

DJ nodded. "For two reasons; I have no doubt that you didn't kill her, and I think you may be the only person who can find her murderer. With my help, of course. How do you like your eggs?"

"Soft scrambled."

DJ rose and turned the heat on under the frying pan. "Good choice. Make the toast and pour the orange juice. It's in the fridge. And you may want to turn on the radio. Commissioner Key's opening volley in the war on police corruption is headline news on all the stations."

A home-cooked breakfast and a body that was beginning to feel less achy put Sam into a good mood. DJ pushed him hard about helping with the investigation. He suggested that she follow up with the school she'd attended with Laura. As a former student, it would give her an advantage. Sam would check on Susan Cogan to make sure she was okay and find out what was happening with Johnnie Turner. After last night, he didn't want that thug roaming the streets free. If they met again, somebody could get killed.

They agreed to compare notes later in the day. At the front door, she held him back. "You can stay here anytime, Sam. I'll leave the porch light on."

Sam smiled. "That's a tempting invitation."

"I mean it."

He hit the pavement and headed home, rested, fed, but in need of a shave, a hot shower, and a change of clothes. What was it Laura had wanted to say to him? Her murder must somehow be tied to him, but how?

CHAPTER 8

SPECIAL EDITION MORNING NEWSPAPERS BALLYHOOED THE decision of a district court judge to release without bail all the suspects who'd been swept up in the commissioner's sting. Speculations by pundits suggested ties between the judiciary and the mob. Lawyers for the accused officers called it a witch hunt and demanded Key's resignation. Citizen advocacy groups applauded the operation but clamored for more to be done to purge the city of all its dirty cops. Quotes from Commissioner Key and the DA praised the work of the dedicated officers and personnel who had spearheaded the operation. Commendations and promotions would be forthcoming.

Sam didn't care about any of it. Only the troubling reality of Johnnie Turner being back on the streets made him jumpy. His call to Mike Dalton from a public pay phone raised his anxiety. The judge's swift action had been so unexpected, surveillance on the perps hadn't been set up. Where Turner might be was anyone's guess, but Dalton said the task force would eventually find him. Sam wasn't reassured.

He decided to forgo a side trip to his apartment and instead went straight to Susan's flat. Out in front, he was detained by a uniformed cop on duty until he could be cleared to enter the building. Susan, looking completely drained, let him in. On the easy chair was her suitcase, partially filled with clothes. An official from the commissioner's office had appeared at her door earlier demanding she surrender the ten-thousand-dollar payment agreement Key had cosigned. She'd been told to either do as asked or face arrest and prosecution on her old drug possession charges.

"I can't stay here," she announced desperately, wrapping her arms around Sam. "I can't stay in this city another minute. I've got to leave. I need the money that was promised to me."

"Calm down." Sam slipped out of Susan's embrace and sat with her on the couch. "You have police protection outside, so give me some time to straighten things out. I'll talk to Commissioner Key personally."

"What good will that do?"

"I witnessed the agreement he made with you. I doubt he'd want word to get out that he reneged on it."

"Are you sure that will work?"

"I know Key. He's trying to cover his ass, not hurt you. He may not pony up the full amount, but I'll try to squeeze him for enough cash so you can get away safely. Once this mess gets sorted out, you can return. Treat this like a well-deserved vacation."

Susan smiled and clutched Sam's hand. "Where were you ten, fifteen years ago, Sam Monroe?"

Sam thought about it. Where was he then? His mother's suicide jumped through his mind. Not a good memory. He smiled and squeezed Susan's hand. "Sit tight and finish packing. I'll be back."

*

THE GREAT WHITE CASTLE, the police headquarters building in Little Italy, dominated Centre Street. A crowning dome topped the five-story beaux-arts granite and limestone structure. On either side of the arched stone entryway, reclining lions welcomed the public. Commissioner Key's offices were on the second floor. Sam announced himself to the receptionist and was asked to wait. He cooled his heels for hours before being ushered into Key's private office. Key was on the telephone at a large desk that former police commissioner Teddy Roosevelt had used before the turn of the century when he worked out of the old police headquarters building on Mulberry Street.

He waved Sam in the direction of a pair of rolled armchairs positioned facing the desk, hung up, and cut Sam off before he could begin his pitch. He knew why Sam was there, and no way could he put ten thousand dollars of city money into the hands of a known prostitute.

One whiff of it would create a scandal for him and bring everything he was trying to do crashing down around his ears. He didn't like deceiving Cogan, but he was a cop, not a welfare worker. He'd done what he had to do.

"Well, what are you willing to do for her now?" Sam asked gamely.

"A couple hundred, just to make it right."

"I can get at least that much selling her story to Walter Winchell or some other gossip columnist."

Key scowled. "Five hundred."

"Three thousand," Sam countered.

"I can get her a grand out of a discretionary fund, but that's it."

Sam did the math in his head. It was barely enough to cover Cogan's living expenses for several months. "Fifteen hundred, plus an extra hundred for a plane ticket," Sam proposed. "You want her gone for a while, don't you? But the DA may want her back if he decides to go to trial. Think of it as procuring some goodwill."

Key stayed silent, tapping his fingers together in thought.

"I came here as a friendly acquaintance," Sam added. "But I can leave as Cogan's lawyer. It's up to you."

"Come back tomorrow."

Sam shook his head. "No, today. Cogan wants to go right now. She's worried for her safety, and I don't blame her. She's packed and ready to leave."

Key nodded, made a quick phone call, dropped the handset in the cradle, and told Sam an assistant would accompany him to accounting. "What's your cut, counselor?" he asked scathingly. "One-third?"

Sam got to his feet. "That's uncalled-for, Steve. But the answer is zero."

It took accounting an hour to produce an envelope with the cash. While waiting, Sam called Susan's number several times but got no answer. He'd asked her to sit tight. Had she bolted? He grabbed a taxi on Centre Street and told the cabbie to floor it to her address.

*

THE BEAT COP IN front of the building had just come on duty. He was a young rookie fresh out of field training. He told Sam that Susan was in her apartment, and that the officer he'd relieved had reported all was quiet. Pleased with the news but concerned she hadn't answered his calls, Sam hurried up the stairs hoping all was okay and she'd be happy with what he'd managed to squeeze out of Key.

He found her clubbed to death on the bathroom floor. Several fatal blows to the head had almost exploded her skull. Blood from the wounds had matted her hair and seeped under the claw-foot tub. It had the stamp of a killer who'd enjoyed it. Someone like Johnnie Turner with his trusty police nightstick.

Seeing her dead filled Sam with disgust. He stepped back from her warm body into the front room, his rage building. He'd been a witness to the aftermath of the murder of two women, both of whom had touched his heart in different ways. He no longer wanted just to find the killers; he wanted vengeance. To hell with a judge and jury. Damn the law.

In Susan's open purse on the couch, he found a pocket-sized address book with the name of a Sarah Cogan in it, along with a Tulsa, Oklahoma, address and phone number. Sam wrote the information down, called NYPD to report the homicide, and left the apartment. Outside, he informed the rookie cop that Cogan had been murdered and ordered him to stand guard at her apartment door until the detectives arrived. Stunned and anxious, the young officer raced into the building.

Likely to become a suspect in another homicide, Sam wasn't about to stick around to be grilled by detectives. The only person he could think to turn to was DJ Ryan. After what had just happened, would she still be willing to help? Under a depressing gray sky, he hightailed it through crowded sidewalks and heavy traffic to her office.

*

DJ TOOK THE NEWS of Susan Cogan's murder with a deep sigh of regret. "I liked her. She had a good heart. What are we going to do about it?" she asked.

"Nothing, right this minute," Sam answered, relieved by DJ's reaction. She didn't ask him to explain himself. "First we need to learn who Sarah Cogan was to Susan and tell her what's happened."

"Her daughter, I bet," DJ said as she dialed the Tulsa phone number. Sam picked up the extension in DJ's bedroom to listen.

Calling as Sam's legal assistant, she spoke to Ellen Cogan, Susan's sister, who wanted to know why a New York City lawyer's office wanted to talk to her. DJ informed her of Susan's death and offered her condolences. "Mr. Samuel Monroe will be managing your sister's estate," she added.

There was a long silence before the woman asked what had happened. DJ explained that Susan had been murdered.

"I'm not surprised," Ellen replied, after a long silence.

DJ asked why.

"New York is an evil, sinful place. Susan had wanted to be an actress; instead she became a whore. I found out when I went to visit her and bring her baby daughter home with me. It mortified our parents until the day they died."

She explained Susan's baby had been born out of wedlock. She'd asked Ellen to take the child until she got financially back on her feet. That day never came, and for fifteen years Ellen had raised Sarah as her own.

"When can I expect some money?" she asked. "Susan never sent me enough. I barely get by on my typist's salary."

"Mr. Monroe will send a Western Union money order to you tonight," DJ promised.

"How much?"

"Enough to last for a while."

"Will there be more?"

"Perhaps." She gave Ellen her contact information in case she had any questions and hung up. "Unbelievable."

"The typical American family exists only in a Norman Rockwell painting," Sam commented.

"Don't be such a cynic. Some families are almost normal. I'll call Commissioner Key and tell him what we're doing with the money. He'll understand."

"Let him know you're collaborating with me to solve the murders. It might give me a little breathing room."

DJ smiled sweetly. "I've already done that."

"What happened when you visited your old school?"

"We can talk about that when you get back from Western Union."

"First I need to go to my apartment, clean up, and change."

"There's no need. I've laid out some clothes in the spare bedroom that my ex-husband left behind after we separated. You're about the same size."

"You have an ex-husband?"

"It's a sad tale of love gone stale."

"I want to know all about it."

"No, you don't." She pushed him in the direction of the door. "Go send the money order."

*

AT WESTERN UNION, Sam sent the full amount to Susan's sister. He should have taken the time to verify what the woman had told DJ, but he wanted the money out of his hands and gone. By dragging Susan in on his scheme to bring down Johnnie Turner, he'd caused her death. He had no way to make amends. It wouldn't be easy to wash the guilt away. At DJ's, he showered, changed into the clothes that she'd laid out for him, and joined her in the living room.

"You look better in Frederick's clothes than he did." She handed him a glass and held up a bottle of expensive scotch. "One shot or two?"

He sat next to her on the couch. "One. I can't picture you with someone named Frederick."

"In retrospect, neither can I." She poured and raised her glass in a toast. "Cheers. Never married?"

"Guilty. What did you learn about Laura at the school?"

"Aren't you going to press me about my failed marriage?"

"I imagine it was Frederick's fault, not yours."

DJ laughed. "You do have some redeemable qualities, Mr. Monroe. I was able to track down the retired head of the school, Irene Rehorn. She recalled that Laura's father withdrew her from the school just before the start of the tenth grade. Laura had spent the summer at her mother's family farm in Stillwater, New Jersey, along with another girl who supposedly was there for having gotten into trouble at home."

DJ refilled Sam's glass. "Miss Rehorn wasn't told who the other girl was but recalled that, at the time she met with Laura's father, he had just learned of the situation and seemed agitated and distraught. She transferred Laura's academic records to her new school, and that was the end of it. I have the name and address of the school."

"You knew Laura. Care to speculate about the trouble?"

"At that age, every teenager is overwhelmed by raging sexual hormones. It causes them to act out in strange ways."

"But not you?"

DJ squared her shoulders. "Certainly not me. Are you hungry?"

"Yes, I am."

"Me too. My favorite Chinese restaurant is a short walk away. Let's go, I'm buying."

"That's unacceptable."

"You're unemployed, if I'm not mistaken. You can treat after you find a new job."

*

DINNER AND SOME CASUAL small talk eased Sam's guilty conscience about Susan, but it couldn't erase the image of her lifeless on the bathroom floor. When he ran out of things to say, DJ wisely called for the check, and they walked back to her apartment in silence. Over a glass of port, they talked about possible next moves. Sam was determined to find Johnnie Turner before Turner found him. He'd seek the help of his old boss at the department store, George Lemond, a retired NYPD detective, who'd spent over thirty years on the force and knew every underworld snitch in the city. If there were even an inkling of Turner's whereabouts, George would know who Sam should talk to.

DJ decided a drive to New Jersey to sniff around the Kittatinny Valley Farms was worth a shot. Whatever happened to Laura that summer had caused a tremendous change in her. But until they learned more, they wouldn't know if it had anything to do with her murder.

Sam declined the offer of a second port, excused himself and tried unsuccessfully to go to sleep in the spare bedroom. Visions of Laura strangled, Susan bludgeoned, and a young soldier dying in his arms on a frozen hill in Korea, chased away any chance of that. Deep into the night, the bedroom door opened. DJ slipped under the covers, pressed her naked body against his, and without saying a word soon had his full and undivided attention.

*

GEORGE LEMOND, A LEGEND at the NYPD, had retired with more commendations and citations for bravery than any other detective in the history of the department. He stood five-foot-nine, weighed two hundred and fifty pounds, and had a small office in the executive suite at the Best & Company department store, where he oversaw security and loss-prevention operations. Sam found him behind his desk dawdling over coffee and the morning papers and asked for his help. He explained who Johnnie Turner was and what had happened to Susan Cogan.

"He's on the lam from Commissioner Key's sting operation and I need to find him before he finds me."

"I've been reading about it. Sounds like a botched job. Johnnie Turner, you say? I knew his old man, Julian Tartaglione, before he legally changed the family name to Turner and joined the force. He was a frigging disaster as a cop. Like father, like son, the old saying goes."

"How do I find Johnnie?" Sam asked.

"I'd start with Salvatore Silano, the best pickpocket in the city," George replied. "He's known on the street as Mano. That's the Italian word for hand. He lost an arm in France during World War I, but that hasn't slowed him down. Cops and crooks treat him like a lucky charm. But be careful, he's protected."

George wrote an address and passed it to Sam. "Hangs out at Dino's Diner. You can't miss him, late fifties, skinny, six feet tall, and only one arm—the right one. Tell him I sent you. He owes me a favor or two."

"You're the best, George."

"Come back and see me when you want your old job back."

Sam laughed. "I may just have to do that."

*

DINO'S DINER DOMINATED A corner of a busy Little Italy intersection. Parked outside were a variety of late-model Cadillacs and Lincolns, all in showroom condition. Salvatore Silano occupied a corner barstool with a clear view of the street and entrance. He wore an expensive Brooks Brothers suit, the empty left sleeve neatly pinned to the jacket pocket. Looking younger than his late fifties, he had graying hair, a long Roman nose, and a high forehead that gave him an aristocratic air.

Sam introduced himself by way of mentioning George Lemond as a mutual friend.

Sal eyed him suspiciously. "George never called in a favor for someone else before. You got his phone number?"

Sam rattled it off. Sal used the bar phone to call George, confirmed Sam and the favor were legit, hung up, and said, "What is it you need?"

"The whereabouts of Police Officer Johnnie Turner. He'd like to kill me, and I don't want that to happen."

"You gonna kill him?"

"Not if I can help it. Getting him sent to prison for life on a murder one conviction would do."

"And what if he gets out?"

"Then I might have to kill him."

Sal didn't flinch at the idea. He eyed him up and down. "Okay, buy me a drink and tell me why you think this might happen. Leave nothing out."

Sal liked good scotch. Sam called the bartender over, ordered two straight shots with a water chaser, and told Mano his story. It took two more rounds to finish it.

He was paying the tab when Richard Carlin, the playboy from Laura's list of lovers, walked in and went to a back booth where four men sat in quiet conversation.

"Do you know Richard Carlin?" Sam asked.

"Sonny Carlin? Sure, everybody knows him. He used to come in here all the time with the dame you're suspected of murdering. Did you kill her?"

"No, but maybe Sonny did. What's his story? I thought he came from Wall Street money." ֵ

Sal nodded. "His family owns a big construction company, Edifice Partners. It's building subdivisions up and down the Northeast coast. They started out in commodities and trucking. His father sits on the stock exchange board."

"Any connection to Havana?"

"You ask too many questions." Sal handed Sam a business card. "Call me in twenty-four hours. I'll have something for you by then."

"Thanks."

"Thank your friend," Sal replied. "Because of him, we've been talking."

Sam walked to Wall Street, the sky overcast and the air thick and humid. He covered the distance thinking about the things Sal had said about Sonny Carlin and his family. It was commonly known that the mob had ties to construction, commodity, and transportation companies—no major surprise there. But Dino's Diner wasn't a venue where one would normally find Wall Steet executives conducting business. Unless, of course, it was something shady and illegal.

Sal had warned him off about Havana, a city that thrived on gambling, drugs, and women, all established, profitable mob enterprises. He decided to learn more about the Carlin family business and dig a little deeper into Sonny's Havana alibi. But where to start?

*

THE HUMIDITY MADE SAM'S shirt cling to him like a limp rag. He entered the stock exchange and at the research office asked to look at the most recent quarterly filings for Edifice Partners, Incorporated. As expected, Sonny was on the corporate board of directors, along with several well-connected businessmen with ties to City Hall. Also unsurprisingly, the company was cash-rich, and its stock price was rising. And, according to the accounting firm that had audited the books, Edifice Partners was totally on the up-and-up.

So much for believing in truth and honor among cops, crooks, and capitalists. He asked a passing stock market analyst if he knew the name of the preferred travel agency Wall Street movers and shakers liked to use, and was directed to the nearby branch office of a prominent establishment.

The walls of the agency were decorated in nicely framed reproductions of Hudson Valley landscapes and furnished in expensive leather chairs grouped around substantial walnut desks. It looked more like a gentlemen's club than a business. Sam was greeted by Margie Rose, a full-figured woman with spectacular gray eyes and a slightly seductive smile. He introduced himself as a freelance writer doing a magazine story on the up-and-coming sons of Wall Street moguls and their glamorous lifestyles.

"Maybe you've read some of my pieces in *Esquire*," he said, easing into a chair next to Margie's desk. "Or *Redbook*. I did a piece last year on Tony Curtis and Janet Leigh."

Margie's smile brightened. *Redbook* was her favorite women's magazine. "Oh, yes, I think I may have read that article. How can I help you?"

"I'm doing research for an upcoming interview with Mr. Richard Carlin. He's on the board of Edifice Partners. I wonder if your firm has had any business dealings with him."

"Edifice frequently uses our services. I've often booked Mr. Carlin's travel arrangements personally."

"Excellent," Sam said. "Young lions like Mr. Carlin make for interesting reading. Has he been traveling lately? I'd love to be able to ask him about where he's been going, what he's been doing. You don't need to be too specific. I just want to get a sense of it. Will you look it up in your records?"

Happy to oblige, Margie pulled the Edifice billing statement. In the past month, Richard Carlin had made one trip to Las Vegas, and stayed at the brand-new Riviera Hotel for a week. He'd also reserved four tickets to the Liberace show during his stay. She gave him the dates. He'd been in New York the night of Laura's murder.

"Any out-of-the-country trips?" Sam asked.

Margie shook her head. "No."

"Any gossip you're willing to share?"

Margie smile faded. "Certainly not."

"Had to ask," Sam said apologetically. "Thanks, Margie, you've been a tremendous help. I'll drop by a complimentary copy of the magazine article when it's published."

Margie's smile returned. "That would be swell."

He left wondering why Carlin had lied to him both about being out of town *and* his whereabouts. He made a call to George Lemond and laid it all out.

"Back off, buckaroo," George cautioned. "Richard Carlin is part of the Carlucci family. They were a small, independent Mafia family that changed their identity and went mainstream-legitimate in the mid-forties. Edifice in Italian means building. From what you're telling me, if there is a Las Vegas connection, they're not completely legit. Be very careful."

"Thanks, boss," Sam said. If he remembered correctly, one of Laura's past lovers currently living out of state resided in Las Vegas. He consulted the list of her lovers that he'd copied. Tony Carlucci, now of Las Vegas, had been next after Richard Carlin.

A cousin? An uncle? Who? Then there were all these Italian names. Julian Tartaglione, Salvatore Silano, Tony Carlucci. Were they all connected? As George suggested, had he unexpectedly walked into the middle of a rebranded Mafia family?

Sam stopped short on the sidewalk. Jesus, had he totally been misled by Laura? Had she been nothing more than a crazy sex junkie? He would follow George's advice and tread lightly. Starting with taking a closer look at what he'd taken from Laura's apartment. He headed to Penn Station to retrieve the stolen stash.

CHAPTER 9

MIKE DALTON SAT DOWN NEXT TO SAM AT THE AUTOMAT AND gazed at the address book and appointment calendar on the table. "Those must be the items Neilson's maid reported missing from the apartment," he commented.

Except for Laura's diary, which was still in the Penn Station locker, Mike was right. "How did you find me?" Sam asked.

"You're not in hiding, are you? Besides, why should I share my trade secrets with a murder suspect who has stolen documents in his possession that might further implicate him?"

"What are you going to do?"

Mike picked up Laura's address book and thumbed through it. "What do you think I should do?"

Sam shook his head. "Do the right thing, Mike. You've already cut me enough breaks."

Mike stood up. "Stay put while I get some coffee." He returned with coffee and a fresh cheese Danish. "I've read the statement you gave the detectives at the Bronx precinct. Fill me in from there. What more have you learned?"

Sam frowned. "Aren't you going to arrest me?"

"Probably, but first things first. Talk."

Caught flat-footed with no way out, Sam talked. When he finished, Mike knew everything, right down to the reason for DJ's planned trip to Stillwater, and the discovery of Laura's past personal connection to a Mafia family.

Mike didn't even look mildly impressed. He waved a hand over the incriminating evidence spread out on the table. "Are you finished with all of this?"

"Pretty much," Sam answered. He'd memorized Tony Carlucci's Las Vegas contact information, and he still had his copy of the list of Laura's lovers. "What's next?"

"The mayor's office has made an appointment for you to meet with Laura's parents this evening at their town house." Mike handed him a note with the address, a phone number, and the time. "Don't be late."

"Can I bring a friend of the family?"

Mike scooped up the books and stood. "Don't be such a wiseass. If you mean DJ Ryan, call the number on the note I gave you and ask."

"Thanks, Mike."

"Consider yourself lucky that I don't take you back into custody, and don't even think about flying to Las Vegas to talk to Tony Car- lucci. You're grounded, got it?"

"Are you having me tailed?"

Mike smiled. "What do you think?"

"Has anybody spotted Johnnie Turner?"

"Not yet."

"I'll find him."

Mike scoffed at the idea and left.

From a pay phone, Sam reached DJ, who had just returned to her office from New Jersey. He told her of their unexpected evening invi- tation to visit the Neilsons.

"I'll call and let them know that I'm coming with you," she said. "Stop by my office so we can fill each other in. I've learned a few things of interest."

"Me too," Sam said. "I've got one more call to make on Staten Island, so it will be a while before I get there."

HE MADE IT TO the tip of Manhattan in time to catch the next ferry a few minutes before it departed, looking for a tail along the way. He didn't spot anyone either onshore or onboard. He stopped looking.

The ferryboat, a two-stack behemoth, lumbered through heavy waters, spewing black smoke into a murky sky. Sam felt a lot better when it docked. Timothy Baldwin opened his front door with a surprised look on his face.

"I didn't expect to see you again."

"If it's not a bother, I'd like to take a second look at your uncle's files," Sam said apologetically. "It won't take long."

In the basement, he retrieved Laura's file and quickly read Baldwin's background report on Tony Carlucci. There was no mention of a family relationship to Richard Carlin, only that Carlucci had been introduced to Laura by him at her request. According to Baldwin's investigation, Tony owned an import-export company that operated in Hoboken, on the New Jersey side of the Hudson River.

Sam scribbled down the business name and address. There was the usual other stuff in the report. Carlucci was single, well-off, and a respected member of the business community.

Upstairs, Sam thanked Tim. "Your uncle must have been quite a successful shamus," he added. "Not many private dicks get to retire on a boat and go sailing up and down the East Coast."

Tim's genial expression dimmed. "I wouldn't know about that."

"And to have such a complete repository of his case files is truly remarkable," Sam continued. "Think of the secrets he must have discovered over the course of his career. I bet some people would love to know that this treasure trove exists."

"You'd better leave," Tim grumbled.

"I'm not here to cause trouble," Sam soothed. "How you and your uncle conduct business is none of my concern."

"Then what is it you want?"

"Are you tied to the mob?"

Tim laughed. "If that were the case, Uncle Everett and I would both be dead."

Sam smiled. "Fair enough. That's all I wanted to know."

He said goodbye and made his way to the ferry station. Uncle Everett and his nephew were living off the proceeds of a hefty blackmail operation. He wondered how much they were raking in. It was a bulletproof, invisible criminal enterprise, and in spite of himself Sam was impressed.

Tugboat horns moaned through the mist, the ferryboat's engine coughed and chugged. The Statute of Liberty was nothing more than a vague and threatening shape. It was a perfect setting for the opening credits of a 1940s crime noir movie featuring a flawed protagonist who courts disaster and in the end dies. Roll the credits. Sam hoped for both a different outcome and a more promising future.

*

DJ USHERED SAM INTO her office, settled back behind the desk, and made her report. In late August, during Laura's summer vacation at the New Jersey farm, she and a girl named Jeannie had gone on a hike to a remote swimming hole on the property that was off-limits but popular with the local kids. It was an abandoned stone quarry surrounded by a dense stand of trees that had flooded years ago when the mine operator hit an underground spring. With a fifty-foot drop from the summit of an almost vertical cliff to the deep pool below, only the bravest, or those who gave in after being relentlessly bullied, risked the jump.

When the girls arrived, they'd discovered the body of Allen Quick, a popular high school athlete, floating dead in the water. Hysterical, they hurried back to the farm and called the local sheriff.

DJ had located the retired elderly lawman living in a nearby township and spoke with him. He remembered the incident well. "He says the accident never made any sense," DJ said. "The boy was an excellent swimmer. He even had a summer job as a lifeguard at one of the bigger lakes in the area. The assumption was that he'd died when he dove headfirst from the lip of the quarry and crashed into a rocky ledge that juts out ten feet above the water. The sheriff personally retrieved his body. The boy's head wound was major, but there was no evidence he'd crashed onto the ledge."

"Could he have hit the side of the quarry wall higher up?" Sam asked.

"The sheriff wondered that also. He used a rope and pulley to lower himself down to examine the quarry rock face. He found no impact evidence. The coroner ruled it an accident."

"But was it?"

NIGHT IN THE CITY

"The boy was well liked, had no known adversaries or rivals at school, and had never been in trouble with the law. According to the sheriff, Laura's family paid a fairly hefty sum of money to compensate Allen's family for his death. They put up a fence around the quarry almost immediately and posted it against trespassing. To this day, kids still try to sneak in for a swim."

"How much money did the family shell out?"

"Fifty thousand dollars."

Sam whistled. "That's serious money. Who was the girl with Laura?"

"Jeannie. The sheriff said she wasn't a local and he couldn't recall her last name. He thinks she was a guest at the farm. At the sheriff's office in Newton, I asked to see a copy of the incident report and was told it had been destroyed years ago. The farm manager told me no one who currently works there, including himself, was employed at the time of the accident, although the tragedy is still remembered as part of the local lore."

"I guess we'll have to ask Laura's parents who this Jeannie was when we meet with them," Sam reflected.

"Yes, we will. What about your day?"

"Other than the deep dive I took into some murky Mafia waters, there's not much to report."

DJ laughed. "That's a great introduction, but don't tease me with it. What have you got?"

Sam told her most of it, including about the Carlucci family and their ties to Las Vegas, Sal, aka Mano, and Baldwin's blackmail scheme.

"Do you think he was blackmailing Laura?" DJ asked.

"That's iffy," Sam answered. "Laura didn't care much about what other people thought of her."

"I agree. But she might have paid him off to protect someone she cared about." DJ sat across from him, took off a shoe, and ran her bare foot up his pants leg to his zipper. "Let's change the subject."

Now he understood why she'd locked her office door behind him.

"Remember, we're meeting with Laura's parents," Sam cautioned.

"We've plenty of time," DJ replied.

They used it wisely.

*

DIRK AND ELIZABETH NEILSON'S Upper East Side town house was three blocks away from the Carnegie Mansion and a step or two down in opulence. However, the land under all of the houses on the block was part of the original New Amsterdam homestead that still remained in the family, and, according to DJ, generated sizable income.

Dirk Neilson greeted them at the front door. Of average height, with a receding hairline, he had the bearing of a strict headmaster who brooked no foolishness. He did, however, manage to give DJ a bit of smile.

He ushered them through the spacious entryway to a beautifully appointed library with floor-to-ceiling bookshelves filled with rare first editions, and memorabilia and artifacts from past and more recent world travels. From an Italian leather chair, Elizabeth Neilson politely rose to meet them. Slightly taller than her husband, she had an angular face and body that reminded Sam of Katharine Hepburn.

Sam got a handshake and DJ a hug.

Mrs. Neilson returned her attention to Sam. "We've been encouraged by the mayor and the authorities to believe you are innocent of our daughter's murder."

"I am determined to find Laura's killer." Sam turned to DJ. "We're determined."

"Why?" Dirk asked flatly. "DJ, we can understand. She's a friend of the family."

"I loved your daughter," Sam answered. "Until I met her, I didn't realize how lonely I'd been. Not just for anyone, but for her."

DJ looked surprised, and her glance at him was full of questions.

Elizabeth raised an eyebrow. "You knew of her inclinations about men?"

"Laura held nothing back from me."

"Are you one of those so-called free thinkers?" Mr. Neilson queried.

"Only in certain circumstances," Sam replied graciously, brushing past the implied criticism. "Can you recall what happened to Laura the summer before you sent her away to school in New England?"

Dirk colored slightly. "I see no point to your question."

"She changed that year, Mr. Neilson," DJ interjected. "I saw it. Everyone who knew her did."

Elizabeth's expression tightened momentarily and then relaxed. "Oh, yes, the terrible accidental drowning of that boy at the quarry. Finding him there dead devastated Laura."

"Of course," Mr. Neilson said, relief flooding his voice. "It disturbed her greatly."

"It must have," DJ replied. "As well as the girl who was with her that day. Jeannie, I believe, is her name. What can you tell us about her?"

"How does this relate to my daughter's murder?" Mrs. Neilson countered.

"It might not," Sam soothed. "But surely you'd want us to pursue every avenue of inquiry."

"Yes, of course," Dirk replied. "The girl was staying with our farm manager's family. But I don't recall if she was a relative or a friend."

"And his name?" DJ asked.

"Huizinga," Elizabeth replied. "Lars, but everyone called him Lee. He was with the farm until he passed away. His wife and children relocated, but I don't know where."

"Do you know a private investigator named Baldwin?" DJ asked.

"No, why do you ask?" Dirk inquired.

"It's possible he was blackmailing Laura," Sam noted.

Mr. Neilson almost laughed. "I doubt it. Laura flaunted her love affairs to us whenever she had the chance."

"Maybe it wasn't about that."

"I think that's quite enough questioning," Mrs. Neilson said as she stepped to the library door. "Thank you for coming. Find our daughter's killer, if you can, Mr. Monroe. We would be more than grateful."

With a promise to keep them informed, DJ got another quick hug from Elizabeth. Sam got a nod and stiff handshake from Dirk.

"Now what?" DJ asked as they walked to the avenue in search of a cab.

"We find Lars Huizinga's family. With a name like that, the odds should be in our favor. Did you notice we weren't invited to sit?"

"It certainly wasn't a social call, was it? Up for a short road trip to northern New Jersey in the morning?"

"What have you been driving?"

"My father's brand-new Thunderbird hardtop. I've promised not to wreck it."

"I'm your man."

DJ stopped in midstride and flashed a smile. "I like the sound of that." Her smile faded. "Inside, you said that before you met Laura you were lonely for her but just didn't know it."

Sam nodded. "It takes a certain person to fill some of the jagged empty parts of who you are. Laura did that."

"I've never heard love explained quite that way before. Does this only happen once?"

"I certainly hope not."

DJ's smile returned. "I'm relieved. Are you coming home with me?"

Sam nodded. "Only if I can raid Frederick's left-behind wardrobe in the morning."

DJ reached for his hand and pulled him along. "It's a deal."

Sam held her back. "One question. You said Irene Rehorn, the retired headmistress at your and Laura's old school, got no explanation from Dirk Neilson for her abrupt transfer."

DJ's eyes widened. "That's right. Why wouldn't he want to explain what had happened to traumatize his daughter?"

"And as if one shock isn't enough, why add to it by pulling her out of a familiar environment to send her to a strange boarding school hundreds of miles away from family and friends?"

"We have been lied to," DJ said.

"Let's find out why."

CHAPTER 10

THE ALMOST EMPTY TWO-LANE ROAD SIXTY MILES NORTHWEST of the city took them past tidy farms, pastures filled with lounging cows, roadside stands offering fresh produce, and occasional small rural schoolhouses that anchored the surrounding tiny townships. Northern New Jersey was a different, more peaceful world, and Sam didn't miss the soot, smoke, noise, and madness of New York. He rubbernecked all the way to Newton, the Sussex County seat, while DJ wheeled the Thunderbird skillfully on the curving, sometimes hilly country roads.

Newton, a pretty little village with a towering Civil War monument on the town green, looked like a New England hamlet magically transported to New Jersey. They ate an early lunch at the Cochran House hotel in a dimly lit dining room designed to resemble a log cabin. The food was no more inspired than the setting.

With the help of a clerk at the hall of records, they found two property tax records listed under the name of Huizinga. Sidney Huizinga operated a farm in nearby Fredon Township, and Sofia Huizinga owned a house in Stanhope, a borough at the southern tip of the county. With directions supplied by the clerk, they made the short drive on a county lane to a hilltop farm set back from the road, bordered on two sides by second-growth woodlands. A gentle breeze rippled through acres of field corn ready for harvesting. The old farmhouse and barn were lovingly cared for, with a flower garden in front of the house and a large vegetable garden to the rear. A sturdy chicken coop was steps away from the barn.

DJ eased the Thunderbird to a stop. A stocky middle-aged man with a weathered face Rembrandt could have etched stepped out of the barn.

"My wife has no eggs today," he said. "Try the Kinsey place, up the road."

"We're looking for anyone who knew Lee Huizinga." DJ stepped out of the car and flashed her PI license. "He managed the Kittatinny Valley Farms. Are you Sidney Huizinga?"

"I'm Sid Huizinga. Lars was my uncle. What can I do for you?"

"We'd like to talk to a woman who once lived with your uncle at Kittatinny. She would have been a girl back then, in her early teens."

Sid Huizinga shook his head. "You're asking a lot."

"What do you mean?" Sam inquired.

"Uncle Lars and Aunt Lotte only had one child, my cousin Sofia, who has never been right in the head. To make up for it, they fostered dozens of children, mostly girls."

He went on to explain that they'd done it primarily for Sofia's benefit, hoping it would help her get smarter and learn how to get along with other children. Over the years, at least thirty youngsters had been placed with the family, and as Sofia matured, boys were no longer accepted out of fear she might be taken advantage of.

"Did you know any of the girls?"

"I met a few when we visited, but I don't recall their names. Some were mousy and quiet, and some were on the wild side."

DJ asked Sid if he'd met a foster girl at the farm named Jeannie around the time of Allen Quick's drowning at the slate quarry. The name didn't register. Sam asked Sid about his cousin's slowness. She was mentally retarded but functioned well enough with some support from the state to live alone in a small cottage inherited from her mother. Sid hadn't seen her in several years, but his wife called regularly to check up on her.

With thanks for his help, they left with directions to Sofia's home in Stanhope.

*

SOFIA HUIZINGA'S TWO-STORY HOUSE with clapboard siding was part of a working-class neighborhood close to a scattering of village businesses along the main street. She was in her front yard sitting on a swing attached to a substantial limb of a large sycamore tree. She waved and smiled cheerfully as Sam and DJ approached.

"I don't know you," she said guilelessly. Dressed in bib overalls, she was bulky, with a short neck, broad shoulders, and thick arms.

"We know your cousin Sid," Sam said.

Sofia nodded. "That's right, Sid's my cousin."

"I'm Sam and this is DJ."

Sofia looked DJ up and down and giggled. "That's a funny name, DJ."

"I think so too," DJ replied. "We wanted to ask you if you remember Laura Neilson."

Sofia's smile brightened. "She was my best friend. You know her?"

DJ nodded. "Yes, I do, and I'm trying to help her. Do you remember the summer when Allen Quick drowned at the slate quarry?"

Sofia shook her head. "No, I don't remember that."

"What do you remember?" Sam asked.

"He died."

"How?" Sam prodded.

Sofia's expression clouded. "I don't know. I was just told. He was bad."

"Was he bad with you?" DJ asked.

"No." She grabbed the ropes, pushed off with her feet, and started slowly swinging. "I just heard he was."

"Heard from who?"

"I don't know."

"Was he bad with Laura or Jeannie?"

"Not Jeannie," she said.

"Not Jeannie?" DJ probed.

"No, Jeannie wasn't the name she used," Sofie answered. "She didn't like it."

"What was her name?" Sam inquired.

"I don't remember."

"Was Allen Quick bad with Laura?" he asked.

"I don't know that. You should leave now."

"Try to remember Jeannie's real name," DJ pleaded. "It would help Laura a lot."

Sofia hopped off the swing. "Go, or I'll yell loud, and Mrs. Lorenzen will call the sheriff."

There was movement at a window in the house next door.

"We didn't mean to upset you," DJ said soothingly.

Sofia smiled benignly. "That's okay." She pointed toward the street. "You go."

They left Stanhope and headed for the city. Sam proposed a stop in Hoboken on the off chance that Tony Carlucci might be at his company's offices.

"Why not, the day's been a washout," DJ replied, frustrated. "Let's go oh-for-three."

THE AROMA OF CUPCAKES and coffee signaled their arrival in Hoboken, a waterfront city that flaunted its ragtag countenance at the soaring Manhattan metropolis across the Hudson River. It was home to a commercial snack food bakery, several coffee and tea producers, a steel company, and a major shipyard strung out along a row of piers on the river.

Downtown looked busy, but in spite of a strong economy and plentiful jobs, parts of the cramped residential neighborhoods were run-down, and there wasn't any beauty to be discovered in the boxy industrial buildings that proliferated on the waterfront.

The Carlucci import-export company warehouse and offices sat back from the river on a wide alley where a small fleet of large trucks were parked. There were no gunsels in sight and Sam and DJ were greeted by a buxom young secretary who inhabited a small reception room that, from the looks of it, had seen few visitors. Other than the secretary's desk, the only piece of furniture was an armless chair that sat forlornly against the wall. Office adornments consisted of two framed enlarged photographs on the walls, featuring the nearby Lackawanna railroad station and the aging Hoboken ferry terminal.

The secretary seemed surprised when they asked to speak to Mr. Carlucci. "He's never here. May I ask the nature of your business?"

DJ flashed her PI badge and license. "We're investigating a murder."

She reached for the desk telephone. "I'd better call him."

"Ask if we can speak to him for a few minutes," DJ added.

"I'll ask, but don't count on it." She turned aside, cupped her mouth over the phone, and whispered into it. She listened, nodded, hung up, and smiled brightly. "He'll be here in five minutes. Have a seat."

"Thanks," Sam said. They remained standing.

Carlucci arrived in less than five minutes. Hopping out from behind the wheel of a new Cadillac Coupe DeVille hardtop, he entered in a hurry.

"What murder?" he asked without preamble, glancing from DJ to Sam. "Let me see some ID."

"Laura Neilson," Sam answered, holding out his PI credentials.

Tony Carlucci shook his head and laughed in exasperation. "That bitch, dead? I could see it coming from a mile away."

"How so?" DJ asked.

Carlucci opened the door to the inner office and gestured them inside. He was tanned, slender, and wore a white shirt open at the collar and black slacks. Six feet tall, he had dark curly hair and deep blue eyes. In looks, more a pretty boy than a mobster.

"Because she was just asking for it," he answered, closing the door.

The office was no more attractive than the front reception, except there were two visitors' chairs instead of one, and the wall art consisted of two large maps, one of Hoboken and the other of Italy. Sam and DJ stayed standing.

"How so?" DJ inquired again.

Carlucci settled behind his desk. "Did you know her?"

"You didn't ask us how she died," Sam countered.

"I didn't have to, it was in the papers. Did you know her?" Carlucci repeated.

"Well enough to know she had certain proclivities."

Tony laughed. "Proclivities. I like that. The woman was sex-crazed, always pushing it to the edge. Once she followed me into the men's room at a Greenwich Village jazz club demanding sex right then and there, grabbing at me. I had to push her off. Another time, on the balcony of a hotel where we stayed, she wanted it in full view of anyone watching. I had to slap her to make her stop. Even with all her money, that dame had no class."

"But why would that get her killed?" DJ queried.

"Because, like I said, she was a crazy piece of ass and a thrill junkie. Sooner or later, somebody would off her, and someone did."

"You, maybe?" DJ speculated.

Carlucci's expression turned frosty. "You should watch what you say to people you don't know."

"Let's change the subject slightly," Sam proposed. "Can you account for your time on the night Laura was murdered?"

"I was in Las Vegas. Ask anybody."

"That shouldn't be too hard to do," Sam mused sarcastically.

Carlucci pushed back from his desk and stood. "I've been polite, but now you're forgetting your manners. See yourselves out and don't come back, capisce?"

DJ smiled winningly. "Thank you for your time."

Carlucci followed them to the front door and watched as they drove away.

"You didn't ask what Mr. Carlucci imported and exported," DJ chided jokingly.

"It didn't seem prudent," Sam replied. "Did you buy what he said about Laura?"

"Isn't that a question you should ask yourself?"

Sam sighed. "I'm starting to believe she was a chameleon."

"Different with each lover," DJ added.

"Exactly."

"That doesn't explain you."

"Yes, it does. I was her brief foray into normalcy. With me, she could make-believe about being happy with an ordinary lover—just a meat-and-potatoes-type guy."

DJ laughed and wheeled the T-Bird in the direction of the George Washington Bridge. "There's nothing ordinary about you, counselor. Let's take the long way home."

Twilight scattered the last of the sunset across the Hudson River, the backdrop of Manhattan skyscrapers reflecting the dying rays like countless nautical lighthouses. It masked the dirt and dead dreams of the city, made it appear mysterious and beautiful.

The panel truck came out of nowhere and slammed full-speed into the back of the Thunderbird. DJ's head hit the steering wheel as the car spun crazily toward an abutment. Sam reached over, yanked the wheel, and forced his foot hard on the brake. The car wobbled on two wheels momentarily before slamming down on the pavement to a bone-jarring halt.

Traffic paused in all directions, and people piled out of vehicles to witness the wreckage. Sam turned to see the panel truck reverse, spin around, and vanish behind a line of stopped vehicles, the driver's face hidden by a ball cap pulled low over his forehead, the license plates missing.

He pulled an unconscious DJ from the wreckage as gasoline leaked from the ruptured tank. The T-Bird ignited and blew up. The sound of approaching emergency vehicles, their sirens screaming, grew into a crescendo as black smoke and tongues of searing flames billowed into the deepening twilight.

He sat on the pavement with DJ in his arms, rocking her, begging her to wake up.

CHAPTER 11

UNCONSCIOUS AND STRAPPED ON A GURNEY WITH HER HEAD immobilized, DJ was wheeled into an ambulance and driven away. Two cops cleared the traffic congestion from the smoldering crash site in spite of Sam's protests to find and question witnesses about the panel van that had deliberately rammed into them. They didn't seem to care. They told him to tell it to Sergeant O'Reilly, who was en route.

Firemen hosed down and mopped up debris from the crash. A medic patched a cut on Sam's cheekbone, while the recently arrived sergeant stood by ready to take his statement. The medic moved off and the waiting uniformed sergeant approached. No more than five-ten, he had a narrow nose, a prominent chin, and a no-nonsense attitude. He introduced himself as Sergeant O'Reilly and asked Sam for his identification, which he recorded in a pocket-sized notebook.

"Tell me what happened," O'Reilly said.

Sam summarized the event while O'Reilly took notes. He scanned his entries before asking questions. They came in a flurry. Who was driving? What was the name of the woman transported to the hospital? How did the accident happen? What did the panel truck look like? Was there anything distinctive about it? Did he get a look at the driver?

Sam answered quickly, said he wasn't sure about the panel truck, but thought it might have been a Ford, plain white, with double rear doors, each with a small window. He couldn't see the driver's face.

The explosion had melted the T-Bird down to the undercarriage. Burned to ash were the vehicle registration and DJ's purse containing her identification.

O'Reilly noted that Sam's surname was different from DJ's. What was their relationship? Sam wasn't about to be turned away at the hospital when he got there, so he lied and said she was his wife. O'Reilly asked who owned the vehicle. Sam said it belonged to his father-in-law, Dr. Daniel Ryan.

"I need to get to the hospital right now," he added.

"A few more questions," O'Reilly said. "Were you in Hoboken on business?"

Sam explained that they were returning from a northern New Jersey day trip and just passing through. Tired of O'Reilly's questions, he held up his hand to call a halt and demanded to know where DJ had been taken.

Sergeant O'Reilly closed his notebook. "Saint Mary Hospital. I'll have an officer take you there. Thank you for your cooperation." He told a nearby patrolman to drive Sam to the hospital and turned his attention to the crash site

Sam pointed at the roadway. "You do understand the hit-and-run driver deliberately tried to kill us? There are no skid marks on the pavement to show he tried to stop or swerve out of the way. And what about that front bumper he left behind? Shouldn't you take it into evidence? It might help you narrow the search for the vehicle. This was no accident."

Sergeant O'Reilly gazed at Sam as if he were a troublesome child. "I know you're upset, but we're not finished here. Leave the police work to me, Mr. Monroe. I'll be in touch if I learn anything new or need to speak to you again. You did a brave thing saving your wife."

O'Reilly turned away. Sam climbed into the patrol car, rode silently to the hospital, and jumped out when the vehicle stopped at the entrance. The adrenaline rush had begun to wear off and his fear about DJ's well-being intensified as he approached the information desk. He asked the elderly nun where he could find her and was told she'd been admitted to the women's general inpatient ward.

He asked about her condition. The nun dialed the nursing station and reported DJ was unconscious but in stable condition. Yes, of course Sam could see her.

"I'll pray for her swift recovery," the sister added.

Sam thanked her. At a lobby pay phone, he got Dr. Daniel Ryan's

residential phone number from a long-distance operator, who immediately put the call through. Dr. Ryan answered and Sam explained
what had happened. Ryan wanted more information about DJ's condition than Sam could provide. Frustrated and worried, he ordered Sam
to stay put until he and his wife arrived. The line went dead before
Sam could promise to do as he asked.

At the inpatient women's ward, he found DJ in a hospital bed behind
a privacy curtain, watched over by a tall, thin nurse dressed in starched
whites and a bib apron. DJ had a black eye and an angry bruise on her
forehead. An IV in her arm was supplying her with fluids.

He sank into a bedside chair, his spirits dwindling. First Laura, then
Susan Cogan, now this. What if she didn't make it? The thought of it
froze his heart. He summoned the last shreds of his composure to ask
the nurse about DJ's condition. She told him that her respiration, blood
pressure, and heart rate were normal—all encouraging signs. Also,
DJ had opened her eyes briefly in response to a pinch, and her pupils
appeared normal.

"That's all very positive," the nurse said reassuringly.

Sam wasn't comforted. He wanted DJ to wake up, right away. He
reached for her hand.

The nurse smiled, said she was nearby if needed, and straightened
DJ's bedcovers before leaving to continue her rounds.

Sam felt light-headed, sleepy, and woozy. The cut on his cheekbone
throbbed. Time passed and he dozed off. When he opened his eyes, DJ
was sitting up, clutching his hand.

"Nice to see you, husband," she said jokingly.

At the foot of the bed were a man and a woman he took to be Daniel
and Jacquelyn Ryan. Sam got to his feet. They were late-middle-aged,
fit, and attractive. It was easy to see where DJ got her looks. Neither of
them smiled at him.

"Explain yourself," Dr. Ryan ordered.

Before Sam could answer, DJ spoke up, explaining she'd told her
parents about their day outing to New Jersey and that the accident had
happened out of the blue. She made no mention of Laura's murder or
their run-in with Tony Carlucci.

Dr. Ryan gazed intently at Sam. "Have you anything to add?"

"Except for the fact that we're not married, she has covered the events nicely," he replied without flinching. "When I arrived at the hospital, I needed to make sure she was going to be all right, so I lied about our relationship."

Mrs. Ryan looked relieved, Dr. Ryan less so.

"He's a good guy and I like him," DJ announced. "Can we leave it at that?"

Dr. Ryan nodded. His wife smiled tightly and was about to say something when the admitting physician arrived.

He examined DJ and recommended keeping her overnight for observation. The shock of the accident was cause enough to merit caution. Over DJ's protests, Dr. and Mrs. Ryan agreed. They would stay at a local hotel, shop for any necessities DJ needed, and keep her company until visiting hours ended. In the morning they would take her to their Connecticut home to recuperate under their watchful eyes for at least several more days—no disagreement allowed.

DJ wrinkled her nose but didn't pout.

The physician arranged with the nurse to have DJ moved to a semi-private room. He promised to return in the evening and departed. Dr. Ryan didn't say a word about his new Thunderbird getting totaled. That showed class. Sam was about to leave so DJ could have time alone with her parents when Sergeant O'Reilly arrived fresh from the crash scene.

O'Reilly introduced himself to DJ's parents, found out who they were, and said he needed a few minutes alone with Mr. and Mrs. Monroe to ask them some questions. Mrs. Ryan quickly corrected him about DJ's marital status.

DJ covered her mouth to hide her laugh as Sam's tenuous credibility with her parents nosedived again.

"Wasn't it simply an accident?" Dr. Ryan inquired.

"I'm afraid it's become more complicated than that," O'Reilly replied.

Dr. Ryan glared at Sam, switched his attention back to O'Reilly, and said, "If that's the case, Sergeant, please explain what you mean."

"In due time, sir," O'Reilly calmly replied. "Now, if you'll excuse me, I need to speak to these two alone."

The nurse escorted the Ryans away. O'Reilly waited until they were out of earshot, closed the privacy curtain, and stepped to the side of the bed. In a quiet voice, he told them the burned-out remains of a stolen panel truck with a missing front bumper had been located on a Union City industrial side street. The crash was now officially an attempted homicide investigation. He had questions for Sam and DJ before the detectives arrived, and the answers had better be truthful.

"Why is that?" Sam asked.

"Because it's in your best interest to trust me. You said earlier that you'd just been passing through town. That you'd stopped nowhere in the city." The look on O'Reilly's face made it clear he knew differently. "What were you doing here? Who did you see?"

"Tony Carlucci," Sam answered. "We asked him about his past relationship with a murder victim, Laura Neilson. He didn't appreciate the presumption that he might be a suspect."

"Sweet Mary," O'Reilly cussed. "You're that ex-ADA under investigation for murder." He turned to DJ. "Is what he just told me correct?"

DJ nodded. "Yes, every word."

"Do you know who Anthony Carlucci is?"

"Yes, we do," DJ replied. "We didn't mean to upset him."

O'Reilly shook his head in dismay. "What exactly is your relationship to Mr. Monroe?"

"We're just colleagues," DJ replied. "Also, I'm a licensed private investigator."

Sergeant O'Reilly turned his gaze on Sam. "What else were you doing in New Jersey?"

"We drove to Sussex County looking for a woman who once knew Laura Neilson as a child. We found her, but nothing came of it."

"Is that all?"

Sam nodded. "That's it."

O'Reilly paused to take in what he'd been told. "Okay, don't say anything to the detectives about meeting Carlucci. If he was behind the crash, your silence should make him believe that you got the message and he'll let the matter drop."

"And if not?" DJ asked.

"Then nobody on this side of the Hudson River can help you. Not even me."

"Are you telling us if your detectives learn about our meeting with Carlucci we could continue to be in danger?" Sam proposed.

Sergeant O'Reilly sidestepped the probe. "Just take my advice. It's in your best interest."

Sam backed off. "You've been more than helpful, Sergeant O'Reilly, and I regret being belligerent earlier."

O'Reilly shrugged. "You were rattled. Crashes do that to people. No harm done."

"I have another question, Sergeant," DJ said. "Who got us safely out of the car? I'd like to thank them."

O'Reilly nodded in Sam's direction. "Thank Mr. Monroe. From what the witnesses said, he pulled you from the vehicle just before it exploded."

DJ looked at Sam in amazement.

"Are we about done, Sergeant?" Sam asked, in no mood for any accolades. "I'd like to get Miss Ryan settled in her room."

O'Reilly nodded. "Almost. For your own safety, Mr. Monroe, I suggest you take the next ferry to Manhattan. Better yet, take a taxi."

"That's exactly what I have planned."

O'Reilly turned to DJ. "I'll soon find out if Carlucci was behind this, and let you know. Either way, a patrol officer will be posted outside until your release. It would be wise for both of you to avoid Hoboken for a while."

DJ smiled. "Thank you, Sergeant."

"No thanks needed, Miss Ryan." O'Reilly turned and left.

DJ looked at Sam. "You'll do as he said?"

"I will."

"Don't do anything without me."

"I can't promise you that."

"Thanks for saving me."

"Thanks for still being in the world," Sam replied.

"The world?" DJ questioned. "That's a pretty big place to get lost in."

"I meant in my world," Sam amended with a smile. He kissed her on the cheek and left.

CHAPTER 12

THE KID SITTING ON THE CURB IN FRONT OF SAM'S BUILDING got to his feet when the taxi slowed to a stop. No more than twelve, he looked Sam over as he stepped out onto the sidewalk.

"You Monroe?" he asked, trying to sound tough.

Sam paid the cabbie. "What's it to you?"

The kid didn't flinch. "I got a message for you from Mr. Silano. That guy Johnnie Turner you were asking about ain't with the cops anymore."

"That's it? Where is he?"

The kid shrugged. "I don't know nothing about that. Mr. Silano says don't come around bothering him anymore."

"Anything else?"

The kid nodded and popped a stick of gum in his mouth. "Yeah, he says stay away from Jersey. It ain't a good place for your health."

"Now you tell me." Sam put a fifty-cent piece in the boy's outstretched hand. "Thanks, kid."

The kid nodded and strolled away.

Sam turned and looked up. The lights were on inside his apartment, with a silhouetted figure standing at a front room window. He froze momentarily as the window opened and Mike Dalton of the DA's office stuck his head out. He ordered Sam to get his butt upstairs; he had new troubles.

*

SAM FOUND ABE SILVERSTEIN sitting at the small kitchen table, wearing house slippers, slacks, and a pajama top, so he didn't bother to ask how Dalton had gotten inside. "What kind of trouble?" he demanded instead.

Dalton leaned against the kitchen sink and explained that Sergeant Jerome Aloysius O'Reilly of the Hoboken PD had interrupted his dinner to call and tell him that a corpse had been found in the burned-out panel truck. Allegedly, new witnesses had come forward claiming that Sam had been driving the T-Bird and he had caused the accident.

"Hoboken detectives have asked a judge for an arrest warrant charging you with vehicular homicide," Mike added.

"That's crazy," Sam said.

"That's Hoboken," Mike retorted. "Same mob, just a different corrupt city."

"How did O'Reilly know to call you?" Sam asked.

"Your fame as a prime suspect in a high-profile murder case has spread far beyond the confines of Manhattan," Mike replied half-jokingly. "But on a personal note, Jerome O'Reilly is my brother-in-law, and we've talked about your predicament."

"My predicament," Sam mused. "Nicely put."

"I thought you'd like that," Mike said, laughing. "But there's more: The patrol officers outside the hospital have been pulled. Jerry said Miss Ryan left against medical advice. Her parents haven't heard from her, and he doesn't know where she is."

"I've got to find her." Sam turned for the door.

"Hold on," Mike cautioned. "First, learn what you're going up against. Tony Carlucci didn't like the idea that the family's good name might get dragged in the mud because of a past relationship he had with a high-society, sex-crazed nymphomaniac who got murdered. It's warped thinking, I know, but Tony might reach out to the Manhattan families to quelch your investigation."

"In other words, I could be walking around with a target on my back," Sam concluded glumly.

"Miss Ryan as well," Mike added. "Unless you can convince Tony to back off, I suggest you keep a low profile."

Sam shook his head. "Not without DJ."

"It's your call, but I wouldn't hang around here for too long, if I were you."

"I won't. Tell Marilyn not to give up on me."

Mike headed for the door. "The boss knows what's going on. Stay in touch, okay?"

"I will." After the door closed, Sam waited a beat and turned to Abe. "How much will you give me for everything in the apartment? You can sell it, give it away, or rent the place out furnished, I don't care."

"I'm not doing that," Abe replied. He owned the building free and clear and lived on the top floor in a corner unit. He always treated his tenants like family, and they all loved him back, including Sam.

"I can't lie low until I find DJ, and I need cash to do it."

Abe emptied his wallet and handed Sam sixty-three bucks. "It's a loan, understood? I'll stake you to more if you need it."

Sam pocketed the cash. "You're the best."

Abe waved off Sam's thanks and got to his feet. "Forget it. Just don't get yourself killed."

"That's good advice," Sam replied.

"I mean it," Abe said on his way out the door.

Sam washed up at the kitchen sink, put on a wrinkled but clean shirt, and inspected his face in the mirror by the door. The cut on his cheek looked nasty but wasn't deep. He could get by without scaring people.

DJ's purse and wallet had been consumed by the fire that destroyed the T-Bird. Sam didn't recall if her parents had given her money before leaving to find a hotel room for the night. They'd promised to return with some essentials, so maybe they'd left her a few bucks. Would it be enough for her to get home? What if she'd left the hospital with nothing? Alone and on foot, the only way to cross into Manhattan would be on the George Washington Bridge. No matter if it were day or night, if someone was looking for you, that would be risky.

He cleared his mind of worry. First, find her. The phone rang as his hand reached for the doorknob. Daniel Ryan, his tone anxious and tense, wanted to know if Sam knew where DJ was.

"I don't know, but I'm about to go find her," Sam replied. "Did you leave any money with her at the hospital?"

"No," Dr. Ryan answered.

"Where are you now?" Sam inquired.

"We've just arrived home, hoping she'd be here."

"Stay there in case she calls. You'll hear from me."

"What have you gotten DJ into?"

"She's fine, I promise," Sam replied, praying it was true. He hung up and hurried outside.

CHAPTER 13

IT WAS ONE OF THOSE RARE CLEAR NIGHTS IN THE CITY. A cool breeze swirled lazily off the harbor, coursed up the Manhattan avenues, and brushed aside the remnants of a humid day. Stars were visible in the sky and moonlight dappled the rivers. New Yorkers strolled leisurely along the sidewalks. Stoop sitters lounged and watched the human parade pass by. Kids crowded the fire escapes. Teenage boys on street corners smoked cigarettes and eyed the pretty girls. It was as if a mysterious calm had settled gently over the island.

At any other time, Sam would have loved it. Instead, he hurried to find a cab, biting back his fear that something terrible might have happened to DJ.

At her building, he had the driver wait. There was no answer at her apartment and the two neighbors he spoke to hadn't seen or heard her. On the roof, he found a discarded screwdriver next to an empty can of paint near the door well. He climbed down the fire escape, jimmied open a window to DJ's apartment, and searched every room. There were no signs of a struggle, a search, or a hurried departure. Good news, but not enough to lessen his anxiety.

Traffic was light and the cabbie got him quickly to DJ's downtown Broadway offices. The two street-side businesses were closed, and the separate entrance to the upstairs suites was locked. He leaned on the call button next to her nameplate repeatedly, with no response. He pushed all the call buttons. No luck.

The security system for the entry door operated on low-voltage electricity. The lock released when a button was pushed in any one of the offices. It served as a dead bolt but wasn't difficult to defeat. Sam used the screwdriver to pry back the latch and yank the door open.

Upstairs, the door to DJ's offices was locked. Sam didn't bother with finesse. He used the butt of the screwdriver to break the frosted glass pane, reached in, pushed the release button on the doorknob, stepped inside, and switched on the ceiling lights. Nothing appeared out of place.

DJ's inner office looked the same, but a small, unlocked corner closet held a surprise. Instead of supplies and file boxes, there was a rack of women's clothing, several pairs of shoes, plus a built-in cabinet with a drawer that contained fresh underwear, stockings, a small cosmetic purse, and a Browning nine-millimeter semiautomatic handgun with a full box of ammunition. Underneath it there was an empty case for a purse-sized twenty-five-caliber handgun.

Sam loaded the Browning, stuck it in his waistband, and pawed through the rack of clothes. On the closet floor, hidden by a long wool winter coat, were the clothes DJ had been wearing. Somehow, she'd made it back to the city, changed, armed herself, and left. But to go where? There had to be a clue.

He started with the closet and searched everything. He turned out pockets, shook shoes, and emptied all the cabinet drawers. In her office, he rummaged through the desk and looked behind the framed certificates and diplomas. He was about to move on to the reception room when he thought to look under the leather desk mat. There he found a postcard with a black-and-white photograph of the Eiffel Tower.

It was addressed to DJ, postmarked from France, and written by someone named Bunny who had just moved into a small flat on the Rue Popincourt.

The cursive handwriting was dainty, suggesting a woman, and the postcard had been mailed less than a month ago. Bunny wrote she was enrolled in a Paris art school and taking private lessons to improve her French. She thanked DJ for being such a dear and sent along hugs and kisses.

A "dear" about what? Sam wondered. And who was Bunny? Sam paged through an address book from the top drawer of the desk and found a listing for Beatrice "Bunny" Terrell on a Greenwich Village side street close to Washington Square. Her phone was no longer in service.

He hopped a taxi, had the cabbie drop him off a few blocks from Bunny's address, and approached it with caution. It was on a narrow street that contained a row of four-story, mid–nineteenth century Greek revival town houses. Lights showed in the windows on all the floors.

Sam climbed the ornate wrought-iron staircase to the front door expecting to find a number of apartment call buttons, but there was only one. He pushed it and DJ opened the door.

"What took you so long?" she teased.

Sam waved Bunny's postcard at her. "I'm just a slow learner. How the hell did you manage to get back into the city?"

"I traded the night nurse my diamond stud earrings for a twenty-dollar bill and the promise that I wouldn't ask for them back." She hurried him inside and closed the front door.

Rooms radiated off either side of the spacious circular foyer, and two large abstract paintings dominated the walls, one by Jackson Pollock, the other by Willem de Kooning.

"Exactly who is Bunny Terrell?" he asked.

"Her mother is a Guggenheim," DJ replied.

"That explains a lot. How did you know to run?"

"Sergeant O'Reilly left a message for me with the charge nurse that the officers outside were no longer there. That's all I needed to hear."

DJ led him into a large reception room filled with comfortable chairs arranged around a Danish modern coffee table piled high with art books and gallery exhibition catalogues.

"We're safe here," she added, as she sank into a chair. "I need to stop talking for a while."

"Are you all right?"

"Tired. Hungry. A little shaky."

"Where's the kitchen?"

"Cross the foyer, through the dining room. Can't miss it. You can cook?"

"I'll see what's in the pantry. Stay put."

"I'll be right here," she replied wearily.

The kitchen was large enough to accommodate a half dozen chefs and their assistants. As he expected, there was nothing useful in the refrigerator. Sam explored the walk-in pantry and gathered up all that he needed to prepare a macaroni and tuna salad. An adjacent wine cabinet held an excellent selection of French vintages. He chose a Chablis.

When the pasta was cooked, he put the salad together and brought it on a serving tray to the reception room, where DJ was half-asleep in her chair. They were both hungry and tired, so there was little desire for conversation. The Chablis only added to their growing lassitude.

Sam did a quick kitchen cleanup and found DJ asleep when he returned. He carried her to an upstairs bedroom, covered her with blankets from a hallway linen closet, and stretched out beside her on the bed. Brain-weary, he wondered what he was missing. Impugning the moral character of a mob boss didn't stack up as a sufficient reason to get them killed. There had to be something else going on to make Tony Carlucci want them erased. But what?

And then there was ex-cop Johnnie Turner, who believed he had good reason to kill him. All of it was surely enough to worry anyone. He fell asleep anyway.

CHAPTER 14

DJ WAS STILL SLEEPING WHEN SAM WOKE UP NEXT TO HER. The bruise on her forehead had shrunk, the swelling around her black eye had lessened, and her face had gained good color. Downstairs in the kitchen, he made coffee, splashed water on his face, and left to find a neighborhood market, where he bought enough food to last them a couple of days. As he unloaded the bags in the kitchen, DJ appeared fresh from the shower, wearing a robe, her hair wrapped in a towel.

"I smell coffee," she said.

Sam smiled and poured her a cup. "Good morning. Breakfast will be served in the dining room in fifteen minutes."

"Good. That gives me time to get dressed and put on my face." She turned, cup in hand, and left.

When she reappeared, she was dressed in slacks and a lightweight wool sweater she'd found in Bunny Terrell's walk-in closet, which were a little baggy. In her hand was an antique glass jar filled with coins.

"Pocket change," she said. "I found it in Bunny's bedroom on her dressing table." She dug into her breakfast with gusto, which Sam took to be a particularly good sign.

Finished, she put her empty plate aside and said, "I have to find a telephone and call my parents."

"I called your father on the way to the market. He knows you're okay, but doesn't know where we are. When I refused to explain why, he used some choice words to describe my lineage."

DJ laughed. "He's always been a little overprotective. What is it you're not telling me?"

"A lot." He laid out the discovery of the dead body in the burned-out panel truck, the emergence of *new* witnesses who swore he'd been driving the T-Bird, and a pending warrant for his arrest on vehicular homicide charges.

DJ shook her head. "This is crazy. What did we do to rattle Carlucci's cage? It has to be connected to Laura, but how?"

"Perhaps she had something in her possession that Carlucci doesn't want made public," Sam proposed. "Something tangible he believes may have survived her death."

"Were there any signs of a search of Laura's apartment when you found her?"

"No."

"Can we even be sure Carlucci is behind this?" DJ pondered.

"If he wasn't, everything Sergeant O'Reilly told us would be called into question."

"I think that's improbable," DJ said. "So it has to be Carlucci."

"There's another possibility: Johnnie Turner, who wants to kill me for destroying his career. It's likely he killed Susan Cogan. He's quit the department and gone underground."

"Does he have ties to Carlucci?" DJ asked.

"Unknown," Sam answered. "But his father's name was Tartaglione before he changed it to Turner."

"Let's keep Turner as an open possibility until we find out more," DJ proposed. "We'll start with Laura and dig deeper."

"But not today," Sam countered. "First, we need a plan." He handed her the morning newspaper. "Turn to the police blotter page. There was a break-in at your office last night. According to your secretary, nothing was taken."

"You broke in?"

"I was in a hurry to find you."

"Amateur," DJ chided.

"When it comes to picking locks, I agree. I'll pay you back for the broken window after I get a job. That's if I can stay out of prison. Are you steady enough to pull KP? I need to go out for a while."

"And do what?" she demanded.

"Collect Laura's private diary that I have stashed in a Penn Station luggage locker. I want you to look at it. Maybe you'll be able to catch something I've missed."

DJ cocked an eyebrow. "Never mind, I won't ask how you came by it."

Sam pushed back from the table. "Good. I'm gone, be back soon. By the way, you look good in Bunny's slacks."

"No, I don't, but thanks for the compliment. If she wore my size, I'd loot her wardrobe before we leave. She has so many lovely outfits to choose from that I couldn't possibly afford."

*

SAM MADE A HURRIED trip to Penn Station without detecting any tail or surveillance. Still, he varied his return route and backtracked slightly twice just to be sure. At Bunny's, he sat across from DJ in a cozy, richly appointed study off the reception room as she paged through Laura's diary, responding to her occasional questions.

She wanted to know what the series of small dots meant that were next to the names of Laura's lovers. There were ones, twos, threes, and fours. Sam's entry had only one dot. His was the only one.

"I have no idea," he replied.

"Let's assume one meant the best," DJ suggested.

"I like that idea, but 'best' at what? Being a dupe? Or a plaything?"

"Don't be so self-effacing," DJ chided. "Carlucci earned a four. The only four."

"If your ranking about the meaning of the dots is correct, that can't be good."

DJ tapped her finger on the diary. "The men you spoke to, did any of them other than Carlucci strike you as the violent type?"

"No, and I focused on that possibility, but I could have missed it."

"No gut feeling?"

"Thinking back, no."

DJ drummed her fingers and sighed. "I'm missing something too, but I don't know what."

"Take a guess."

"It's about her, not the men. Her diary entries are so visual, you can picture what she describes." DJ's expression lit up. "That's it; photographs. Did she ever take snapshots of you?"

"Occasionally. She'd had this folding camera, German-made, I think. She'd grab it from a sideboard or a shelf and take snapshots of me. I never saw any of them."

"Why not?"

"She said the lab ruined the prints, or she'd misplaced the roll of film, or none of them came out the way she wanted."

DJ laughed. "That's priceless. Laura's father gave her a camera when she was in fifth grade, and she was soon taking pictures of everything and everybody. She almost never went out without it. She got so good, he bought her a more expensive model and had a darkroom built so she could develop her own prints. After that, she said that she'd never use a commercial film lab again."

She looked at Sam. "I bet she had a darkroom somewhere. At the penthouse, perhaps?"

"It's not there, as far as I know."

"Any framed photographs on the walls?"

Sam nodded. "Several nice black-and-white prints of Central Park and the Hudson River, but she never claimed them as her work."

"I can't imagine a reason for her to stop," DJ said. "She enjoyed it so much. When I was with her during holidays and vacations throughout high school and college, she was always carrying around a camera, snapping street scenes or surreptitiously taking photographs of unsuspecting ordinary people."

"Okay, let's assume Laura took photographs that Carlucci wants found and destroyed," Sam suggested. "We won't know unless we can discover what they might be. I spent a lot of time with Laura in her penthouse, and there was no darkroom."

"No secret hidey-hole that she told you about?" DJ queried.

"No, and I never thought to even consider the possibility. But I recall that Dr. Birkenfield, Laura's childhood psychiatrist, told me Laura's trust owned the entire property. The darkroom could be elsewhere in the building."

DJ's expression brightened. "We have to go and look," she declared. "Aside from Sergeant O'Reilly, who knew that Carlucci might be gunning for us?"

"O'Reilly's brother-in-law, Mike Dalton, was waiting at my apartment to warn me when I got home. He's a DA investigator I worked with. He said my old boss, Marilyn Feinstein, also knew what was happening."

"Are they trustworthy?"

Sam nodded. "Definitely. They've been backing me up all the way since Laura's murder."

"No one else?"

"Sal Silano, a mob-connected pickpocket, sent a kid to tell me it would be unhealthy to return to Hoboken anytime soon. So the word on the street might well be that I don't have a bright and shiny future."

DJ rolled her eyes and wanted to know how Sal figured in. Sam explained he'd cashed in a favor owed to a friend for Sal's help finding the whereabouts of Johnnie Turner.

"The Carlucci incident has derailed that," he noted. "And Sal's pint-sized envoy warned me I was not to bother him again."

"So where do we start?"

"Now that we might have a suspect, we need to concentrate on solving Laura's murder. Besides, Johnnie Turner's going to come looking for me, so why bother looking for him? I'll just have to be ready when he finds me."

"Is that smart?"

"He's a thug and not too bright. I should be able to see him coming. Do you have a better idea?" he countered.

"I do, but it has nothing to do with our current dilemma." She moved to where Sam was sitting and unzipped his fly. He quickly grew hard. "I see that you agree with me."

"Indeed I do."

"I think we should rest up and recover from our recent ordeal before we go to Laura's."

"You make a compelling argument," Sam said, reaching for her.

CHAPTER 15

LATER IN THE DAY, THEY DISCUSSED WAYS TO GAIN ACCESS to Laura's building. DJ asked about the lock to the service entrance door, which Sam described as a keyed doorknob. With a locksmith kit retrieved from her office, she'd have no problem with it.

She wanted to know the layout of the basement. Sam sketched it out. The super's office was just off the entrance, followed by a large mechanical room, a utility closet, a trash and garbage collection area, a lavatory for employee use, and a series of padlocked storage rooms that ran the length of the corridor, which ended at the freight elevator.

DJ consulted Laura's diary. On a page reserved for important dates, she'd recorded a series of three letters and numbers, most likely the combination for a padlock.

"If she did have a darkroom in the basement, she probably kept it secured. She would also need access to water. Chances are it will be right next to a janitor's closet or an employee lavatory."

Sam asked if they'd have enough time to search both the penthouse and the basement. DJ said they should try to do both. Why risk getting arrested on two separate felony breaking-and-entering charges when they could combine it into one?

They waited until nightfall before leaving for DJ's office. A thick carpet of low clouds smothered the island, obscuring the tops of tall buildings, trapping the lingering odor of garbage and pollution. A dusting of soot blurred the streetlights, dulled traffic signals, and blunted the headlights of passing vehicles, making the night appear vaguely mysterious.

The stopped at a pay phone so DJ could call and reassure her parents. They took a circuitous route to DJ's office by subway, taxi, and on foot, looking for a tail and seeing none. Outside the building, before they approached the entrance, they waited in shadows until certain there was no streetside surveillance. Upstairs, they found the broken office door window covered with a thin piece of plywood. Sam pried it off, reached in, and opened the door.

In her office, DJ got a small locksmith kit from a desk drawer and plucked a card for Walt Seaver from her desktop Rolodex. Seaver was private investigator who was expert at tracking people, and she'd used him on several missing persons cases.

"If anyone in the city can locate Johnnie Turner, he can," she explained. "I'll call him in the morning."

Keeping a careful eye out for tails, they walked several blocks before hailing a cab, which dropped them off at the corner of Laura's address. As they strolled past the glass lobby door, Sam expected to see Carl DeAngelo on duty. Instead, it was Albert Guzman, the senior member of the crew who usually worked days.

DJ had no trouble picking the service door lock. Inside, the combination from Laura's diary worked perfectly on the storeroom padlock, and the open door revealed a fully equipped darkroom. A four-drawer metal file cabinet contained folders of photographs which were identified by subject, location, and year. Sam and DJ went through them quickly, one by one, setting aside photos of landscapes, concentrating on those of people and places.

A freestanding bookcase contained various camera lenses, light meters, tripods, and supplies. By the time they were finished, they'd assembled a packet of more than a hundred black-and-white images that stretched from recent times back to Laura's childhood.

Some of the people DJ could identify, most she could not. There were several of DJ that Laura had taken while they'd been teenagers ice-skating in Central Park during a Christmas holiday. One, a close-up, captured DJ's radiant smile and laughing eyes.

There were headshots of Sam, along with some of Laura's former lovers that he could identify, but none of Carlucci. There was nothing amateurish about Laura's work. She had a keen eye for composition and a knack for catching her subjects unawares.

In the back of the bottom file cabinet drawer was a scrapbook filled with commercially processed snapshots taken at the New Jersey farm where Laura had first become interested in photography. It also included some pencil drawings and sketches of places and people on the farm, all carefully labeled in Laura's neat penmanship.

Three cameras on a shelf held no film, and there were no exposed rolls to be found. They gathered everything up, put it in a tote bag DJ had grabbed from under the sink, and locked up. To keep Albert unaware of their presence, they avoided the elevators and took the stairs to the penthouse.

DJ made quick work of the door lock. Inside, the large alcove was empty of furnishings and wall art. A stack of packing boxes lined the entryway wall. In the living area, the couch, chairs, and tables had been moved to the center of the room. Table lamps and shades had been packed in sealed and labeled boxes, and paintings and framed photographs were carefully crated.

"Looks like we got here just in time," DJ said.

They went through the rooms methodically, only to find that drawers, closets, and shelves had been emptied. It made no sense to waste time searching through the packed and sealed boxes. Instead, they concentrated on the furniture, looking for concealed or hidden items tacked or taped to the undersides.

In the back of the empty walk-in master closet, DJ cracked open a locked small wall safe that contained a jewelry bag with five rolls of undeveloped thirty-five-millimeter film. They added it to the photographs and scrapbook in the tote bag and quietly left by the stairwell. To the east, false dawn had touched the sky.

They decided to split up, DJ back to Bunny's with the material they'd collected. She would call Walt Seaver along the way, while Sam tracked down the night doorman, Carl DeAngelo. He had more questions to ask him about the night Laura had been murdered.

"We make a pretty good team, don't we?" she said as they stood at the corner of the block waiting for a cruising taxi to appear.

"I'm beginning to think so," Sam answered. "In more ways than one."

NIGHT IN THE CITY

That earned him a kiss before she turned on her heel and whistled down a cab.

Sam was impressed. He could never whistle like that.

He went back to Laura's building, and walked through the unlocked front door, where Albert Guzman greeted him with a stiff-handed stop-where-you-are gesture. A jockey in his youth, Albert was in his sixties, stood five-foot-five, and was only a few pounds over his riding weight.

"You're not allowed in the building, Mr. Monroe. Orders of management."

"I was hoping to speak to Carl," Sam said agreeably. "He must be off duty. I'll try to see him another time."

"What do you want with him?"

"Just to talk. I'm trying to find Miss Neilson's killer, and he might have some helpful information."

"He's already talked to the police. Everybody that works here has."

"Does that include you?"

"Yeah," Albert answered.

"Did you have anything useful to tell them?"

"Just that I didn't think anybody in the building killed Miss Neilson. You get to know a lot about people as they come and go, ask for small favors, or show their gratitude. None of them had anything against her—and not the employees either."

"Is Carl sick?"

Albert shrugged. "I don't know. I've been covering his shift the last two days. He hasn't called in. That's not like him, and he isn't answering his phone. I'm worried about him. If he doesn't show by tomorrow night, he'll lose his job."

"If you know where he lives, I'll tell him to get in touch."

"That would be great." He consulted a pocket notebook and wrote down Carl's address and phone number. "He lives with his sister. Have him call me right away."

"I will." It was a Queens address, close to LaGuardia Airport. "Thanks, Albert. What's going to happen to Miss Neilson's penthouse apartment?"

"The family is moving everything into storage. It's gonna be put in tiptop condition and then leased. East Side housing is tight and there's already people asking about it. Plus it's a choice location in a good building, with great views."

"Yes, it is," Sam said. He thanked Albert again, and went in search of a cab, thinking that one of the reasons the rich stayed that way was by never being sentimental about anything or anybody.

He flagged a taxi down within a few minutes. Traffic was building but still manageable, and he was quickly in Queens at Carl DeAngelo's residence standing outside a police barricade, looking at the burned-out ruins of a small detached two-story house with a collapsed roof.

It was not what he'd expected. He glanced at the house next door. It was cut from the same working-class subdivision mold that had been carved out of the Queens marshland in the early twenties. The front-room curtains were open, and a visible console TV cast a pale, flickering light across the room. Surely the neighbor would know what had happened.

Sam walked over and rang the bell. The man who answered was short, balding, and middle-aged. He wore fuzzy bunny slippers and held a mug of coffee in his hand. Sam introduced himself and said he was looking for Carl DeAngelo, a friend of his.

"Don't you know what happened next door?" the man asked.

Sam shook his head. He'd skipped over the article in the morning newspaper and hadn't listened to the radio or watched TV since leaving with DJ for New Jersey. "I've been out of town."

"Carl, his sister, her two kids, and her boyfriend died in the fire. Fire department says it doesn't look suspicious. They haven't announced the victims' names yet."

"Did you know Carl well?"

The man nodded. "For years. We'd have a beer together regularly, watch a game at the bar with the guys, and the wife had him over for dinner a lot. He was a good guy."

He said Carl had been about to leave the city for Las Vegas to start a new life. "Tragic for this to happen. You know what I mean?"

"I do. Did he say what he was going to do in Las Vegas?"

"A doorman's job at one of the big casinos. With tips, he'd double his income, and the rents were cheap out there."

Sam asked if he knew who'd offered the job to Carl.

The man shook his head. "He didn't say how he learned about it. How do you know Carl?"

"I'm the property manager of the apartment building where he works," Sam lied. "I've been concerned when he stopped showing up for his shifts."

He thanked the man and left to find the nearest subway station back to the city. On a train crowded with commuters, some still half-asleep, he thought about what Albert Guzman had said. Was he worried about Carl because he was AWOL, or was it something else? He'd have to ask.

He left the train at a crosstown stop and transferred to a downtown local that was filled with noisy teenagers on their way to school.

He stood near an exit door, hanging on to a strap, wondering what memories they'd have when they grew up. His were filled with vague remembrances of frequent moves, new schools, no long-lasting friendships, and the loneliness of being an only child of parents obsessed with their own desires and aspirations.

He shook it off. First Laura's murder, then Susan Cogan's brutal killing, followed by an automobile crash that almost killed DJ, and now Carl, his sister, and her family, burned up in a house fire. What kind of voodoo was going on? It bedeviled him all the way to his stop.

CHAPTER 16

AT BUNNY'S, SAM DISCOVERED THE RESIDENT POPULATION
had doubled. Seated with DJ at the dining room table was Walt Seaver,
the private dick she'd hired to find Johnnie Turner. Also present was
DJ's buxom, middle-aged receptionist, who was introduced as Delores
Stedman. She had the steady gaze of a woman who took guff from
no one.

Walt Seaver was a surprise. No more than thirty, with a wild mop
of curly hair and big ears that looked pinned flat against his head, he
could pass for an underfed graduate student who would fall over dead
if he tried to run a hundred-yard dash. He said that he needed to learn
everything Sam knew about Johnnie Turner in order to get started.
He was eager to begin.

Sam politely put him off and pulled DJ aside to the kitchen. "Why
are these people here?" he demanded. "This is supposed to be a safe
place where we won't be found."

"We *are* perfectly safe, unless you let somebody follow you," she
replied snappishly "Besides, we need their help."

Delores had been recruited to take the exposed film rolls to a commercial lab to have them developed. She would wait there and return
with the prints. Additionally, she'd cash DJ's bank check from the
office account to pay for the quick turnaround service and get them
some money for expenses.

"We can't get by on Bunny's pocket change alone," she noted.

"I'll pony up my share when I can," Sam promised. He filled her in
on the house fire in Queens that killed Carl and his sister's family, and
what he'd learned from the conversation with Carl's neighbor.

"It can't possibly be coincidental," DJ remarked. "Carlucci?"

"He's our strongest candidate."

"God, I hope we're wrong," DJ mused.

"That's a lot of muscle to go up against," Sam noted as he looked at the table in the dining room. The surface had been transformed into a photo gallery of all the prints they had taken from Laura's darkroom, neatly laid out. Studying each one carefully for people and places to identify would take time. Laura's handwritten margin notes on many of them should be helpful.

Walt Seaver stepped in front of Sam to get his attention and asked, "Can I talk to you now?"

"You bet."

They adjourned to a reception room, where Seaver questioned Sam extensively about Johnnie Turner. He took no notes and, when finished, he sat silently staring off into space so intently that Sam felt compelled not to disturb him.

"Several comments," Walt finally said. "If Turner willingly quit the department, he shouldn't be hard to find. Probably he still hangs out at an old haunt or two. If not, then I'll find out who has him on a short leash and where he's parked. That could take some time."

"Understood."

"Additionally, if Turner did kill Susan Cogan as you intimated, why did he act so precipitously?"

"What are you suggesting?" Sam asked.

"It seems to me that he may have been tipped off about the victim's immediate departure from the city. Otherwise, why risk a daylight attack with a police presence outside her building? Who knew of your arrangement with Commissioner Key?"

"You're thinking there was a leak," Sam hypothesized.

"I am," Seaver said. "Any ideas?"

Sam sat back and thought about it. "I'm not sure."

And he wasn't, but there were the others directly involved in the dirty cop sting operation, including Marilyn Feinstein, Mike Dalton, and U.S. Deputy Marshal Eddie Snyder. And what about the detectives who interrogated him right after his initial meeting with Key in his limo? Or the officers on stakeout the night they took Turner and Shift

Sergeant Hanrahan down in Susan's apartment? And then there was Key's headquarters team that coordinated the sweep. Finally, there was also DJ, whom Sam had told everything.

"What are you thinking?" Walt probed.

"The day Susan Cogan was killed, I spent hours waiting to meet with Commissioner Key about her money, and more time waiting to get the actual renegotiated cash delivered to me. If I'd been given the payment promptly, she might have left before Turner showed up to kill her."

"If it was Turner," Walt reminded him. "Do you think Key stalled you deliberately?"

"No, but I'm starting to believe that nobody's trustworthy."

"Among the people who might have tipped off Susan Cogan's killer, does anyone stand out?"

Sam shook his head. "But there are a number of faceless people I never really met who knew exactly what was going down."

Seaver stood. "I'll start at Turner's old precinct. Surely somebody knows where he liked to hang out after work. Do you know anything about his personal life?"

Sam shook his head. "Only that he's Italian. His father changed the family name from Tartaglione to Turner."

"Not unusual," Walt noted. "But I imagine not every Tartaglione anglicized their surname. I'll keep it in mind."

Sam gave Seaver an appraising look. The man was smart, asked good questions, and didn't miss a trick. "What got you into the PI business?" he asked. "You sure don't fit the mold."

Walt laughed. "That often works to my advantage. I dropped out of my Ph.D. coursework in mathematics because of sheer boredom. I may eventually return if I grow tired of finding missing persons. For now, I'm on an extended, all-but-dissertation sabbatical."

"Be careful out there," Sam warned.

"From what you've told me, I'm inclined to take your advice seriously," Seaver said.

"I'm serious, be careful."

"Always," Seaver replied.

*

THERE WAS NO TELEPHONE service at Bunny's. Walt left with a promise to return by nighttime with a progress report. Delores had departed on her errands, and DJ was alone in the dining room studying a black-and-white photograph of a vague outline of an automobile parked at the foot of distant sandhills.

She handed Sam a magnifying glass. "I can't clearly make out the car. You try."

It was a convertible, but Sam couldn't identify it. A sports car, postwar production, not American-made. "Why this photograph?" he asked.

"It's from Laura's Las Vegas file," DJ answered. "And it's the only one different from all the others. The rest are just snapshots of the casinos along the strip. Casual vacation pictures, not at all like her usual carefully composed work."

"Are you sure it was taken in Las Vegas?"

DJ sighed. "I don't know, I've never been there. Are there sandhills in Las Vegas?" She plucked the magnifying glass from Sam's hands and dropped it on the tabletop. "This isn't getting us anywhere."

"Let's keep looking," Sam proposed.

Several hours passed with no success. Delores's return with news that the film canisters could not be developed until the following morning soured their already unhappy mood. She gave DJ her bank envelope of cash and left to supervise repairs to the office door. She'd be back early in the morning with the prints.

They'd been up all the night before, and were bleary-eyed, worn out, and unmotivated. DJ dug in her heels, called for a break, and went off to take a nap. Sam stretched out on a couch in the library and promptly fell asleep. When he awoke, day had turned to night, and he wondered what the fuck he was doing.

Commissioner Key had virtually given him a free pass, the mayor had agreed to stay on the sidelines, the police chief had made it known there were other persons of interest in the case, and the DA had announced that he was currently not prepared to prosecute anyone for Laura's murder.

He could walk away from the whole mess and hope that it blew over. Leave the city and start fresh somewhere else. On his way out of town, he'd get a message to Carlucci and ask him to call off the wolves. He knew nothing—*nothing*—that would ever cause him concern. Ditto DJ.

Sam shook his head. Bad idea. It wasn't unreasonable to believe that the police department might be corrupt all the way up to the commissioner's office. And if Stephen Watts Key, the great hope for reform, was dirty, Sam had simply played into his hand. Was the city's criminal justice system that rotten?

He couldn't stomach the idea of Laura's killer going free. She'd been as flawed as he was, only in different ways. Everybody was broken in one or two places, and the residual damage you carried was always uniquely yours alone.

He was about to go looking through the house for DJ when the front doorbell rang. He opened up to a worried-looking taxi driver pointing at his cab, which was idling at the curb. "The guy's hurt bad," he said. "Said for me to bring him here."

Sam hurried down for a look. Walt Seaver was hunched over on the backseat, face bloody, clutching his gut. He didn't look good.

"Pay the cabbie," Walt whispered, "and take me to a hospital."

"Right away," Sam promised. He told the cabbie to wait, went back inside, grabbed the semiautomatic, some cash from the bank envelope, and ordered the driver to take them to the nearest hospital. On the short drive, he learned Walt had waved the cabbie down near Dino's Diner in Little Italy, crawled into the backseat, told him where he needed to go, and collapsed.

Walt lost consciousness; his pulse was weak and his breathing shallow. In the emergency room, surrounded by staff, he was rushed into an examination room. Sam waited anxiously in the lobby. Long minutes passed before a doctor called him over.

"Your friend took a beating but is going to make it," he said. "He's got some cracked ribs and deep bruises to his torso, along with a broken nose that I reset, and several loose teeth. He's conscious and on a mild painkiller."

"I need to see him," Sam said, relieved it hadn't been worse.

The doctor motioned in the direction of the admitting counter. "He had no identification with him, so first you need to get him registered. He'll be in an observation room down the hall. I'm going to keep him overnight."

"Thanks, Doc."

"We'll take good care of him."

Sam rushed through the paperwork and found Walt alert and coherent, though the bandaged broken nose made it hard for him to breathe and talk simultaneously. He told Sam what had happened in spurts. A trusted police informant had told him that Turner had been on a prodigious drinking spree since quitting the force, hitting all the bars and saloons in Little Italy.

Throughout the day, Seaver had tracked Turner to every dive and beer joint he'd canvassed in the neighborhood until he'd spotted him entering Dino's Diner late in the afternoon. Walt staked out the place, waiting for Turner to emerge, and when Turner failed to show, Walt went inside to investigate, but the man had vanished.

Outside, he questioned two young street kids who loitered at the corner playing pitch-pennies against the wall of the diner. Walt described Turner and asked them if they'd seen him. The older boy nodded and pointed to a service entrance in a narrow alleyway behind Dino's.

Walt threw the kid a quarter, entered the alley, and got knocked sideways by the blow to his belly that put him on his knees. Turner worked him over until Walt admitted he'd been hired by Sam to find him. Turner wanted more information, but Walt clammed up. Turner hammered him in the kidneys, abdomen, and face until he passed out. He woke up face down in his own vomit, his wallet and ID gone.

"Sorry, Sam," he said.

"Don't be. You did great. I'm sorry you had to take a beating on my account." He put a sawbuck in Walt's hand. "The doc is keeping you overnight. When you get released, take a taxi to Bunny's. If I'm not there, fill DJ in on what happened."

"What are you going to do?"

"Pay Johnnie Turner a visit, now I know where to look."

"Be careful."

"I thought you'd say that."

Walt tried to smile, and winced. "I couldn't resist."

At the hospital entrance a fine dark mist had dampened the street. He grabbed a taxi and sat back, the semiautomatic pressing against his spine. Would he kill Johnnie Turner? He wasn't sure, but from here on out, he'd no longer play nice.

CHAPTER 17

IN SPITE OF THE CHILLY NIGHTTIME MIST, MULBERRY STREET in the heart of Little Italy was hopping. Clam shops, restaurants, and pizza joints had people waiting outside for tables. Locals roamed the open markets and drinking establishments. Import stores catering to the tourist trade, many drawn by the lure of the Mafia mystique, were crowded.

If Walt Seaver was right, Johnnie Turner was hiding nearby right under the nose of the chief of police in the Great White Castle. If he was hiding at all.

Pedestrians streamed past Dino's Diner, but there were no anxious patrons waiting for admission. The kid loafing near the entrance was the same tough-acting, prepubescent delinquent who'd delivered Sal's warning message to Sam outside his building. There were no thugs, wise guys, radio cars, or beat cops to be seen, which meant Dino's was police-protected territory.

Before the kid looked up and recognized him, Sam picked him up by the collar, marched him to the middle of the block, and shoved him into a dark recess that led to a closed religious gift shop.

"What's your name, kid?" Sam tightened his grip on his neck.

"What's it to you?" the kid retorted.

Sam showed him the Browning. "Let's try again, and this time be nice. What's your name?"

The boy's eyes widened. "Marco."

"Okay, Marco, make this easy on yourself. Is Mr. Silano inside Dino's?"

Marco shook his head. "No."

"Where is he right now?"

"How should I know?"

Sam returned the Browning to his waistband. "No backsliding, Marco. You only get one more chance. Where is Sal, and don't tell me where he might be."

"Home, I guess."

"And where exactly is that?"

Marco sputtered out an address. "I swear to God that's where he lives. Let me go, okay?"

"Does anybody else live with him?"

"His wife, Lucille. Everybody calls her Lucy."

"Describe her."

"Younger than Sal. Maybe like my mom's age. Pretty. Curly blond hair."

"Is that all you can tell me about her?"

"Her father owns a funeral home."

"What's the name of it?"

"I don't know, cross my heart."

"If you've lied to me, or you try to tip Silano off, I will find you. You don't want me to do that, do you?" For emphasis, Sam patted the semiautomatic with his free hand.

Marco's jaw trembled. "You'd shoot me?"

"Is it worth it for you to find out?"

Marco shook his head vigorously.

Sam eased the pressure. "Go home, Marco, and think about whether you really want to be a watchdog for the mob the rest of your young life." He stuck a dollar bill in Marco's shirt pocket.

Marco scrambled down the sidewalk as fast as he could run. Sam felt a twinge of guilt for his heavy-handed treatment. But he wanted Marco to think long and hard before trying to warn Sal.

The gift shop window contained framed prints of Jesus Christ, the pope, and various important saints. There were statues of the Virgin Mary, scented candles, crosses, wall platters with images of the Holy Father, and icons of other venerated subjects. At the corner of the display, a sign advertised a weekly bingo party in the local parish hall, and tonight was the night.

Korea had wiped out the last remnants of Sam's on-again, off-again childhood exposure to Christianity. But if Marco was religious, by some miracle the kid might turn out all right.

He paged through a directory at a public pay phone; there was no listing for Sal. At the address the kid had spurted out, Sam discovered a small two-story brick town house bracketed by large tenement apartment buildings with upper-floor fire escapes fronting the street.

Sam gave Sal's domicile a good look. He doubted a one-armed pickpocket could afford such a home on the income of wallets and purses clipped from unsuspecting citizens and tourists. More likely, he was a low-level capo in the family, running his own band of merry men, and paying protection to the cops.

There were no lights visible behind the closed window drapes and no sign of a sentry. The few folks walking by didn't look suspicious. He was about to circle the block to avoid drawing any onlookers' attention when three women rounded the corner. They paused briefly in front of Sal's house, where the curly-headed woman of the trio waved a goodbye from the front door, unlocked it, and went inside. Her two companions continued leisurely down the block to the corner and disappeared from sight.

Glimmers of light showed at the fringes of the first-floor window curtains. A few minutes later, lights came on upstairs. He wasn't sure if Sal was home or not. But based on Marco's description, the curly-headed woman was his wife.

Sam had planned to lean on Sal to get to Johnnie. But it would be easier and smarter to get what he wanted, without any muscle, from Mrs. Sal.

He crossed the street, rang the doorbell, and waited. Finally, the woman with the curly blond hair opened the front door. She eyed him curiously.

"Are you Mrs. Salino?" Sam asked.

"Yes." Her expression remained inquisitive. "Who are you?"

"Oliver Chanute," Sam lied apologetically. "I don't mean to be impolite. A young boy on the street told me your name and said you might know the whereabouts of an old Marine buddy of mine, Al Tartaglione."

"What boy?"

"His name was Marco. I didn't get his last name. I paid him a dollar for the information." He added that he was in the city on business for the next two days and had wanted to look up his pal before he left. "I lost his address," he added apologetically. "I was hoping you could help me."

Lucy Silano's expression turned slightly suspicious. "I don't know anyone by that name. You said this kid Marco sent you to see me?"

"No, to speak to your husband. I'm hoping he knows Al. Will he be home soon?"

"I'm sorry, mister, I think Marco took you for a ride." She closed the door in Sam's face.

So much for taking an indirect approach, Sam thought glumly, his stomach rumbling. At a Mulberry Street pizzeria he had a couple of slices and a beer and considered what he'd learned. Exactly nothing, other than that Sal wasn't home and Lucy's family ran a human disposal parlor, which in an ironic way made sense. The mob controlled the Department of Sanitation, so why not the city's funeral businesses as well?

Who would know the most about neighborhood funeral homes? Priests came to mind. He looked at the wall clock. He'd passed a Catholic church on his way to the pizzeria. Chances were good bingo night was still going on.

He got there just as the last of the parishioners were leaving. A middle-aged Franciscan friar sat at the head table packing up and tallying the take for the night.

He smiled pleasantly as Sam approached and asked if he could help. Sam replied that he was looking for an old Marine friend from the neighborhood named Al Tartaglione.

The friar smiled sadly. "No, I'm sorry, I don't know him."

"Do you know anybody else with that surname?"

"Not personally, but Rocco Benedetti might. His departed mother was a Tartaglione before she married." He made the sign of the cross.

"Where can I find Mr. Benedetti?"

"At the Benedetti Funeral Home on Grand Street. He and his wife live above it."

Sam thanked the friar and left, thinking how easy detective work was when you found the right person and asked the right questions.

With the cops looking for Johnnie, a family-friendly funeral parlor might be about the best place to hide out. Sam quickened his pace and headed for Grand Street. Johnnie Turner just might be within reach.

*

THE ORNATE LETTERING ON an awning above an Italianate entrance and a bronze plaque next to the hand-carved double doors discreetly announced the Benedetti family undertaking business. The black hearse parked in a reserved space was locked and empty. A loading dock, an overhead garage door, and side entrance at the rear of the building provided egress for both the living and the dead. Other than the glow from apartment windows above, a dim outside light fixture provided the only illumination. Everything was locked up tight.

Hoping Johnnie Turner hadn't retired early for the night, Sam hunkered down behind several smelly garbage cans. He didn't want to think what might be in them. Time passed slowly. A block away, express trains on the Third Avenue El clanked and clattered until the night deepened. Soon the tracks would be torn down and sold for scrap.

Eventually all the apartments went dark. A languishing chill to the air settled like an invisible weight on his shoulders. The sky, bleak and starless, seemed compressed into a thin ribbon by the height of the surrounding buildings.

Unhappily, he considered the possibility that Turner wasn't going to show. Since he knew Sam was looking for him, the element of surprise was almost nil. He wondered if he'd muffed his only good chance to catch him unawares. Worse yet, what if Turner wasn't bunking at the undertaker's?

Occasional footsteps on the street approached and receded. All fell quiet again, until the sound of a car broke the silence. He called it a night when the lights came on in the apartment above the mortuary. Stiff and sore, and in desperate need of coffee and some food, he walked to Third Avenue in search of an eatery. Sam had his hand on the door of a delicatessen when he spotted Turner inside at the counter paying his bill.

He retreated to the shadows under the El, and when Turner emerged he followed him down Grand Street, heading straight for the Benedetti Funeral Home. Before he could close the gap, a familiar voice rang out from across the street.

"Over here, Johnnie," Lieutenant Jack Osborne said. "You're late."

"Give me a break," Turner griped sarcastically as he hurried across the street. Sam stopped, retreated, and watched the two men talk. He couldn't hear what they were saying, but the conversation appeared amicable. Whatever the subject, it made Turner laugh. Suddenly Osborne shot him twice in the head, checked to make sure he was dead, took his wristwatch and wallet, and calmly walked away.

Sam fled in the opposite direction, found a vantage point on the stairs to a basement apartment, and waited for the cops to arrive. Lights at the Benedetti Funeral Home came on. Residents gathered on the sidewalk, gawking and talking. Parents pulled kids away from Turner's body. Grandmothers prayed, men clustered in tight groups and yammered. Somebody with a camera and flash attachment snapped pictures.

It took thirty minutes for the first radio car to pull up, more than enough time for Osborne to make a clean getaway. That confirmed it for Sam; Turner had been a hit job, and the arriving cops knew it. But why?

He was glad Johnnie Turner was dead. He'd deserved it. He was equally happy not to have been the triggerman. But other than not having blood on his hands, he felt no relief. Unanswered questions remained. Was the hit linked to Susan Cogan's murder? Did it have something to do with Turner's connection to the mob? What was he not seeing this time? It was worrisome, but he was too fog-brained to sort it out.

He turned away from the murder scene and started for Bunny's as the cops readied to begin their canvass. He wanted a long, hot soak in a tub, he wanted to sleep under a pile of warm blankets—and he wanted the whole damn nightmare to be over.

CHAPTER 18

DJ OPENED THE FRONT DOOR, LET SAM IN WITHOUT A WORD, and led him past the dining table, where a fresh batch of photographs from the lab was spread out. In the kitchen, she turned and gave him an icy stare. "I thought we were a team," she finally said.

"We are." Wobbly, Sam leaned against the counter.

She shook her head in disagreement, poured a cup of coffee, and kept staring at him. "You make decisions without bothering to discuss them with me, send a badly battered Walt Seaver as a messenger boy to fill me in on what you're doing, and then go missing overnight hunting for Johnnie Turner. How is that teamwork?"

In the face of DJ's ire, Sam pivoted. "How is Walt? Where is he now?"

"He's at home recovering. Delores is looking after him. Don't change the subject."

"I'm sorry, but I felt I had to act fast."

DJ sipped her coffee and considered his opening argument. The angry bump on her forehead was almost gone, but her expression was unforgiving.

"That's a bunch of crap. I've been here alone all night wondering what the hell is going on and if you were alive or dead, until it struck me that you're impulsively foolish and not worth worrying about."

The well-deserved criticism smarted. "I needed to have Johnnie Turner off my back for good, so we can concentrate on finding out who else wants us dead."

"Well, were you able to sweet-talk him out of gunning you down, or did you have to shoot him?"

DJ's mockery stung. "He's dead. A police lieutenant killed him.

Don't ask me why." He took a cup from the dish drainer, filled it with coffee, and had a swallow. "I haven't a clue yet, although there are some reasonable probabilities."

"Interesting, and I'd love to hear them, but that doesn't solve my problem with you."

"Which is?" Sam asked, dreading whatever DJ's answer might be.

"I thought we were in this together, but obviously I've been mistaken. Either I'm a full partner, or we call the whole thing off. I don't have time to waste on a man who sees me as an interesting distraction or an apprentice helper."

Sam nodded. She'd put her life, money, and reputation on the line to help him, and he'd dealt poorly with her. "You're right, and I apologize. Full partners it is from now on."

"That could be a hard promise for your male ego to keep," DJ challenged.

"I'll keep it in check. You can remind me when I fall short," Sam offered.

"I may just do that," DJ allowed, almost smiling. "Now, tell me exactly what happened last night."

Sam recalled the events in detail as best he could, until his empty stomach and sleep-deprived light-headedness made him stop. "I need something to eat," he announced, pushing the empty coffee cup aside.

"There's the leftover tuna salad you made in the refrigerator."

"You saved that?" he asked in amazement. "It was awful."

"I can fix you something."

"Never mind, I'll grab a nap on a couch."

"The bed is made up."

"The couch will do until I know for sure that I'm out of the doghouse. Or the Bunny house, as it were. We can't stay here indefinitely, you know."

DJ laughed. "In spite of being occasionally hardheaded and foolish, you do have some redeeming qualities."

"I appreciate your restored confidence in me," Sam replied. Too achy and exhausted to defend himself further, he found his way to the nearest couch and collapsed.

*

SAM WOKE UP WITH the day nearly gone and a welcoming cup of coffee brought to him by DJ, who promised him food if he washed up first. Scrubbed clean of Manhattan soot, he feasted on a deli pastrami on rye in the kitchen while DJ retired to the dining room to continue her inspection of the contact sheets and snapshots of the exposed film that had been developed by the lab.

Hoping progress had been made, he hurriedly finished eating and joined her. With a shake of her head, she waved a hand dismissively over the assemblage of photographs spread out on the dining table and said, "All that breaking-and-entering we did was for nothing."

"What about Laura's notes on the photos we took from her darkroom?"

"Unless she was using a secret code or something, they're useless."

"Now what?"

She picked up the photograph of the convertible parked at the base of distant sandhills that she'd set aside.

"We've looked at this before," San remarked.

"Yes, but remember it's an anomaly; the last frame on an exposed roll of film that's completely different from all the other Las Vegas Strip images. In fact, as far as I can tell, it's totally unlike everything else on the table."

"Which means, if Laura took more photographs at the same location, we don't have them."

"Exactly," DJ said. "It's a long shot, but I'd like a blowup of this. The processing lab runs twenty-four hours a day. I'm going to have them do a rush job. It shouldn't take too long."

"Is it worth it?" Sam asked.

"What else do we have?" DJ countered. "You stay here."

"Okay."

"Promise?"

"I'm not going anywhere." Sam looked skeptically at the array of photos and contact sheets. "Maybe I'll spot something you missed. Be careful out there, okay?"

"Always." On her way to the front door, she threw him a kiss.

Feeling half-forgiven and less foolhardy, he turned his attention to the photographs, hoping something would catch his eye. He was eager for someone other than Tony Carlucci to emerge as a prime suspect for Laura's murder. It was hard to believe that a smart crime boss would rashly order a hit when he had no reason to worry.

So why the overreaction? And if it wasn't Carlucci, then who was behind the attempt to kill them? Sam flipped through a pile of photographs and sighed in frustration. So many of them were wonderful landscapes, beautifully composed character studies, captivating street scenes of everyday people, and absolutely no help at all.

Whatever he needed to learn wasn't about to be found spread out on Bunny Terrell's dining room table. The repeated, irritating buzzing of the doorbell made him testy. Thinking DJ might have locked herself out, he opened the front door to find Marco, the budding juvenile mobster-in-training, standing next to a two-hundred-fifty-pound gorilla packing a pistol in a shoulder holster visible under his open sports coat. He looked like he could bench-press twice his own weight. A Lincoln Continental idled at the curb.

"That's him," Marco said.

The gorilla grunted and nodded at the Lincoln. "Get in the car."

Sam stepped back. "First I need my jacket."

The gorilla patted his shoulder holster. "Don't be a dumbass, get in the car."

"Whatever you say."

Marco led the way, with the gorilla close behind, breathing down Sam's neck. Salvatore Silano waited in the backseat. Sam joined him. Gorilla got behind the wheel, Marco rode shotgun, and they drove away, heading uptown. For a brief moment on the western horizon a luminous sunset put the city lights to shame. Sam didn't enjoy it.

"How did you find me?"

"After young Marco spoke to me, I had him follow you," Sal answered. "Why did you rough up the kid? He was just doing his job."

"I didn't rough him up. I just wanted to scare him away from becoming a wise guy."

"You got some balls talking to me like that. You know nothing."

"You don't have to convince me of that. What is it you want, Sal? I don't have much time to waste with you."

"You go to my home, harass my wife, and now you insult me with your rudeness. I should have you driven to New Jersey and shot."

"Just what a mob boss would do," Sam countered.

Sal sat back and shook his head. "You do have a pair, I'll give you that. I send you a warning, but you don't listen. Are you really that stupid?"

"All young Marco said was Johnnie Turner had quit the cops, and I should stay out of Hoboken and leave you alone. I took it to mean that Tony Carlucci was behind the attempt to kill me and my partner. But I've been starting to think that it doesn't make any sense. Just like I've been thinking you're more than just a legendary pickpocket with an illustrious reputation."

"Maybe you're starting to get smart, so let me further your education a bit," Sal said. "You saw a cop gun down an ex-cop, correct?"

"I did."

"Do you think it had anything to do with you?"

"Maybe, I'd be stupid not to."

"Good." Sal tapped Gorilla on the shoulder. He slowed and pulled to the curb.

"That's it?" Sam asked.

"Where do cops and their families live?" Sal asked.

"And that's helpful how?"

Sal reached across and opened the curbside passenger door. "Stay out of Hoboken."

"And leave you alone," Sam added.

Sal smiled. "You're getting smarter by the minute."

*

SAL LET SAM OFF on the outskirts of Spanish Harlem. It was a dirty trick and he deserved it. On the other hand, he was only six blocks away from where Adella Diaz, Laura's former housekeeper, lived. Now that the penthouse was about to go on the rental market, he won-

dered if the Neilson family had found a way to keep her on the payroll.
If not, she might be willing to talk more freely.

He decided to risk the chance of getting mugged to find out. He set
a brisk pace, hoping the growing darkness would mask his outsider's
identity. Besides, what interloper would be stupid enough to walk on
such potentially dangerous streets?

The teenage boy who opened the door to Sam's knock looked fit
enough to throw him down a flight of stairs. Sam introduced himself
and asked to speak to Adella. The teenager told him to wait in the hallway and closed the door. Adella appeared, apologized to Sam for her
son Pedro's poor manners, and sat with him in the small living room.

"Why have you come here?" she asked.

Sam said he knew the penthouse was being emptied of Laura's pos-
sessions so it could be leased, and wondered if Adella still had a job.

She shook her head. "No, I'm looking. The lawyer gave me a letter
of reference."

"Any severance pay?"

"One month's salary."

"May I see the letter?"

Adella retrieved the letter from a table drawer and handed it to Sam.

The letter was signed by one Jeffrey Kaplin, Esquire. There was
nothing heartfelt or warm about it. He memorized his name and the
name of the firm. "How many years did you work for her?"

"Nine and a half. She paid me well for what I do, and there were
occasional gifts and generous bonuses. I have no reason to complain."

"Still, a month's wages for nine and a half years of service," Sam said
sympathetically. "That's small potatoes."

"And it will run out soon. I have little savings." Adella smiled. "But
you did not come here to offer me a job, did you?"

Sam shook his head. "No, I didn't. You often helped Laura when she
had parties and informal gatherings. I remember several myself. If I
recall, some of the other building residents were present. The Millers,
Jay and Janet, come to mind."

"Yes, Laura was friendly with them. I don't think they killed her."

Sam bit back a smile. The Millers were an elderly, childless couple who loved to play canasta and bridge. "I don't think so either. Would it be violating the rules for you to tell me everyone in the building you know who'd been invited to the penthouse?"

"How does that help finding her killer?"

"We all make an occasional slip of the tongue or let our guard down. A drink too many, and something may be said, later to be regretted. Little things like that can point me in the right direction. A list could be very helpful."

"You really do want to find Laura's killer."

"I won't stop until I do."

"Some were there only once or twice, others more often."

"That information would be helpful too," Sam noted. He knew Laura frequently entertained when Adella was off duty, so her list wouldn't be exhaustive. Still, it would broaden the parameters.

Adella wrote out the list and handed it to Sam. "You know, Laura talked to me about you more than any other of her men friends."

"I didn't know that."

"You were special to her."

"I'd like to think so. Was there any other male friend she was talkative about?"

"Only one, back when I first started working for her. Stephen Key, the new police commissioner. He was like a father figure to her. I don't think she was romantically involved with him. He was a detective at the time. They acted like old friends."

"Old friends?"

"Comfortable with each other."

"That is interesting. Have you heard from Laura's family?"

Adella shook her head. "No, and I don't think I will."

"Why do you say that?"

"They disapproved of the way she lived her life, and Laura liked to rub their noses in it every chance she got. She once said to me it was payback, but never told me why."

"Did she ever talk to you about what it was like when she was growing up?"

"I wasn't her confidante. She was always very private about her family, and especially her early years. But several times recently I over-heard her on the telephone telling someone that she was sick and tired of being reminded about the family farm in New Jersey. She said to knock it off. She was upset, almost angry."

"How recent?"

"Within the last six months."

"Any guesses who?"

"No. Do you have someone waiting outside?"

Sam stood and shook his head. "I'll be fine. Thanks, Adella. You've been extremely helpful."

"Pedro will go with you to the subway station."

"That isn't necessary."

Adella paid him no mind and called for her son, who walked Sam safely to the station.

"You shouldn't come up here alone like that again," Pedro warned.

"I'll remember that. Thanks."

"Find my mom a job, okay? I can't get any more hours at the market unless I quit school, and she won't let me. I may have to anyway."

"Do what your mother says and stay in school," Sam counseled. "I'll get her a job, promise. Tell her that."

"When?"

"Soon."

"Okay," Pedro said. "Good night."

Sam sat in the almost-empty train as it swooshed and clattered out of the bowels of Spanish Harlem and into the more civilized reaches of Manhattan, wondering how in the hell he could find Adella Diaz a job. And what was Stephen Watts Key to Laura?

He knew, after promising DJ to stay put, a verbal buzz saw would greet him when he got back to Bunny's. To ease his growing appre-hension, he retreated to the subject that puzzled him most: What was it about the family farm that caused Laura such distress?

CHAPTER 19

THE HOUSE WAS DARK, THE FRONT DOOR LOCKED, AND THERE was no response to the doorbell. Was DJ inside and ignoring him? Was he completely on the outs with her? She could be inside and hurt. Or, worse, abducted.

With her help, Sam had already committed a string of felony break-ins, so why not add one more to the total? An ornate wrought-iron gate at the side of the house barred a narrow passageway that led to an open-air garden at the rear of the building. He jumped the gate, broke the sliding glass door with a rock, and searched the premises top to bottom. No DJ, no sign of a struggle, and the house had been put back into perfect order as if they had never been there.

It wasn't reassuring. Maybe DJ had tidied up, or maybe someone else had, after . . . He didn't want to think about it.

An extra buck tip got him a quick cab ride to DJ's office building, where lights shining in her second-story suite did little to reassure him. Buzzed in, he hurried up the stairs. The glass on the unlocked outer door had been replaced. DJ was in her private office along with her father and an elderly pipe-smoking gentleman. Nobody looked particularly happy to see him. Enlargements of Laura's sandhills photograph were scattered on the desktop.

"Where did you go off to this time?" DJ asked flatly, without emotion.

"I was literally kidnapped. I'll explain later."

"That won't be necessary," DJ replied tartly.

Sam glanced at DJ's father. "Nice to see you again, Dr. Ryan."

Daniel Ryan nodded wordlessly.

"Let's get this over with, so we can move on," DJ said. She quickly introduced the elderly man as Professor Paddock Bennett, a friend of her father's and a fellow of the American Geographical Society. She'd asked her father, a lifelong member of the society, to seek out a specialist in physical geography who could identify the approximate location where the photograph had been taken.

Dr. Ryan had reached Bennett at the society's headquarters in the Washington Heights neighborhood of Manhattan and promptly brought him to DJ's office. She asked the professor to summarize his conclusions for Sam's benefit.

The professor put his pipe aside and said the original photograph had most definitely been taken in New Mexico or southern Arizona. On one enlargement, he pointed out two distinct types of shrubs found only in the northern reaches of the North American Chihuahuan Desert, which spread for thousands of square miles over the Mexican border into both states. He used another enlargement to identify an alkali flats area common to the topography. He speculated that the time of year might have been late spring, but, as he was not a botanist, he couldn't be certain. However, he was convinced the photograph could not have been taken in or around the Las Vegas, Nevada, area.

Sam found it all very interesting, but what jumped out at him was the fact that the convertible at the foot of the sandhills was a Porsche identical to Laura's model, and someone was in the passenger seat.

"Can we get a closer look of the passenger?" he asked.

"Not without the negatives," DJ replied. "What are you seeing?"

"The automobile is the exact make and model as Laura's. She drove it on an extensive western road trip some time ago. For at least part of the journey someone went with her, but I don't know who. It might be the person in the ragtop."

Seeming disinterested, DJ gathered up the enlargements, put them in a desk drawer, and locked it. "When you can pay back what you owe me, the photos are yours."

She handed him an itemized, typed-up bill, which included the cost of the new glass in the outer office door and the money he'd taken from the bank envelope.

"You are no longer my client. Good luck, Mr. Monroe. Please leave."

"Come on, DJ, don't do this," Sam protested. "Laura meant something to you, I know she did."

"You heard her, Mr. Monroe," Dr. Ryan said.

Paddock Bennett fiddled quietly with his pipe. Icy stares from DJ and her father froze any further objection.

"I broke the patio door at Bunny's looking for you," he confessed. "I was worried about you. I'm glad you're safe."

"I'll add the repair cost to your bill and mail you a revised invoice," DJ said, skipping over Sam's expression of concern. "Pay me when you can."

"Fine." He backed out of her office and walked aimlessly down the street, not sure what to do next. Twice he stopped and turned around to go back and explain himself. Both times he hesitated. He thought about returning later to wait outside and talk to her as she was leaving. But that wouldn't work until she stopped being angry.

He turned crosstown to go home, but it could hardly be called that. More a place to hang his hat on a crowded, noisy, sooty island that only occasionally seemed peaceful deep in the night before predawn woke the city up.

He had never felt lonelier. He sucked it up and laughed at himself for feeling so misunderstood. A passerby ducked his head and hurried on. Sam quickened his steps. He'd started out alone to catch a killer and he'd soldier on alone as long as it took. It might take days, weeks, or months, but he'd find a way to keep at it. Laura deserved that much.

The mailbox at his building held a final paycheck from his job that included a sizable chunk of unused vacation time. It bolstered his resolve to keep going. He needed to interview all the people on Adella Diaz's list of building residents Laura had socialized with. How and where to do it was the question. But first he wanted to give Laura's Porsche a thorough search. Last time, he'd done a quick lick and a promise.

He called the parking garage and spoke to the late-night attendant. The vehicle in space 117 had been picked up that afternoon by someone from a Park Avenue car dealership. The man didn't know where the Porsche had been taken. It was too late to call the dealership. But when the doors opened in the morning, Sam would be there, hopefully before anything had been done to it.

After that, he'd contact Mike Dalton and ask him to help set up interviews with the tenants on Adella Diaz's list. Surely he'd be willing to help if there was the chance that the new information might bring a break in the case.

Sam also wanted to know about the dead body found in the burned-out panel truck. Had it been identified? If so, was there a mob connection? If not, he'd be almost willing to completely discount Carlucci as a threat. Sergeant O'Reilly might know. Since Mike frequently spoke with his brother-in-law, he'd ask him to find out.

It was a plan. He slept until Department of Sanitation workers woke him up banging the garbage cans and grinding the trash into the back of their truck on York Avenue.

AT THE REQUEST OF Laura's trust, the Porsche had been picked up by the dealer to be serviced and put in tip-top condition. If everything checked out, there was an eager buyer for it. No one at the dealership had a name for the buyer. The car had been taken to a service facility near Eleventh Avenue.

The building was a two-story former warehouse within sight of the Hudson River. It had few windows but a large garage-door drive-through entrance that opened onto a series of service bays lit by rows of overhead fluorescent lights. The rear engine compartment hood of the Porsche was up, and a mechanic was giving it the once-over. Sam introduced himself as a representative of the deceased vehicle owner's family and explained that he needed to do a complete visual inspection for insurance purposes. He assured the mechanic it would only take a few minutes. The man nodded agreeably and went off for a quick smoke.

Sam saw nothing of interest in the engine compartment. He moved on to the cabin. The pull-out ashtray above the cigarette lighter held two crumpled receipts. One was for the repair of a flat tire in Prescott, Arizona. The second was a signed Western Union receipt for five hundred dollars paid to Laura Neilson at its Albuquerque, New Mexico, office. Both were dated a few days after the airplane tour of the Grand Canyon.

There was nothing he'd missed in the glove compartment. He wondered if the Grand Canyon, Prescott, and Albuquerque stops had come at the tail end of Laura's road trip. Had she dropped off her travel mate in New Mexico on her way home? There were too many blank spots that needed to be filled in.

An empty black clamshell eyeglass case from Marshall Field & Company was wedged under the passenger seat. He wondered if it went with the broken frames he'd found in the small luggage compartment. Tucked into the driver-side visor was an unused postcard picturing the La Fonda Hotel in Santa Fe. Had she stayed there alone or with her friend? He'd call the hotel long-distance and ask.

He set everything aside for another careful look. Satisfied that he'd missed nothing, he pocketed his findings, waved goodbye to the returning mechanic, and walked to the nearest branch of his bank. He cashed his check and wrote a note on borrowed bank stationery explaining to DJ what had happened to make him leave Bunny's. He signed it with affection and regrets, put it in an envelope with enough cash to pay her bill, including the estimated repair cost for the broken patio door, and caught a bus that let him off three blocks from her office.

In her building, he opened the outer office door, where Delores Stedman looked up from her reception desk, shook her head sternly, and told him not to enter.

"You're not welcome here," she added.

Sam approached anyway with a smile. "Just dropping something off. Give DJ my love."

He put the envelope on the desktop, turned quickly on his heel, fled down the stairs, and jaywalked across the street before looking back. Someone was standing at DJ's office window, and it wasn't Delores.

He'd shot a large part of his wad to square things with DJ. It might not have been the smart thing to do. From the moment he'd found Laura's body, he'd been on the edge of financial catastrophe. He was still tottering on the brink, but it felt good to settle the account with a woman who had quickly come to mean a great deal to him.

Sam was hungry. A neighborhood diner advertised a great price for breakfast served twenty-four hours a day. He hurried inside.

*

BELOW CANAL STREET, a large number of federal, state, and local government buildings dot the landscape of Lower Manhattan. Sam spent the morning hopscotching from one building to another, sometimes steered to the wrong agency, occasionally backtracking to uncover more information. By late afternoon, he'd learned that a senior principal partner in the law firm that administered Laura's trust was her father's first cousin. Two other partners had married into the family. Additionally, Laura's trust funds were disbursed by Kittatinny Valley Farms through a privately owned bank. Laura's parents and ten other extended Neilson family members were owners of both the farm and bank.

Kittatinny Valley Farms was also registered as a privately owned corporation in the state of New York. Among its many holdings was the entire city block of buildings on the street where Laura had lived, minus hers, which was held in trust. The trust had been established to take effect on her twenty-first birthday. Sam wondered if Laura had left a will. If so, would it go through probate? It was another question that needed answering.

As with the land under the Neilson mansion, the corporation owned it under all the buildings on the block, plus some nearby buildings, including the parking garage where Laura had housed the Porsche. Several of the buildings fronted busy Madison Avenue, where retail space was at a premium.

Property records for the land predated the Revolutionary War. All property taxes were up to date. Sam figured the same would have been true on the New Jersey side of the Hudson, but he made a note to check it out when he could.

He tried hard to find a way to take a look at Laura's financial records, but it was a no-go, as were whatever stock holdings or additional assets she owned. It would take more time, expense, and expertise than he had. But he had learned that, unlike many of the city's nineteenth-century robber baron descendants, the Neilson clan was particularly gifted at keeping their gilded wealth a private family affair.

Sam finished in time to hightail it to the Criminal Courts Building, which housed the District Attorney's Office, before quitting time. He'd always loved going to work in the seventeen-story Art Deco skyscraper with its limestone façade. Built at the end of the Great Depression, the grand entrance of two freestanding columns provoked a feeling of solemnity, which was continued in the two-story marble lobby with a hanging clock as the centerpiece, and the two magnificent staircases that embraced the lobby and pulled all who entered inside.

He had a ten-minute wait in the lobby before Mike Dalton appeared. He spotted Sam, hurried over, and clapped him on the back.

"Good to see you. How are you holding up?"

"I'm okay. I've a question for you: Did O'Reilly ever learn the identity of the dead man in the burned-out panel truck?"

"I don't know, but I'll ask him. Is it important?"

"If it was one of Carlucci's mob goons, it could be. Either way, it would be helpful to know."

Mike nodded. "That makes sense. I'll talk to him tonight. Where can I reach you?"

"I'll be at my place. But I also need a favor, Mike. I have a list of people I need to interview, but I'm not going to be able to talk to them without some official backup."

"What people?"

"Residents of Laura's apartment building who were her friends or social acquaintances."

"Everybody in that building was interviewed by detectives."

"I know, but I'd like to go into greater detail with the people in the building who knew her on a more personal basis."

"I get where you're going with it, but, sorry, no can do," Mike replied. "New orders have come down regarding your situation. It's hands-off. Not prosecuting you is as far as the DA is willing to go, and he's keeping his options open. Any assistance that's given to you could taint a potential court case. I'd face disciplinary action if I helped you."

"I understand."

"But I'll talk to Jerry and get back to you."

"I appreciate it."

Mike nodded and moved on. Sam was disappointed but understood. The odds had been against him from the start. Since face-to-face interviews were out, he needed to find another way to follow up, and that was a head-scratcher. He dropped the idea temporarily and thought about Police Commissioner Stephen Watts Key. His connection to Laura might be pertinent to her murder.

He knew the basics of Key's professional rise through the ranks to become the city's top cop, but nothing about his early years. How to fill in the blanks? In law school, one of Sam's favorite instructors had been Nicholas Reddy, a visiting lecturer. After serving in the Judge Advocate General's Corps during World War II, Reddy had been hired by the *New York Herald Tribune* to report for the newspaper on major criminal court cases and significant judicial decisions. As his encyclopedic knowledge of the New York City criminal justice system grew, he'd earned his own regular opinion column. His byline sold papers.

After his lectures, Reddy occasionally would buy a round of drinks at a neighborhood bar for the veterans in his class. It was clear during those informal gatherings that Nick Reddy and Steve Key had a friendship that went beyond that of teacher and student. If anyone could tell Sam about Key's life before the NYPD, it would most likely be Reddy.

He was a bachelor and a workhorse who didn't believe in the eight-to-five routine. Although it was after hours, Sam took a chance and called the *Tribune.* Reddy was at his desk and would be glad to see him, but only if Sam agreed to an exclusive interview.

Rush-hour traffic slowed Sam's arrival at the *Herald Tribune* building near Times Square by a good ten minutes. Nick was in his cubbyhole office pounding away on his typewriter, a cigarette dangling from his lips. He was burly without being overweight and always looked a little bit crumpled and sleepy-eyed.

"So, what do you want to know about our police commissioner?" he asked.

"What do you know about his early years?"

Reddy snuffed out his cigarette in the desk ashtray. "First, tell me why you're interested."

"Key personally knew Laura Neilson, and some years ago was a frequent and welcomed guest at her apartment. I'd like to know how they are connected."

"You're not thinking he murdered her?"

"No, but when I talk with him, I want to ask the right questions. How, when, and where did they first meet? What was the nature of their friendship? How did it evolve?"

Nick leaned back in his swivel chair. "After you telephoned, I pulled my file on Steve for a profile piece I'd written some years ago when he'd started to make a name for himself as a cop. He was born in Manhattan but raised in New Jersey after his mother divorced his father. He grew up in Sussex County on a horse farm called Tranquility Ranch that his mother owned. She was originally from out West and had money. He was a spoiled only child. She sent him off to an Ivy League college, but he dropped out after his freshman year, bummed around Europe, got married and divorced with a girl from Sweden—no kids—and burned through a lot of his mother's money. When the stock market crashed, his mother's inheritance dried up, so she sold the ranch for a pittance and returned to Wyoming."

Nick paused to light a fresh smoke. "Steve stayed in Jersey. Because he was local and knew about horses and animals, et cetera, he got some temporary farm jobs. After a fall harvest, he got laid off, moved to the city, and applied to the department. His father had some pull with the mayor's office, and that, except for his war years' service in the Army, was the beginning of his brilliant rise to the top."

"Did he say where he worked in New Jersey?"

"No. Is that important?"

Not sure of Nick's current friendship with Key, Sam was unwilling to share all the thoughts that were rattling around in his head. "Maybe not," he said. "What you've told me makes me think it's very likely Steve knew Laura from the time she'd spent as a child at the Neilson family farm in Sussex County."

"And what would be the significance of that to Miss Neilson's murder?" Reddy asked.

"I'll have to talk to Steve before I can answer that question for you."

Nick nodded and reached for a pad and pencil. "Okay, fair enough, now it's your turn. I want your story, starting with your childhood, right up to your torrid affair with Laura Neilson and your hunt to find her killer."

Sam groaned.

"Fair is fair," Reddy reminded him.

"You're right."

Nick stubbed out his butt and said, "Where were you born?"

"Panama. At the time, my father was an artillery officer stationed at the Canal Zone."

"Where are your parents now?"

"Both dead. My father, retired Lieutenant Colonel Asher Sherman Monroe, of a heart attack. My mother, Catherine Mulvaney Monroe, by suicide."

"Suicide?"

"Sleeping pills. Six months after my father's death. She missed him."

Nick scribbled a note and looked up. "Any siblings?"

"None."

"Where did you grow up?"

"I was an Army brat. You want the complete list?"

"Of course. I want it all, and everything you tell me is on the record. Okay?"

What the hell, why not? Sam thought as he settled back in his chair. There was no one else he knew who was interested enough to ask. "Except for what I've learned about Stephen Key's personal relationship to Laura Neilson. Agreed?"

"For now," Nick answered, handing Sam his business card. "But I have first dibs if and when there's anything newsworthy about it."

NICK WAS A SKILLED interviewer and Sam didn't hold back. He told Reddy everything, right up to that moment. Surprisingly, he felt refreshed when it was over. It helped him temporarily derail the emotional roller coaster he'd been on since Laura's murder, including DJ symbolically kicking him in the seat of his pants and out the door. Not even Nick's probing questions about the currently stalled status of the investigation drained Sam's revived spirits.

In the lobby, Nick said it might take a while before the column appeared. "I'll be fact-checking some of what you've told me."

"I understand."

"But you'll like it." He smiled, waved his hand across an imaginary theater marquee, and said, "The headline will read: 'War Hero Vows to Catch Socialite's Killer.'"

"Isn't that a bit much?"

"Not at all. It's a murder case wrapped around a steamy love story. That's good copy." Reddy said he would call if he had any follow-up questions, waved half-heartedly, and retreated in the direction of his office.

The moon was up, splashing vague skyscraper shadows across the avenue. It reminded Sam of the atmospheric images of the city he'd seen at an exhibition of Alfred Stieglitz's photographs that he'd attended with Laura.

Back in his apartment, he was too antsy to settle down. The phone rang as he was about to leave for Stamm's Bar and Grill. Mike Dalton had heard from his brother-in-law that the body in the panel truck remained unidentified. However, he didn't think it had been a soldier from the Carlucci family. All the local goons were accounted for. But it didn't rule out someone being brought in from the outside. He had feelers out about any known street punks looking to win favor with the family who might have gone missing. Mike would keep Sam posted.

It was Tuesday night, and Stamm's was busy with locals who religiously convened for the ever-popular weekly schnitzel and potato salad dinner special. There was enough room at the bar for Sam to slide in and order a drink from Alfonso, who was too busy to gab. By the time he'd finished his second scotch, the crowd had thinned out and there was elbow room at the bar. Alfonso stopped by for a brief chat, wanting to know what was up with the case.

Sam was about to launch into a nickel tour of his flawed hunt for Laura's killer when DJ appeared at his side.

"I got your love note," she said. "Did a twelve-year-old really abduct you?"

"I'm not sure of Marco's age, but yes. How did you find me?"

"It wasn't hard. Remember, I'm a private investigator. Nicholas Reddy called me."

"He said he would."

"After we finished talking, I realized I know so little about you."

"I'm an open book."

"Don't be flippant. I'm sorry I didn't trust you. I've been stung too many times by unreliable males."

"My luck with women has been no better."

"Can we start over?"

"I'd like that."

"Tell what you've learned."

At an empty table at the back of the dining area, Sam summarized Salvatore Silano's oblique message that the attempted Hoboken hit that destroyed her father's T-Bird was the work of corrupt cops, not the Carlucci family.

"Which means they were after me, not you," he concluded.

"What do we do about it?" DJ asked.

"Nothing, right now."

He told her about Adella Diaz's list of building residents Laura had seen socially, Laura's personal friendship with Stephen Key, and the background information Nick Reddy had shared about the commissioner.

"We have to go back to New Jersey," DJ proposed.

"I agree it may be necessary, but not immediately. First we need to find a way to interview the people on Adella's list. If we can catch the killer without implicating Key, I'd rather go that route. But Mike Dalton can't risk his job to help out."

DJ drummed her fingers on the tabletop. "Something bad happened to Laura in New Jersey when she was young. We know that. What we don't know is if it had anything to do with the drowning of the teenage boy at the quarry. I think it's time to put some pressure on Laura's parents and ask them to help us schedule the interviews. Let's meet with them again as soon as possible. I'll set it up."

"Good."

"Also, I've been thinking about Osborne, the police lieutenant who gunned down Johnnie Turner," DJ said. "What if Osborne killed him because he didn't want you to get to him first?"

"Johnnie might have told me something Osborne didn't want me to know."

"Exactly. Let's put Walt Seaver on it and see if he can connect Turner and Osborne to Salvatore Silano's not-so-subtle hint of dirty cops in Hoboken. He's brainy and loves solving puzzles. I'll ask him to start with Turner and see if he can spread a web to snare Osborne and any others. Besides, he needs something to do while he heals up."

"You're some cookie," Sam said adoringly.

"No, I'm a seven-course meal at Delmonico's," DJ replied. "Take me to your apartment and I'll treat you to dessert."

"I love it when you talk dirty."

THEY SNUGGLED IN BED after making love, talking for hours. DJ asked about Sam's life growing up. He talked about being yanked out of schools repeatedly whenever his father got transferred to a new Army post. How the constant upheaval had turned him into a loner and an outsider throughout high school and in college. He told her about his parents' deaths, his combat experiences in Korea, and the rare camaraderie he'd found with his brothers-in-arms amid the insanity of war and its devastation.

DJ wanted to know how Laura had come into his life. Laughingly, he told her about Laura shoplifting at the department store to get his attention. How she'd quickly filled some of his broken and missing parts with her fierce passion, intelligence, and excitement for life. Then they slept. When he awoke in the morning with DJ beside him, he felt fully rested for the first time in a very long while.

CHAPTER 20

DIRK NEILSON AGREED BY PHONE TO MEET WITH THEM MID-morning. He greeted them at the door, made excuses for his wife's absence, and guided them into his library with its view of Central Park. With the autumn sun lower in the sky and the trees dressed in bright colors, the park appeared idyllic, disturbed only by the traffic noise that floated up from Fifth Avenue.

"What news of your investigation do you have for me?" Neilson asked DJ.

Sam ignored the subtle snub and answered. "We believe Laura's murder is tied to something that happened years ago at the farm. Something other than the accidental death of the boy at the quarry."

"We've been over this before," Dirk retorted.

"And, somehow, Stephen Key was involved," DJ added.

Neilson arched his eyebrow. "You've spoken to him?"

"Yes," Sam replied, hiding behind the half-truth of his answer. "We'd like your version."

Dirk gestured for DJ and Sam to sit in chairs arranged in front of a wall of leather-bound books. "I still don't see the relevance of this line of inquiry."

"Laura is gone, murdered," DJ said softly. "Help us find who killed her."

Dirk took a deep breath. "By now you know that Stephen found her after she'd been raped."

"Go over that for us, please," DJ urged, restraining her surprise.

Dirk explained that Key had been visiting his mother at Tranquility Ranch when Laura's saddled and riderless pony arrived, lathered and agitated. He'd ridden out, found her at the side of a bridle path, half-naked and badly beaten, and carried her home to the farm.

"We were called to come immediately from the city," Dirk added. "After the doctor examined her, we asked what had happened. All she said was that she didn't know her attacker and hadn't seen his face. When she spoke with the sheriff, she was unable to give him any helpful identifying information. She'd been knocked unconscious, and when she came to he was gone. We repeatedly asked her to remember what had happened, but her story never changed. After that, she completely shut down."

"Of course, she was traumatized," DJ said compassionately.

Dirk nodded. "When we found out she was pregnant, we made the decision to remove her from school until after the baby's birth and then place the child up for adoption. But that never happened. Laura miscarried in her first trimester and almost died."

"How terrible," DJ said.

"The whole experience changed her," Dirk said. "She became more impulsive, less concerned about what people thought. She was frequently dismissive of people she'd once liked, including of course Elizabeth and myself. Soon after, she started carrying on with boys."

"Carrying on?" DJ inquired.

"Yes, blatantly at times, to the point of embarrassment."

Sam didn't bother to ask who was embarrassed. "Laura wasn't able to provide any information about her attacker?" he queried. "Height, weight, the sound of his voice?"

Dirk shook his head. "Nothing, and I questioned her carefully many times."

"What did she tell you?"

"That she blacked out, and when she came to, he was gone."

"Where and when exactly did the attack happen?" DJ asked.

Dirk noted the day and year, and described the bridle path that bordered the family farm and continued on to Tranquility Ranch. "It's used mostly by locals, summer cabin owners and occasional vacation hikers," he added. "I've told you all that we know."

"And you've been helpful," Sam said, wondering if that was true. "Does the bridle trail extend beyond Tranquility Ranch?"

"Yes, and to the south as well, but I can't say where exactly. Stephen would know, he rode it often." Dirk glanced from Sam to DJ. "I expect you both to keep what I've told you confidential."

"Of course," DJ replied. "We'd like you to arrange for us to speak to some of the residents in Laura's building. Only those she knew socially. It could be important to learn a little bit more about her recent activities."

"We'll be discreet," Sam promised.

Dirk thought about it and huffed. "All right. I'll speak to the attorney and have him contact you."

"I think Jeffrey Kaplin is the lawyer handling Laura's trust," Sam offered. "He's the man to talk with."

It earned him a piercing, questioning glance.

Dirk ushered them to the door. On the street, DJ paused and asked Sam why he'd let on that he knew the name of Laura's lawyer.

Sam laughed. "I'm impulsive, but you already know that. Laura's parents covered up what happened to her, and she paid a heavy price to protect the family's precious reputation. Now that she's dead, she's still paying. That angers me. I want Dirk and his wife to know that the Neilson armor isn't impenetrable."

"Why?"

"Because they didn't love her well enough, and I want to rub it in their faces."

"You truly did love her."

"You already know that," Sam retorted. "What about you?"

DJ nodded and got teary. "For a time, she was a sister to me. I loved her dearly and was heartbroken when she went away."

Sam gave her hand a squeeze. "That's why we're in this together."

*

DELORES GREETED THEM AT DJ's office with a message from Jeffrey Kaplin. He'd called to say that without a court order they would not be allowed in the apartment building to interview any of the residents.

Additionally, all residents were being advised to seek legal counsel before agreeing to talk to them either by phone or in person.

"That torpedoes that idea," DJ said, looking at Adella's list. "What jerks."

"I think the Neilsons need a new inscription for the family crest," Sam said. *"Pride Above All Else.* What would that be in Latin?"

"I can't help you. Language was never my strong suit. Did you ever meet any of the people on this list?"

"Yes. Unless I'm the worst judge of mankind, we can cross off Jay and Janet Miller. The few others I met only briefly, perhaps once or twice at a large penthouse gathering. I did talk with Julia Anderson, who's a recent resident. She struck up a friendship with Laura after moving to the city. She seemed okay when we talked. One of Laura's ex-lovers is an old college friend of Anderson's and confirmed her story."

"That's it?"

"There's Laura's therapist, Erica Birkenfield, but she no longer lives in the building. She refused to tell me anything about Laura's childhood, other than to say that she needed to escape from everything. I took it as a euphemism for her parents."

"How can we possibly get to the other people on the list?" DJ asked in frustration.

"We could stake out the building and waylay them when they emerge," Sam offered half-jokingly.

DJ shook her head at his sorry attempt at humor and reached for the telephone. "Or we could twiddle our thumbs. We need to talk with Stephen Key right now."

She called his office and was put through to a secretary. Key was out of the building until late afternoon and unavailable that evening. DJ emphasized that she needed to speak to him about his personal relationship with the murdered socialite Laura Neilson, and it could not wait. She was promised a call back.

Ten minutes later the phone rang. Key would see them in his office at six o'clock.

They spent the remainder of the day in DJ's office telephoning the people on Adella's list, hoping to reach them before Kaplin's warning kicked in. Some had already heard from Kaplin and were heeding his advice. Some calls went unanswered. Only three individuals agreed to talk. Each of them freely described their social contacts with Laura, spoke affectionately about her, and expressed sorrow about her murder. Without hesitation they detailed their whereabouts on the night of the murder and provided names of persons who could corroborate the information. Follow-up phone calls to those witnesses verified their accounts. Although their innocence was not an absolute certainty, Sam saw no reason to view them as suspects.

DJ agreed, made one last call to a local deli, and ordered delivery of a late lunch. "No sense going up against the police commissioner on an empty stomach," she declared.

While they picnicked at DJ's desk with Delores joining in, Sam decided to backtrack with the Millers, Erica Birkenfield, and Professor Anderson. He dialed each one. Janet Miller was devastated about Laura's death. She reminisced about the small surprise eightieth birthday party for Jay that Laura had thrown, and Sam had attended. It reminded him how sweet and caring Laura could be.

His attempt to pry more information from Dr. Birkenfield with his newfound knowledge of Laura's rape gained almost no traction. "If only that had been all that happened to her back then," she said with finality. "I do hope you find the killer. I cared for her very much."

He hung up wondering what he needed to know about Laura's childhood he wasn't paying attention to. He placed the question on hold and dialed Anderson, who wasn't answering at home or at her faculty office.

When it was time to leave, they cleaned up the remains of the picnic and left Delores behind to close up shop. A layer of smog had settled over the island and the smell of gasoline, diesel fuel and the stink caused by the activity of millions of people was almost unbearable. New Yorkers on the street were toughing it out.

"We need a break," Sam remarked as he waved for the attention of a passing taxi.

"From?" DJ asked.

"Everything," he replied moodily. Something had to give.

*

STEPHEN KEY'S SPACIOUS, nicely appointed office contained the centerpiece desk Theodore Roosevelt had used during his tenure as police commissioner. A dark burgundy carpet was offset by cream-colored curtains that covered the long windows. Matching side chairs were positioned on either side of the desk, and off in a corner an arrangement of comfortable chairs was grouped for conversation.

Key's secretary guided Sam and DJ to the conversation area, invited them to sit, and said the commissioner would be with them momentarily. Stephen arrived shortly after and joined them, folding his lanky body into a chair. From his days as a department store detective, Sam knew good-quality men's clothing compared to off-the-rack apparel. Key's shoes were Italian, his suit customed-tailored, and the dress shirt was of the finest cotton, probably Egyptian.

Key flashed a friendly smile. "Now, what do you want to ask me about Laura Neilson? I can get the chief of detectives here if you need a progress report on the homicide investigation."

Sam leaned forward in his chair, decided not to attack, and leaned back. "Do they have any creditable suspects?" he asked.

"Other than yourself?" Stephen replied without missing a beat. "No. I understand the DA hasn't completely let you off the hook."

"So it seems," Sam replied, no longer willing to play nice. "But what I *can't* understand, Commissioner, is why a seasoned law enforcement official with your experience and qualifications would fail to mention his personal relationship with a New York socialite murder victim. Explain that to us."

Key stiffened. "It's old history, not relevant."

"It is relevant, especially if the homicide is connected to past events in the victim's life," DJ counterpunched. "And we believe that might be the case."

Key pursed his lips. "What have you learned?"

"You found and rescued Laura after she'd been raped," DJ answered. "Tell us what you know about that event."

Stephen shook his head at the memory. "When her pony arrived at the ranch with an empty saddle, I went looking for her. I found her incoherent, barely alert. Her jeans had been thrown aside, her underpants had been ripped off, and she'd been beaten badly around her face."

"Incoherent?" Sam probed.

'She kept saying, 'He, he,' over and over again, but never a name. I asked her who, and all she did was shake her head. It wasn't until later at the farm that she told me she'd been attacked from behind, knocked unconscious, and never saw her assailant."

"What do you think?" Sam pushed.

"I found her near the bridle path in an open field. There was nothing around her that could have been used as a club and no evidence of a struggle, although the grass was matted. I only saw one set of hoofprints. I don't think she was mounted on her horse when she was assaulted. I'm almost certain she saw him."

"And knew him?" DJ submitted.

"A rendezvous that went bad," Key proposed. "But she never gave him up, and I asked more than once."

"What stopped her?" DJ wondered.

"Heaven knows," Key answered.

Sam asked Stephen about the bridle trail. Key took a writing pad from his desk and sketched it. From Tranquility Ranch it ran north through some swamplands and on to the Kittatinny Valley Farms, where it joined with an abandoned railroad bed.

"There are dozens of thickly forested places where you could step off the trail and be virtually invisible," he noted. "But not in that meadow."

"What do you know about Laura's time at the Kittatinny Valley Farms?" Sam asked.

Stephen crossed his legs and sat back. "Not much. When I worked at the farm she was hardly there."

"You worked for Lee Huizinga," Sam offered.

"You've done your homework," Key said. "Lee did all the hiring. A good man to work for."

"What about Allen Quick?" DJ said.

"The boy who died at the quarry. I don't think he ever worked there."

"A girl named Jeannie?" DJ asked.

Stephen shook his head, uncrossed his legs, and stood. "Doesn't ring a bell. Look, you're both obviously committed to going down this rabbit hole, and I commend you for it. Leave no stone unturned. But I can't manufacture a suspect for you."

"Thanks for your time," Sam said.

"Still, you may be on to something," Key allowed. "I suggest you go back to the farm and ask to look at the ledger books. Over the course of the two centuries the farm has been in existence, I don't think a single penny has gone unaccounted-for."

"That's a good idea," DJ said.

Commissioner Key gestured at his closed office door, inviting departure. "For the record, Sam, I believe that you're not Laura's killer. I hope you can get that monkey off your back."

"I appreciate that. Any leads on the Johnnie Turner homicide?"

"Apparently a gangland hit disguised as an armed robbery. Someone was staked out overnight waiting for him to show. Too bad, alive he could have given us more rotten apples to round up."

"Too bad," Sam echoed.

*

THEY RODE THE SUBWAY UPTOWN, got off at Seventy-Seventh Street, and walked to Sam's apartment. Inside, Sam made a pot of coffee, and they sat in the front room debating their next step. They liked Key's idea of searching through the Kittatinny Valley Farms ledger books, but what exactly would they be looking for? Something unusual wasn't enough of a reason. Had there been a hidden message in the commissioner's suggestion? Unless they knew where to focus, it would be an exercise in futility. They'd need to backtrack and start over in order to unravel it.

They jumped from that bothersome quandary to the question of how to delve into Laura's personal finances. All along they'd been assuming Laura's fortune was secure. What if they were wrong? And again, what would they be looking for? Laura's sexual excesses and risky behavior could have easily led to extortion demands. Did she have gambling debts? Had she lost money with unsound investments?

DJ stopped lounging on the couch and sat up straight. "We still don't have a clear-cut motive for her murder, do we?"

"No, but I'm certain it's something unusual."

"Why not stick with the New Jersey idea that Key proposed and return to the farm?" She yawned and stretched.

"To do what, without legal authority? Did Key dangle a carrot for us to go back to Jersey and get shot? Remember, we've been warned about returning."

"Are you serious?"

The yawn was catching. Sam stifled his. "If the mob isn't trying to kill us, who is? I don't know. And I don't know if there's a connection between Jack Osborne and Johnnie Turner that goes all the way up to Stephen Key. When we asked, he said it was a hit job and brushed if off. Does he know I witnessed Osborne kill Turner?"

"You suspect everybody," DJ announced.

"Everybody who might have had a motive to kill her," Sam amplified. "Until we come up with an alternative, like Key said, I'm the only credible suspect."

"What do you want to do?" DJ asked.

"We can't go back into hiding," Sam answered. "If I can confirm Tony Carlucci wasn't behind the attempt to kill me, that will whittle down the list of threats."

"Don't you mean *kill us?*"

"No, you've never been the target."

"How are you going to do that?"

"I'm going to ask the man who introduced Laura to Tony to act as my intermediary and find out." Sam reached for his jacket. "It may take me a while to track him down. You stay put."

"Who is he, in case I have to rescue you?"

"Richard Carlin."

"Can I sleep in your bed?" DJ asked.

"Anytime," Sam replied. "No, correction, all the time."

CHAPTER 21

RICHARD CARLIN WASN'T AT HIS CENTRAL PARK WEST PENT-
house and the doorman was mum about his whereabouts. At a nearby
cab stand, Sam talked to a driver who frequently took Carlin to the
Copacabana on East Sixtieth Street. Sam decided to give it a go. A fin
on top of the fare got him to the club just as the first show let out.
Comedian Jimmy Durante was headlining, and it was opening night.

The lights were up, the house band was playing a watered-down
version of a Duke Ellington tune, and the lovely, costumed Copa Girls
were slinging drinks for the after-dinner crowd. Carlin was at a table
sandwiched between an Ava Gardner lookalike and a blonde with a
Jayne Mansfield figure.

Sam reintroduced himself and asked for a moment of Carlin's time.
Carlin told his companions to pay a visit to the powder room and told
Sam to sit.

"I need to know if Tony Carlucci wants me dead," Sam said.

Carlin smiled. "Are you a numbskull? Get lost."

"You don't want me to do that unless you'd like to see your name
in tomorrow's *Herald Tribune* as a person of interest in Laura Neilson's
murder."

"You don't have that kind of pull."

"Call Nicholas Reddy at the *Trib* and ask him."

"I was out of town when she got murdered."

"So what? As an officer in Edifice Partners, you've got a reputation
to protect. The firm could lose business if it got tarnished. Call Nick."

Sam gave him Reddy's business card, said to mention his name
and ask if Nick was working on a column about the murder. Carlin

motioned to a Copa Girl to bring him a telephone and dialed the number. He turned away, covered the mouthpiece with his hand, and mumbled something Sam couldn't make out.

When he finished, he glared at Sam and handed him the receiver. "The guy won't tell me what he's got. He wants to talk to you."

Nick asked what was going on. Sam promised to get back ASAP, disconnected, and smiled at Carlin.

"One question, and I'll leave you alone: Does Tony Carlucci want me dead?"

"You wouldn't be here right now if he did."

"Fair enough." Sam reclaimed Nick's business card. "What do you know about dirty cops in Hoboken?"

"You said one question."

"Humor me. Salvatore Silano thinks there's something fishy going on, and I bet you know something too. Do you know of any city cops living there? I thought they're required by law to be New York residents."

"There's rumors about some cops that got something going on that's not legit," Carlin replied. "It's been happening for a while."

"Like what?"

"That's all I know. "

"How long is a while?"

Carlin shrugged. "Who knows? I haven't been to Hoboken in the last three years."

"Maybe I should ask Tony," Sam proposed.

"And maybe you should let sleeping dogs lie. You got what you wanted, now do the same for me."

"I'll tell Reddy it was a false lead." The ladies returned from the powder room and Sam got to his feet. "Your name won't be mentioned."

On his way out, he spotted comedians Red Skelton and Morey Amsterdam at a table with a Hollywood ingénue he didn't recognize. Dean Martin and Jerry Lewis sat nearby. Sam shook off the celebrity glitter and called Reddy from a pay phone by the coat stand to explain the false alarm.

"Not a problem," Nick replied. "My column on the Neilson murder will run in the morning. Get ready to be in the spotlight again."

"I'll keep my head down."

He called DJ to say Carlucci was not looking to kill him. She was pleased to hear it but unconvinced that they could now rest easy. She said Mike Dalton had stopped by to report that the body in the panel van had been identified as a nineteen-year-old Puerto Rican male recently arrived from the island who had no known priors. Hoboken detectives were unable to locate any immediate family. Puerto Rican authorities had been asked to assist.

With Tony Carlucci cleared of suspicion and Turner dead, only Johnnie's assassin, Lieutenant Jerry Osborne, remained a possible threat.

"That we know of," DJ cautioned.

"I think it's time I checked in with Walt Seaver," Sam said.

"I'll go with you."

"It's late. Just give me his address."

"Where are you?"

"At the Copacabana."

"Wait outside for me."

DJ hung up before Sam could coax her into giving him Walt's address.

SEAVER LIVED IN A Morningside Heights five-story walk-up a block away from the university. His top-floor, one-bedroom bachelor apartment showed an undisciplined sloppiness in direct contrast to his analytical mind. A large blackboard filled with mathematical hieroglyphs dominated a wall. Below it, on a shelf made of stacked concrete blocks and plywood, sat a hi-fi record player. There were milk crates filled with long-playing jazz and classical albums, and what appeared to be every college textbook Walt had ever owned crammed on a freestanding bookcase within reach of a raggedy easy chair.

A round café-sized table was jammed next to a passageway to a small galley kitchen. Walt cleared off stacks of books from matching chrome chairs and made coffee. It was almost undrinkable.

Sam brought Walt up-to-date on his meeting with Carlin, noting

once again the recurring message that not all was on the up-and-up
with the cops in Hoboken.

"Interesting," Walt said. "I doubt anyone in the department would
believe that you saw Lieutenant Osborne kill Turner in cold blood.
He's a twenty-five-year veteran with a stellar reputation. We don't
know exactly why he did it, but clearly it was preemptive. I've assumed
Turner could have directly implicated Osborne in criminal activities if
the commissioner's task force picked him up, or talked to you—if you
got there first."

"Any idea what cookie jar Osborne has his hand in?" DJ asked.

"If my analysis is accurate, he's far craftier than that. His entire
career has been first as a robbery detective and later a task force supervisor in Central Robbery. Without access to his personal and financial
history, my only avenue of inquiry has been public information. And
there's quite a bit there."

Using his university teaching assistant credentials, Walt had pre-
sented himself to the chief's administrative aide as a Ph.D. graduate
student writing a dissertation on the history and development of sci-
entific policing within the Detective Division. He had asked to review
pertinent department PI documents and press clippings.

"Boy, did he come through," he added with a laugh. "The possibility of some potentially good press in the face of the current corrupt
cop scandal was almost irresistible."

Walt passed around a number of police press releases of major robbery arrests and convictions spotlighting Osborne's successful investigations. He'd spent an entire afternoon going through the files and
even talked the aide into loaning him some copies, which he'd analyzed
more carefully at home. He had discovered a glaring anomaly. During
the last decade, a major robbery in the city had gone unsolved every
year, each of them six-figure hauls. The heists included a major whole-
sale gem and diamond dealer, the payroll at an international shipping
company, ticket and concession receipts for a major league baseball
double-header, a jewelry heist at a luxury department store, the theft
of world-class contemporary art from a Manhattan gallery, and a half-
million-dollar coin collection stolen from a prominent numismatist.

"And the MO is always the same; three armed men, a driver outside, and only one of them talks or gives orders during the heists."

"No banks?" Sam asked.

"No banks, no feds," Walt explained. "Also, no violence, and no repeat performances—a different target each time. And get this: all the investigations were headed up by Lieutenant Osborne and his team, and not once did he request outside agency assistance."

"Has every robbery occurred during Osborne's work shift?"

"Yes."

Sam took a sip of coffee and tried not to grimace. "It's plausible, but unprovable."

"Dangle a carrot in front of him," Walt suggested. "I bet he'll nibble."

"It doesn't connect with Hoboken," Sam said.

"I can't give you everything," Walt answered. "But each crime was committed by an expert team of three men and a driver, all described as dressed in black, wearing masks, and approximately the same in height and weight. And on three different occasions, witnesses reported the getaway cars had New Jersey plates. All of the vehicles stolen, of course."

"And what about Turner?" DJ asked.

"One of the team?" Walt replied.

"He wasn't bright enough to be on the inside," Sam said.

"A lookout, maybe?" Walt offered.

"Or the driver," DJ suggested.

"If none of the above, maybe he just learned about the gang through his connection with the Carlucci family," Walt proposed. "Let's say Hoboken is a safe, convenient place outside the city to fence stolen merchandise. Who better to handle the transactions than a Mafia capo with connections who operates an import-export company?"

"It's a stretch," Sam countered. "Why would Carlucci be willing to burn the robbery operation to me if the family was making easy money fencing stolen merchandise? What have you learned about the heist team?"

"Statements by the victims describe that they were carefully organized, precision operations. I'm thinking cops, some or all with military service. A look at the personnel files of Osborne's present or past detective roster might prove interesting."

"Do you think Osborne planned the robberies?" DJ asked.

"Possibly. He was conveniently on duty during each heist, so he'd know what to expect upon arrival. He'd be the first on scene and could immediately control the investigation. Everything was carefully orchestrated, so I'm assuming he'd have a field subordinate to run the operation."

DJ bit her lip and looked at Sam. "Unless we can bring him down, you'll remain a target."

"If Osborne is as crafty as Walt says, I doubt he'd react precipitously if I baited him. But for now, I'd rather not."

"Let me see what more I can finesse out of the chief's assistant," Walt proposed. "I'll suggest doing a series of interviews with Osborne and his team. If I'm given names, I can start cross-checking to shake loose some more helpful information."

Sam looked at DJ. "Meanwhile, we'll go back to New Jersey."

"Where you might be more or less likely to get us killed?" she replied.

"We agreed, no more hiding, remember?" Sam glanced at Walt. "Find us a way to bring down Osborne."

"That could be beyond the realm of probability."

"You'll think of something," DJ said.

"What I'm thinking is that this is much bigger than Osborne," Walt cautioned. "Somebody thinks Sam knows something. Whether he does or doesn't isn't important. That's enough to have him silenced."

"Stop trying to scare me," Sam said with a smile. "I'm already halfway terrified. Don't overplay your hand at the Great White Castle, Walt. We don't know how far up the chain of command the cancer has spread."

"Don't worry, I won't." He waved good night as DJ and Sam stepped to the door.

*

OUTSIDE, AS THE LAST hour of the day fast approached, no cabs cruised the avenue or the crosstown streets, and the few pedestrians who hurried along appeared to be college students. Lights were on in many of the walk-up apartments, and the soft sound of a jazz album drifted down from an open window.

"Do you ever miss the carefree college years?" DJ asked.

"It never once felt that way for me," Sam replied. "And you?"

"I don't know how I survived it," DJ answered. "It would be closer and more convenient to stay overnight at my place."

Sam reached for her hand. "I'd like that."

CHAPTER 22

BEFORE FALLING ASLEEP, SAM AND DJ TALKED ABOUT WHERE to start in the morning. What Dirk Neilson and Stephen Key had separately said helped them to piece together a timeline that suggested Laura had been raped approximately two months prior to the drowning of the teenage boy at the stone quarry swimming hole. Combined with the retired sheriff's firm belief that the boy's death might not have been an accident, they decided to dig deeper into the incident.

With the morning sun at their backs, they left the city in a rented Chevrolet and drove to Newton. The daily newspaper, the *Town Crier*, had offices in a three-story building on Spring Street near the county courthouse. Inside they were greeted by a man who sat alone at a small desk behind a counter that had a sign listing various advertising and custom printing rates. A gooseneck lamp on the desk next to a typewriter provided the only light. Behind the desk a passageway opened onto a composition area and printing press. On the walls were framed front pages of several important historical events, including the sinking of the *Titanic* and the surrender of the Japanese to end World War II. The place smelled of printers' ink.

Sam asked if the editor was available. The man stood and introduced himself as Gideon Hollander, publisher and editor.

In his sixties, Hollander had a gravelly voice, a grouchy expression, and a head of gray hair in need of a trip to the barbershop. He looked like a character in a Damon Runyon short story. Sam explained they were investigating the murder of socialite Laura Neilson and wanted to learn more about the drowning of Allen Quick at the Kittatinny Valley Farms stone quarry.

Hollander chewed over the request and asked, "What's that got to do with the murder?"

DJ smiled sweetly. "That's what we're here to find out. Do you have archived copies of your newspaper?"

"Over a hundred years' worth. But you don't get to take a look without telling me why you think what happened to the Quick boy is important."

"You know about the drowning?" Sam asked.

"I covered it. I've known the family my entire life."

"Tell us about the family," DJ prompted.

Hollander motioned for them to join him and returned to his squeaky desk chair. "Not so fast. You go first. What does a drowning that happened years ago have to do with the murder of a Manhattan socialite? And don't leave anything out."

DJ told Hollander everything they'd learned about Laura's rape, pregnancy, and nearly fatal miscarriage. "We know she discovered Allen Quick's body in the quarry and would like to find out if she'd had any personal contact or involvement with him prior to that time."

"The sheriff didn't believe it was accidental," Hollander said cautiously. "Although he asked me not to print that because he'd been overruled by the coroner."

"Yes, I know. I spoke to him," DJ said.

"You think Allen raped her?"

"Possibly. You don't seem surprised by the idea."

"I'm not. The girl may have known or met him. At that time, his parents owned the largest farm supply store in the county, and he'd often help his father with deliveries to the local farms. They did a lot of business with Kittatinny Valley. After they got the settlement from the farm, they sold out and moved to Florida."

"Tell us about Allen," Sam encouraged.

"Good-looking, high school football and baseball all-star. Got scouted by a New York Yankees farm club. Was a bit of a bully but got away with it because of his athletic ability and popularity. Not a whiz kid by any means, but the girls went for him. Give me a minute."

He disappeared into a side room and after some time returned with a copy of a past issue of the newspaper. The sports section contained an article about the high school baseball team that included a photograph of Allen Quick in uniform standing at home plate holding a bat and smiling at the camera.

"We need to connect Allen to Laura at the farm," Sam said, passing the newspaper to DJ. "Otherwise, it's pure speculation. Did you ever talk directly with Laura or the girl who was with her when they found his body?"

"I tried, but her parents wouldn't let me near her. As for her companion, she was a minor in foster care, and child welfare removed her from the home almost immediately. They wouldn't even reveal her name. Where do you go from here?"

"To talk to Sid Huizinga and his cousin Sofia again." Sam stepped to the front of the counter. "Then to the farm if necessary to see if we can look at their books."

"No matter what you find out next, I'm opening my own investigation and printing this in tomorrow's paper," Hollander announced, not looking grumpy anymore.

"Be our guest," DJ said.

"Are you sure you want him to do this?" Sam asked DJ.

DJ nodded. "You bet I do. Dirk Neilson broke his word to us, didn't he?"

Sam nodded.

"Let me know if you learn anything new," Hollander said. "Otherwise, I'll go with what I've got. And thanks for the story. It's going to scoop both the *Times* and the *Herald Tribune.*"

THEY FOUND SID HUIZINGA at the side of his barn replacing spark plugs in a Dodge three-quarter-ton truck. "I wondered if you'd come back around," he said.

"Why is that?" DJ inquired.

"After we talked, I got to thinking. That summer when the boy drowned, I was at the farm more often because Uncle Lars had hurt his back. After school let out for the year, the Neilson girl came to stay with her parents, but they often went back to the city and left her under my aunt's care. She was always hanging around with one of the foster girls, a tomboy sort who was a little too flirty with the boys Lars hired every year as summer help. Aunt Lotte probably let them run free more than she should have because she didn't want to discipline the owners' daughter."

"The girl's name?" DJ asked.

Sid shook his head. "For the life of me, I can't remember her name."

"Did you ever see Allen Quick at the farm that summer?" DJ asked.

"I don't recall, but it's likely. He was a big kid for his age and often helped his dad with deliveries."

"We hope to speak to Sofia again," DJ said. "Is there anything we could say that might put her at ease with us?"

Sid rubbed his chin and smiled. "Ask her about Duchess. It was her favorite dog and followed her everywhere. That might get her talking, but remember . . ." He made a circling motion with a finger next to his head.

"We'll go easy," DJ said. "Gideon Hollander from the local paper might be calling you. He's planning to print a story about our investigation."

"All this about an accidental drowning years ago and the recent murder of a rich woman in the city?" Sid wondered aloud. "Seems like a wild goose chase to me."

"I hope you're wrong," DJ countered with a smile. "Thanks for your time, Mr. Huizinga."

*

"WHAT IF SID HUIZINGA is right?" Sam asked as they left Fredon Township. "And we're marking time, going nowhere?"

"We're going to Stanhope," DJ replied. "Have you noticed that even the smallest cottage looks neat and tidy? Everything is so well tended. There must be something in the water."

"You don't want to tolerate the thought of it."

"And until you drop into the valley, it feels so hidden away from everything, like a secret world."

"You don't want to talk about it."

"I'm talking about secrets," DJ said. "Magic words that get someone talking. Parents that hide the truth. Children that bear the scars.
Memories that jar more memories." There were tears in the corners
of her eyes.

"Are you all right?" Sam asked.

"I was remembering when I first got together with Laura after she
came home from private school in New England. We'd always loved
going to the movie matinees together, so we went to a neighborhood
theater that showed second-run features. It was a silly film about
three sisters who schemed to reunite their divorced parents before
their father made a huge mistake and married a gold digger. I can't
remember the title, but it was nothing more than a fluffy, lighthearted
comedy."

She slowed the Chevy and pulled off the highway. "Near the end
of the movie Laura started sobbing. She sat there in the dark theater
almost frozen, shaking her head and whispering to herself, 'I hate
them, I hate them.'"

DJ stared out the windshield. "I didn't know what to say or do.
Finally, I said we should leave. She got up, walked out, and never
looked back. When I caught up to her, she put on a phony, cheerful
face and apologized for making a scene. I asked what was wrong, but
she wouldn't say."

"What happened in the movie that triggered it?" Sam asked.

"It was a scene where the parents were playfully arguing about getting back together."

"Erica Birkenfield told me that Laura needed to escape from her parents," Sam recalled. "Not in so many words, but that's what she meant."

"I should have known something terrible had happened to her."

"How could you?"

"Because nobody breaks down over a silly movie," DJ answered,
her voice full of self-reproach.

They drove the rest of the way in silence without another mention
of the neat and tidy family farms that dotted the narrow valley floor.
When they arrived, Cousin Sofia was on her swing in the front yard

wearing a scarf around her neck, a baggy, faded gray sweatshirt, and blue jeans with the cuffs rolled up.

She smiled as they approached. "I know you!"

"Hello, Sofia," Sam said. Next door at Mrs. Lorenzen's house, the curtain in the window moved. "Nice to see you."

Sofia pouted. "Don't ask me bad questions."

"We won't, I promise," Sam said. "We came back because your cousin Sid said you could tell us a story about Duchess."

Sofia beamed. "Duchess. Best dog in the whole world. Laura found her and gave her to me."

"That must have made you happy," Sam said.

Sofia smiled broadly and nodded. "She was a runaway dog. Mother said I couldn't keep her, but Laura said I could, so she said yes. She lived a long, long time. I still miss her. But now I have a cat, I call her Lady."

She jumped off the swing. "Come inside, I'll show you a picture."

The sparsely furnished front room contained a console radio, an elderly easy chair with a matching footrest, a floor lamp, and a small bookcase. A framed photograph of Sofia sitting on the lawn holding a scruffy, long-haired, medium-sized dog in her lap was prominently displayed on the top shelf. Lady the cat was nowhere to be seen.

"That's Duchess. Laura took it, and she gave me the camera she did it with."

"Do you still have it?" DJ asked.

Sofia nodded and left the room, returning quickly with an old Kodak Brownie. She handed it to DJ and said, "It's broken. I tried, but I can't make it work."

"Have you used it since Laura gave it to you?"

"No, it's broken," Sofia replied, perturbed that she had to repeat herself.

The crank to advance unexposed film was jammed. "If you could trade the camera for one thing, what would that be?" DJ asked.

Sofia made a face and thought hard. "A television set. My welfare worker says they're too expensive, and Mrs. Lorenzen sometimes doesn't let me watch hers."

"If we went and got you a TV today, would you let us have the camera?"

Sofia nodded and beamed. "It would be the best day ever."

DJ handed Sofia the camera. "We'll wait together while Sam gets you one. Is a smaller TV for your bookcase okay?"

"Yes. How long to wait?"

"Not long." DJ motioned for Sam to join her on the porch. "There's film in the camera, I'm sure of it," she whispered. "Can we do this?"

Sam considered the currency in his wallet. "Barely, but yes."

"On your way, you better tell Mrs. Lorenzen what we're doing so she doesn't call Sofia's welfare worker to come with the sheriff."

"Good idea."

"And be quick."

"I will. And remember, don't ask Sofia any bad questions."

DJ smiled sweetly. "Girl talk only."

MRS. LORENZEN, A STOUT elderly woman who wore her years proudly, slowed Sam down with pointed questions until she was sure he and DJ were on the up-and-up. Because TV reception in the county could be spotty, she recommended that he buy a good antenna to go with the TV. She also suggested not to bother shopping in Stanhope as it had no appliance store, and instead drive to Morristown in the adjacent county.

With twice the population and less than half the quaintness of New-ton, Morristown boasted several appliance stores. Sam picked out a tabletop television and indoor antenna that didn't leave him penniless. Back at Sofia's, he was greeted in the kitchen by Sofia, DJ, and Mrs. Lorenzen, who'd convened a lunch party with sandwiches, cookies, and a pot of coffee. However, he wasn't allowed to eat until the TV was up and running.

After lunch, Mrs. Lorenzen and Sofia settled in to watch a soap opera. Sam and DJ drove to Morristown, where Sam had spotted a photography studio on the main street. Business was slow and the pro-prietor readily agreed to develop any exposed film inside the Brownie. When he came out of the darkroom, he handed over six good images.

"That's all there was," he said, explaining that the remaining unexposed film had been jammed up against the winding mechanism, causing it to malfunction.

They paid the man, retrieved the camera, sat in the rented Chevy, and examined the snapshots. Three were of farm animals lounging in a pasture. Another captured Sofia's dog, Duchess, romping on grass outside a cottage. There was also one of a smiling teenage girl leaning against a mailbox at a farm road entrance. The final frame showed Allen Quick unloading a delivery truck in front of a barn with *Kittatinny Valley Farms* painted in bold letters above the open doors.

"Now what?" DJ asked.

"We call Mr. Hollander to tell him we're on our way with the proof we were looking for. If he can't identify the girl, hopefully Sid Huizinga can."

"We're not going to ask Sofia?"

"Not if we don't have to. I promised her no bad questions."

"You're right." DJ put her hands on the steering wheel, leaned back, and sighed.

"What is it?"

"My sudden feeling of accomplishment just evaporated. Proving a theory doesn't solve Laura's murder."

"Finding new bits and pieces always helps," Sam consoled, feeling equally frustrated.

HUNCHED OVER A TYPEWRITER, Gideon Hollander barely looked up when Sam and DJ entered. He hammered at a few more keys, pushed back from his desk, and read what he'd typed. "'The recent murder of Laura Neilson, a Manhattan heiress, may be tied to the decades-old drowning of a local high school athlete.'"

"It hasn't been proven," DJ protested.

"Nor disproven," Hollander rebutted. "Plus, no libelous accusations against any person living or dead have been made, unless you've got something new to report."

"Nope," Sam answered, offering Gideon the snapshot of the girl at the mailbox.

"Jeannie?"

"We think so. Do you have anything at all about her?"

"Not a thing. Sid Huizinga called just before you got here. Said to stop by again when you have the chance."

Sam reclaimed the photo. "We'll go there now."

*

PART OF SID'S BARN functioned as a toolshed. A small wooden trunk with the name *Huizinga* hand-painted on the side stood open on a worktable.

"I inherited it when Aunt Lotte died," he said. "Put it on a top shelf and haven't looked at it for years. It's mostly nostalgic stuff about when the family came from the old country, and reminiscences about the early years in New Jersey where the Huizinga boys had settled. Unless you're a Huizinga, all in all it's pretty boring."

He handed DJ a leather-bound journal. "But this might interest you. Aunt Lotte kept a record of every foster child they took in from the state. Earlier, you'd asked me about a girl named Jeannie. Her name is in there, along with the dates she lived with Lars and Lotte."

The girl's name was Jeannie Babcock, and the dates she was at the farm lined up perfectly with Laura's rape and Allen Quick's death. DJ showed Sid the girl-at-the-mailbox snapshot.

"Jeannie?" she asked.

"Yep," Sid answered.

"Can we use your telephone to call Gideon Hollander?"

"Sure, but I still can't figure how this helps solve a murder."

"We're still trying to sort that out," Sam answered.

Sid returned the journal to the trunk, latched the lid, and lifted it. "Promised the wife to take it inside so we can both go through it again," he explained with a smile.

"It's good to be reminded once in a while where you come from," Sam said.

At the house, Sid introduced them to his wife Patty, a pretty woman with big blue eyes. After they'd called Hollander with their latest findings, she offered coffee, which they couldn't refuse. For the next little while, they sat with Sid and Patty at the kitchen table listening to stories about the Huizinga family in northen New Jersey.

They left with heartfelt thanks for the coffee and conversation, and returned to the city, carefully avoiding Hoboken. Supposedly, Tony Carlucci wasn't coming after Sam, but no matter what had been said, he wasn't completely sure. It was Carlucci's move to make, and Sam could do nothing about it.

CHAPTER 23

AT DJ'S OFFICE, WALT HAD LEFT A MESSAGE WITH DELORES that Commissioner Key's staff had interceded in his plan to "study" the successes of the Central Robbery Unit and canceled it. Thus, he was stalled. Undaunted, he was searching for another way in and would report back when he found it.

"I love his 'can-do' attitude," DJ said as her desk phone rang. Mike Dalton was calling for Sam. She gave him the handset.

"Nick Reddy's story on you in this morning's *Tribune* has people in the office talking, and it isn't complimentary," Mike said.

"I haven't seen it yet," Sam replied. "Does it say nice things about me?"

"That it does, but it also slams the DA, and I quote: 'Former ADA Sam Monroe and his private investigator partner, DJ Ryan, have done more to try to unravel the circumstances surrounding the murder of socialite Laura Neilson than either the District Attorney or the cops.' Then he asks: 'What's wrong with this picture?'"

"Very nice," Sam said, grinning into the handset.

"Don't be a wiseass," Mike cautioned.

"Why not?" Sam replied. "Nice hasn't gotten me anywhere. Is that all, Mike?"

"No, Jack Osborne wants to talk to you. Give him a call."

"What does a robbery lieutenant want to talk to me about?"

"He didn't say, but it may have something to do with what a priest told him. He said you'd asked questions about Johnnie Turner's old Italian family name on the night he got iced. Play nice. Osborne tried to keep you out of Rikers, remember?"

It was an overstatement, but he went along with it. "I'll call."

"You need to stop snooping around and muddying the waters," Mike advised. "You're still a person of interest in one murder, why make it two?" He gave Sam the phone number and hung up.

Sam put the phone down and gazed at DJ. "Did you get that?"

"You're being set up," DJ answered, "and either Dalton knows it, or he doesn't."

"If he does, it would be stupid of him to do it while I'm with you."

"Perhaps, unless it was meant for both of us. Give him the benefit of doubt, but no meeting with Osborne for now, okay?"

"Yes, ma'am." He pulled out Nick Reddy's business card and dialed his direct number. "Are you ready for what I've got?" he asked when Nick picked up.

"What have you got for me, hotshot?" Nick demanded.

"I want to fill you in before you get scooped," Sam said.

"Scooped by who?" Nick replied. "About what?"

Sam summarized what Gideon Hollander, publisher of the *Town Crier*, was about to do, what they'd discovered about Stephen Key's past involvement with Laura Neilson, the violent rape that occurred when she was young, the maybe not-so-accidental death of Allen Quick, and the search for a witness who may be the only person who knows exactly what had happened. All of it possibly tied to the strangulation of Laura in her penthouse apartment.

"Slow down, cowboy, and give it to me one bullet at a time," Reddy said.

Sam broke it down item by item. Nick didn't interrupt, the background sound of the typewriter accompanying Sam's narrative. When he stopped talking, Reddy asked if he was finished.

"Not quite. I'd like a friend of mine to have access to the paper's microfiche records."

"Tell me why."

"Over the past decade, ten major robberies in the city have gone unsolved, and we want to learn more about them and the detectives who investigated the cases."

"Is there something fishy going on?"

"It's just a theory for now," Sam answered, leapfrogging the question. "His name is Walt Seaver. I'll give him your direct line. And do you know anybody in need of an experienced housekeeper? I promised this lady's son I'd find her a job."

"Who is it?"

"Adella Diaz, she worked for Laura Neilson up to the time of her murder. She's topnotch." He summarized what he knew about her: single mother of two great kids, Puerto Rican, Spanish-speaking, bilingual, high school graduate, reliable and honest.

Reddy sighed. "I'll ask all my hoity-toity friends."

"I'm serious," Sam admonished.

"So am I," Nick retorted. "If you ever decide to switch careers, let me know. In the meantime, keep your eye out for tomorrow's paper and stay in touch."

The line went dead.

"You didn't tell me about Laura's housekeeper needing a job," DJ chided.

"It slipped my mind."

"Tell me about her."

Sam gave DJ his brief. She called her mother and asked her to help a trustworthy woman with two teenage children find a housekeeping job. She gave particulars and stressed that Adella had been literally kicked to the curb by a lawyer for Laura's trust with little compensation. After a promise to help was given, a mother-daughter chat followed. Eavesdropping, Sam learned DJ had no intention of ending her relationship with him.

"So, you still like me," he joked when she disconnected.

"I do, but you may become too expensive for me to keep," DJ replied.

"I'll work for food and do the dishes."

"It's a lowball offer, but I'll consider it."

LATE AT NIGHT IN DJ's apartment, Sam couldn't sleep no matter how hard he tried. He got up quietly so as not to wake her and sat in the dark front room listening to the muffled night sounds of the city, a pulse more mechanical than rhythmic. He was baffled about Mike

Dalton. Was he an innocent messenger, unaware that Osborne had gunned down Johnnie Turner, or a party to the crime? Had Osborne followed him the night he'd gone looking for Turner? Did he suspect Sam had witnessed the murder?

There was only one way to find out. If Osborne's intent was to do him in, it wouldn't matter what time of the day or night Sam called. He dressed in the dark, took DJ's .38 Colt pistol from her purse, left the apartment, and dialed Osborne's number from a public telephone. He answered on the third ring.

"You wanted to talk?" Sam asked.

"This is a helluva time to call me."

"Go back to sleep, I'll call later."

"No, no, I'm awake. We need to meet."

"About?" Sam queried.

"Mike Dalton," Osborne answered. "He's not who you think he is."

"Then who is he?"

"I can't go into it on the phone. Where are you?"

Reluctant to reveal his whereabouts, Sam said, "In Jersey. Sussex County. I can be back in the city in a little over an hour."

"That'll work." Osborne gave him the address of an all-night greasy spoon in Hell's Kitchen and said he'd be there waiting for him. On foot, Sam easily made it long before the hour was up. Through the diner's plate-glass window, he saw two men sitting at the lunch counter, an elderly woman eating alone at a table, and a bored waitress behind a cash register reading a magazine.

There was no sign of Jack Osborne. Everything inside looked copacetic. He moved on, alert for any unusual activity. A working-class Irish neighborhood with walk-up apartment buildings, small mom-and-pop stores, and commercial businesses scattered along the avenues, it had an unusually large assortment of saloons that catered to serious drinkers and dedicated drunks.

He found a good vantage point away from streetlights, and waited and watched as a dribble of customers came and went. After a half hour, a man entered and claimed an empty stool at the counter with the best view of the street and entrance. He lingered over coffee refills and a slice of pie well past Sam's promised arrival time before using the pay phone and leaving on foot.

Sam followed. The man led him out of Hell's Kitchen to a precinct house in the Garment District. After he entered, Sam walked to a corner newsstand, where the vendor was arranging the early morning edition of the *Herald Tribune* on a rack.

Nick Reddy's column was on the front page, with a headline that read: "Major City Heists Go Unsolved for Years." Followed by the lead: "Police drop the ball on ten high-profile robberies."

The story dug into the crimes one by one, detailing the how, what, when, and where of each, and put a spotlight squarely on Lieutenant Jack Osborne's failure to successfully close any of the robberies.

Nick normally didn't share his byline, but this time there were two additional contributors to the column. He had called in reserves to help break the story. Sam wanted to forgive him but couldn't quite muster the enthusiasm to do it. At heart, Nick was more reporter than lawyer, and although Sam had asked for a favor, he'd said nothing about keeping it hush-hush. Nevertheless, it stung and made Sam's circumstances suddenly more dangerous.

Were that the end of it, it would have been bad enough, but a page two headline made Sam groan: "Police Commissioner Tied to Murder Investigation." Again, Reddy had shared his byline, this time with Gideon Hollander of the Newton *Town Crier.*

Sam didn't bother to read it. Down the block, Jack Osborne had emerged from the precinct house accompanied by the man from the diner. Sam stuck the newspaper under his arm and turned away. It would be nonsensical to go up against two corrupt, armed cops. Besides, if he hurried, maybe he could return to DJ's before she woke up.

*

SAM DIVERTED TO A small French café and bakery in DJ's neighborhood that opened early, bought fresh croissants, and had breakfast ready when DJ wandered out of the bedroom, sleepy-eyed and barely clothed. He particularly admired her long legs and nicely shaped bottom. Her subdued look vanished when Sam described Jack Osborne's failed assassination plot. In an attempt to deflect any lectures about his foolhardy impulsiveness, he gave her the *Tribune* morning edition to read.

The intercom buzzed. Walt Seaver waited at the building's front door. DJ glared at Sam, buzzed Walt in, and left the room to bathe and dress. Walt had bags under his eyes and two copies of the *Herald Tribune* under his arm. He spotted the open newspaper on the kitchen table and sank wearily into a chair.

"You've already seen it," he grumped. "Reddy would only give me access to the archives if I agreed to help with the story. He wanted to include me on the byline, but I said no. He sends his thanks and apologizes for screwing you. His exact words."

Walt handed Sam a business card. "He wants to meet with you at his club today for lunch at one p.m. The address is on the back. Jacket and necktie required."

"Do you know what for?"

Walt shrugged. "He didn't say, but he's planning a whole series of in-depth articles on the heists. He'll probably get a Pulitzer when it's finished."

"Did you learn anything that's not in the story?" Sam asked.

Walt nodded. "The department's accounting bureau keeps a record of pay slips for every officer in every precinct, division, and support office. I looked up Jack Osborne's first assignment as a patrolman and checked the precinct payroll records for Michael Dalton and Jerome Aloysius O'Reilly. Both walked the same beat as Osborne early in their careers. Later both served with him in Central Robbery. O'Reilly resigned to join the Hoboken PD as a detective sergeant and later transferred to patrol duty. Dalton gave up his detective shield to join the DA's office as a senior investigator. What's more interesting is their timing: they both left the police department exactly one month after the first heist at the Forty-Seventh Street Diamond Exchange."

"Were they part of the investigating team?" Sam asked.

"That I haven't confirmed."

"What about Eddie Snyder?"

"He was a transfer into Robbery as a plainclothes officer from a

Brooklyn precinct. He resigned to join the U.S. Marshals Service six months after Dalton and O'Reilly left. It would be interesting to see if there has been staff turnover like that in Robbery after every heist."

"I doubt it," Sam offered. "That wouldn't go unnoticed."

"I agree, it's like a limited partnership. But how does Johnnie Turner fit in?"

"What's your best guess?"

"Turner was about to transfer to Central Robbery when you caught him falsifying evidence, which got him booted back to patrol," Walt replied.

"So he really did have cause to hate me. Supposedly he had an uncle at headquarters who saved him from being fired. Did you share all this with Nick Reddy?"

"I saw no reason not to. But more than that, I'm thinking Turner was like a junior partner who was a weak link in the operation."

"A wheelman with a temper and no morals," Sam proposed.

"Exactly."

"Well, at least now I have a clearer idea of why Jack Osborne wants to kill me. He's afraid I know about the operation."

Sam described how Osborne had set him up for a hit by a cop he couldn't ID from the Garment District precinct. "It's time to give him another opportunity."

"Is that smart?" Walt asked.

"Probably not." He dialed Jack Osborne's number. There was no answer, so he called Central Robbery and got put through right away.

"Sorry I couldn't make it last night," he said cordially. "You were going to tell me something about Mike Dalton. What is it?"

"Nothing I can discuss over the phone," Jack replied. "When can we meet?"

"I don't know," Sam replied. "Tonight, maybe."

"Call me at home."

The line went dead. Sam looked at Walt. "Can you stay here and look after DJ?"

Walt grinned. "I'd wait on her hand and foot if I thought it would get me anywhere. What do I tell her?"

"Tell her everything we know, ask her to sit tight, and say not to worry." He slid DJ's Colt revolver in Walt's direction.

Walt shook his head. "You don't make it easy on yourself, do you?"

Sam nodded in agreement and stood up. "Try the croissants. They're made by a French Algerian couple and are the best in the city."

"How do you know that?"

"It says so on their menu." He turned to leave. "See what else you can find out about Eddie Snyder. And good work," he added.

*

SAM'S FORMER SUPERVISOR, Marilyn Feinstein, lived alone in an East Village apartment building within easy walking distance to work. He'd been a guest in her home at dinner parties, staff gatherings, and several holiday celebrations. A widow, she'd lost her husband some years ago in a tragic boating accident, and her two grown daughters had moved away, busy with lives filled with family and their husbands' careers.

He parked himself on the front steps of the building and watched the trees that lined the quiet residential street drop lazy autumn leaves on the sidewalk. It was a picture-perfect postcard morning.

When she came out the door and saw him, she showed no surprise. "Well, if it isn't the talk of the town."

"And good morning to you, as well," Sam replied. "I'd like you to find out where Lieutenant Jack Osborne lives, and please let me know as soon as possible."

"Why should I do that?"

"Because he murdered Johnnie Turner in cold blood and tried to have me killed last night. I witnessed both events."

"Did you tell the commissioner about the hit on Turner when you met with him?"

"Other than you, I've not been inclined to be overly trusting of members of the law enforcement community."

"You do know that he believes in your innocence."

"He has said that."

She took his arm. "Are you walking me to work?"

"It would be my pleasure."

"As we stroll along, tell me everything that Nick Reddy hasn't printed in the *Tribune* about this alleged police robbery ring, and leave nothing out."

They ambled at an unhurried pace, but when Sam brought up Mike Dalton, it stopped Marilyn her tracks.

"Unbelievable," she muttered, searching his face. "You have no proof."

"I want him to be innocent as much as you do, but there is an interesting link between four old friends early in their cop careers: Dalton, his brother-in-law Jerry O'Reilly, Jack Osborne, and U.S. Deputy Marshal Eddie Snyder."

"A link to Nick Reddy's story of a cop robbery ring?"

"Yes."

"You're speculating."

"Yes, but not about Osborne's murder of Johnnie Turner, who was about to be transferred to Central Robbery when I caught him falsifying evidence that cost him his chance for a detective's shield. Or about Osborne's attempt to have me killed last night using Mike Dalton as bait for the reason to meet."

"I still don't see the connection."

"Do you know that he came to my apartment several times, offering support and advice?"

Marilyn nodded. "I put him out there as an unofficial lifeline in case you needed one."

"Did he tell you that he knew I had in my possession items I'd taken from Laura's penthouse the night she was murdered? And answer how was it that Susan Cogan got killed before she could leave town with the money Stephen Key had promised her?"

"I didn't know that," Marilyn replied. "And your question about Cogan's murder is speculation."

"Somebody on the inside of the task force tipped off Johnnie Turner about it, otherwise Cogan would be alive today."

"You're serious?"

"Finally, how did Turner avoid getting rounded up with all the other dirty cops? Pure luck? A coincidence? Supposedly a ranking uncle in the department saved his job once before. But maybe this time it was someone else who made sure he avoided the dragnet. It would be nice to know."

"You're persuasive, but unconvincing."

"I've survived two beatings and two attempts on my life by officers of the police department. Do I need to get shot in order to convince you?"

They were a block away from the district attorney's offices, standing in the middle of the sidewalk as pedestrians streamed around them. "What are you planning to do with Lieutenant Osborne's home address?" Marilyn asked.

"Keep him in my sights until you can unleash some backup."

"That may take some time."

"I've got plenty of it."

"Call me on my direct line later in the afternoon." She stepped away and vanished into the flow of civil servants hurrying off to do the public good.

*

SAM RETURNED TO DJ'S to find a partial dossier on Eddie Snyder waiting for him. Walt had contacted one of Nick Reddy's coauthors of the unsolved heists story, who'd searched archives and learned Edward Snyder had served in the Navy prior to becoming a police officer. DJ had used her naval intelligence contacts to find out that he was an honorably discharged petty officer third class who had served in the Pacific Fleet as a master-at-arms, the equivalent to an Army MP. His active-duty separation papers showed an enlistment address in Hoboken, New Jersey. Ma Bell information had a Richard Snyder currently living at that address.

"We should go there and talk to him," DJ declared.

"Let's slow things down until after my afternoon meeting with Nick Reddy," Sam suggested.

"I agree," Walt said, yawning. His all-nighter at the *Herald Tribune* had worn him down. He made his excuses and left.

"We can't just do nothing," DJ complained.

Sam reached for her. She looked too good, and he was too wound up to feel tired. "That's not what I had in mind."

*

NICHOLAS REDDY'S PRIVATE CLUB was a six-story limestone town house with a Madison Avenue address in the Murray Hill neighborhood of Manhattan. Inside, Sam announced himself to the receptionist, an elderly gentleman in a suit who could easily pass for an English butler except for his slightly discernible New York accent. He directed Sam to a private upstairs dining room and pointed to the elevator at his immediate left. Sam took the grand staircase instead, so he could glance at the portraits of the club's founding fathers that climbed the wall; a who's who of pedigreed nineteenth-century New Yorkers. Among the group, a bearded Reddy and a mustached Key ancestor looked down at him as he passed by. Therefore, he was not surprised when their progeny, several times removed, rose to warmly greet him as he was ushered into the room. Marilyn Feinstein was present, although she remained seated.

"I didn't think you'd be pleased to see me," Sam said as he shook Stephen Key's hand.

"You read Nick's piece?" Key asked.

"No, just the headline."

"Well, he was very generous in describing my alleged rescue of Laura and my old friendship with her and her family. There was nothing to hide."

"The benefits of friendship can run deep," Sam replied with a sharp glance at Reddy. "You've already apologized to me through an intermediary. Is there more you want to say?"

Nick smiled. "We've all been wondering how you got on to this robbery scheme."

Sam took an empty chair next to Marilyn. "I was trying to find Johnnie Turner before he found me, and stumbled on to it. More accurately, the mob pointed me in the right direction."

"Why, I wonder?" Marilyn said.

"I imagine they didn't like competition, especially from crooked cops," Stephen suggested.

"You may be right, but I initially thought the opposite," Sam replied. "Otherwise, why brother to tell me there were rotten cops in Hoboken?"

"Exactly," Key said.

Sam looked at Marilyn. "Do you have an address for me?"

"She does not," Key said emphatically. "We need to move carefully on this. Assemble a small investigative task force to build a case against Osborne and his accomplices. Work with the U.S. Marshals Service and New Jersey law enforcement to tighten the noose around Snyder and O'Reilly's necks."

"Then why am I here?" Sam inquired.

"The district attorney will clear you of all charges and reappoint you as an assistant DA effective immediately, if you take point on the task force," Marilyn replied.

"We need you on the team," Key added.

Sam thought it over. "I'll take a get-out-of-jail card but pass on the job."

Marilyn registered surprise. "This isn't a negotiation."

Sam rose from his chair just as a waiter opened the door to deliver lunch. It smelled delicious. "You're right, it's more like a plea-bargain deal. Count me out."

Nick approached with a business card in his outstretched hand. "Before you leave, my publisher's daughter-in-law is seeking a Spanish-speaking, bilingual housemaid. She wants her two young children to learn a second language. If this woman is all you say she is, it might be a perfect fit. Have her call to make an appointment."

Sam took the card. Mrs. Joan Carson lived on Fifth Avenue in one of the last of the Gilded Age mansions that had once been part of Millionaires' Row. "I certainly will, and thanks."

Stephen Key made a stop gesture with his hand. "What are you planning, Sam?"

"I'm not sure, but whatever it is, I'll do it as a private citizen and not as an officer of the court."

"You're making a rash mistake," Marilyn warned.

Sam paused and smiled. "It's something I've recently been told that I'm good at."

In the grand reception hallway of the mansion, the elderly gentle-man at the reception desk detained him. "The lady asked me to give this to you if you left the meeting early," he said, handing over an envelope.

It was addressed to him in Marilyn's handwriting. He stuffed it in a pocket and waited to read it on the subway ride to Spanish Harlem. She wrote: *Ask George Lemond.*

Of course, his old boss at the department store. If anyone had the juice to milk information out of the department, it would be Lemond. He called George at work as soon as he got off the subway and told him that he needed Lieutenant Jack Osborne's home address, pronto.

"What do you got?" George asked.

"A real bad apple with a badge," Sam replied, adding a quick run-down that included witnessing Osborne's murder of Johnnie Turner.

"Call me at home tonight."

George hung up before Sam could say thanks. He walked toward Adella's apartment thinking he needed a gun, and fast. One that couldn't be easily traced back to him.

CHAPTER 24

ADELLA DIAZ WAS GROCERY SHOPPING WHEN SAM ARRIVED, but Pedro, her son, and Veronica, her daughter, were parked at the kitchen table doing homework. Veronica, a tall girl with a refined tilt to her pretty head, left to give her mother the exciting news of a job interview. Sam used the interlude to ask Pedro if he knew anyone in the neighborhood who had a handgun to sell.

Pedro vigorously shook his head. "No way."

"I'm not asking you to do anything wrong," Sam clarified. "Someone's trying to kill me, and he's a cop."

"That's for sure?"

"Yes. You know the neighborhood, point me in the right direction."

"Two blocks west of the subway station there's an old Mercury parked in front of a barbershop. Stand by the right rear fender of the car and wait. Someone will come out to talk to you."

"Someone?" Sam queried.

"One of the barbers. Younger than you and skinny. He has a teardrop tattooed under his right eye. Bullets cost extra."

"Does he have a name?"

"He wouldn't want you to know it."

"Thanks, Pedro. Don't mention this to your mother."

"Don't worry, I won't. Does this job for her you told us about look good?"

"Real good," Sam answered, wondering what it would take to get Adella, Pedro, and Veronica out of Spanish Harlem.

Adella and her daughter arrived, both out of breath. Adella dumped the groceries on the kitchen counter and started peppering Sam with questions. He slowed everyone down. When they learned who the woman was and what she was looking for in a housekeeper, Adella's smile almost matched that of the Alice in Wonderland Cheshire Cat. She would call for an interview right away.

"I need to get going now," he said.

Adella insisted that Pedro accompany Sam to the subway but had one more thing to tell him. "After I gave you that list of residents you'd asked for, it made me remember that sometimes Laura called Julia Anderson by a different name."

"Do you remember what name?"

"No, but sometimes she gave people nicknames. I think that's what it was."

"Did I have one?"

"Shamas, because she had to shoplift something in order to get your attention."

Sam laughed. "Yes, she did. Do any other nicknames come to mind?"

"Not for people in the building. Mostly she used them for old friends and family members."

Sam handed Adella one of DJ's business cards. "You can reach me at this number, and I'll want to hear how your interview goes."

"You'll be the first to know." She kissed Sam on the cheek as he opened the front door.

*

GRAY AFTERNOON CLOUDS PREDICTED a cold, windy night. With Pedro taking point, Sam walked in the direction of the barbershop and stopped half a block away. "This is where you leave," Sam said.

"I should stick around maybe, make sure you're okay."

"You should do as I say and go home."

Pedro hesitated.

Sam grabbed him by the arm and spun him around. "Go."

He waited until the boy was out of sight before taking a position at the right rear fender of the Mercury. A man eventually came out. He was older, overweight, wore a white barber's smock, and looked somewhat perplexed.

"What do you want?" he asked abruptly.

"Not a haircut," Sam said half-seriously. He'd let Barney, his neighborhood Yorkville barber, deal with his shaggy mop sometime when he had the time and could spare the money.

The barber's gap-toothed smile wasn't friendly. "Then why do you stand there?"

"You know why."

"Go away." The barber turned on his heel, went inside, and drew the shade to the shop window.

An hour passed before the barber returned. "What do you want?" he demanded again.

"A revolver, preferably a Smith & Wesson, plus cartridges."

The barber hesitated and looked at the shop window. When the shade was raised, he shook his head. "I only have a Ruger, twenty-two. Brand-new."

"Never heard of it. How much?"

He quoted a price that was twice Sam's monthly rent. Reluctantly, Sam said okay.

"Go inside." The barber motioned for Sam to precede him.

Sam obliged. It was a two-chair shop, with posters on the wall illustrating the popular hairstyles for men and the best-selling hair-grooming products. A young, skinny guy with a teardrop tattoo under his right eye frisked him, took the cash, and handed over the Ruger and a handful of loose ammunition, saying, "Don't come back here."

"I won't," Sam promised as he walked to the door, the Ruger in his pocket, thinking a pistol is a pistol no matter the caliber.

"I mean it."

"So do I."

*

HE MADE IT TO the subway and out of Spanish Harlem without being robbed or mugged, and relaxed in the safety of the half-empty train as it pulled out of the station. He'd been deliberately vague with DJ about what he planned to do after meeting with Nick Reddy. Sidetracking to Adella's apartment had slowed him down, but it didn't matter.

It was too early to call George, so his next stop would be Hobo-

ken and the Richard Snyder address. DJ would probably dump him
for going it alone and keeping her in the dark, but he'd rather lose her
affection than put her life at risk again.

From a midtown subway stop, he walked crosstown to Penn Station and bought a bus ticket to Philadelphia at the Greyhound terminal, a modernistic building outside the sprawling commuter railroad
hub. Hoboken was the first stop.

Waiting to depart, he dialed Richard Snyder's number, but nobody
picked up. There were racks of free area city maps for travelers. Hoboken was a compact city of slightly more than one square mile, with
shipping, commercial, and manufacturing enterprises dominating the
riverfront. Snyder's address was in the southwest quadrant of the city
within easy walking distance of the bus stop. He didn't know what
might be in store when he knocked on the door, but the Ruger in his
pocket made him feel a little less apprehensive.

A loudspeaker announcement called for departure to Philadelphia,
with Hoboken as its first stop. Sam boarded. He'd deliberately chosen
Greyhound and bought a ticket to Philly in case he needed to hide his
tracks. He'd use the Port Authority to return.

He was in Hoboken within minutes. He moved quickly away from
downtown to a residential neighborhood and found the cross street
that cut through the heart of row houses and long, narrow shotgun
apartment buildings, featureless except for centered front doors and
windows aligned above like stepping stones.

The Snyder address was no different. A light behind a second-story
window curtain was the only evidence of occupation. Sam found a
dark corner with a good line of sight and watched for any unusual
activity. Satisfied that all looked normal, he approached and rang the
doorbell. An elderly woman in a housedress answered and gazed at
him inquiringly. Sam apologized for the interruption and asked to
speak to Richard Snyder.

"Oh, he's long dead," the woman replied. "He was my brother."

"I'm sorry to hear it. The phone book still has him listed. I called but
nobody answered."

The woman nodded. "I know, I heard it ring upstairs on the third floor. I never go up there. My nephew won't change it and I don't answer it. I have my own phone down here."

"I didn't know he had a son," Sam said, hoping for a name.

She nodded.

"Nobody lives with you?"

"Oh, no, I get along just fine on my own."

"Does your nephew live upstairs?"

The woman's expression grew less friendly. "Why did you want to see Richard?"

"I may have come to the wrong address. I'm looking for Richard William Snyder."

She shook her head. "My brother's middle name was Edward."

Sam smiled ruefully. "I'm sorry to have troubled you."

"No bother," the woman said as she closed the front door.

Sam stepped away from the house thinking chances were good Eddie's aunt was on the phone reporting his snooping. But beyond that, he couldn't help but wonder what was on the third floor where Eddie's aunt never ventured.

Sam smiled. Want a legitimate-looking front to mask your criminal enterprise and hide some of the spoils yet to be fenced? What better than an elderly, pleasant old lady living alone in an inconspicuous house on a street in an ordinary working-class neighborhood?

He caught a late evening Port Authority bus back to the city, which, under a darkening sky, looked like a gigantic fortress with a thousand watchtowers warning all who approached to stay away. Sam had no choice; there was nowhere else for him to go if he wanted to find Jack Osborne.

IN MANHATTAN, SAM STEPPED off the bus, called Marilyn Feinstein, and asked if any of the targets in the unsolved robberies had been advised that they were under investigation. Fortunately not. Facts in the cases were still being assembled. He reported his conversation with Eddie Snyder's aunt in Hoboken and his concern that it might have triggered a warning call to Eddie. Marilyn would follow up with the commissioner to have Snyder put under surveillance immediately. She'd didn't chide him for the misstep. He also mentioned the mysterious third floor of the Hoboken house where Eddie's aunt never ventured. Marilyn agreed it needed to be watched.

He dialed George Lemond. Osborne owned a home in Yonkers, a small city thirty minutes north of Manhattan. However, during the work week he stayed in the city with a girlfriend, a nurse who worked at New York Hospital and lived in a Sutton Place co-op building. George was still waiting on the name of the woman and her address. He'd know more in the morning.

Sam hung up, glad to stop for the night and pleased that Osborne was spending his off-duty hours with a woman who lived close enough to walk to from his Yorkville apartment. It almost made him smile.

After getting no answer when he called DJ, he hotfooted it to her apartment, hoping she'd buzz him in. No such luck. At his place, a note from her was tacked on his door. It said she wanted nothing more to do with him, ever again. He shitcanned it and called Walt Seaver, who had no idea where she was, just that she was really pissed that he'd disappeared again without any warning.

He warmed up a can of beans for dinner and then fell asleep in the front room dreaming of Korea. It woke him up and he had a hell of a time getting back to sleep.

CHAPTER 25

IN THE MORNING, ABE SILVERSTEIN KNOCKED ON SAM'S DOOR with a message that some detective had been around yesterday to see him, and it wasn't Mike Dalton. The description matched Jack Osborne. Sam asked Abe to lie to any cops who came around again, including Dalton and Osborne, and say that he'd moved out and Abe didn't know where.

Abe shook his head in dismay. "You've got to get this murder mess cleaned up before you get killed."

Sam smiled anemically. "I'm trying."

He called George, who'd just heard back from his source. Osborne's girlfriend was Amanda Daner, a surgical nurse. The Sutton Place building she lived in had been built during the Roaring Twenties and had fourteen floors and only ten apartments. There was no way a surgical nurse could afford such luxury.

"If Osborne has been smart, he's hidden his ownership of the co-op behind a dummy corporation, using this Daner woman as his beard," George suggested. "It shouldn't be too hard to find out."

"I'll pass the information along," Sam promised.

He went to see what Sutton Place luxury looked like. The building faced the East River, with a view of the Queensboro Bridge. A three-story limestone base anchored the red-brick façade. A gloved and liveried doorman stood under the canopied entrance.

He asked the doorman to ring Miss Daner. The man didn't budge. Miss Daner had left for the day. Sam inquired if any apartments were available. The doorman eyed him up and down before responding. A two-story, six-thousand-square-foot unit had just been listed.

"Ten people could live in it and still have elbow room for everybody," he said in a thick Brooklyn accent. He sounded both sarcastic and amazed at such luxury.

Sam laughed, allowed that it might be out of his price range, and moved on. Interestingly, the building was within walking distance to Duffy's Pub & Restaurant, Dalton's favorite watering hole. Sam wondered if Mike lived nearby. He called Marilyn from a drugstore phone booth with news of the co-op and asked for Dalton's address. Mike lived nowhere near Sutton Place, and he was at work, unaware of any pending doom.

"You need to back off," Marilyn counseled.

"I can't do that," Sam replied. "Have you seen Nick Reddy's newest installment of the cold-case robberies?" Nick had dived headfirst into the heists with an in-depth analysis of the biggest haul, the diamond caper.

"I have, but it's being dismissed by the brass as journalistic sensationalism, to keep it from spooking our targets."

Sam asked about Eddie Snyder. So far, he was adhering to his normal routine. Nothing had been done yet about a search warrant for the Hoboken address, but it was under surveillance.

"You can still change your mind and come back to work," Marilyn proposed.

"I can't do that either," Sam replied. "I'll be in touch."

He stepped outside into the noise from the Queensboro Bridge that ebbed and flowed with the constant hum from two tiers of endless traffic. New Yorkers grew oblivious to such noise. In fact, many embraced it as part of the city's fabric. Sam wasn't one of those. No matter how long he lived in the city, Manhattan continued to jar his senses. He didn't think he'd ever get completely used to it.

He decided to make another try to reconcile with DJ. Her office was closed, there was no response at her apartment, and she wasn't answering her telephone. His best guess was that she'd left town to spend time with her parents in Connecticut.

At a stationery store, he purchased a note card and a stamp, wrote an apology for his erratic behavior, and mailed it. He doubted it would do any good, but at least he would bow out of her life like a gentleman.

Before returning home, Sam went back to Sutton Place, cased the neighborhood around Duffy's, and selected the most likely subway stop Mike Dalton would take to get from work to the pub. He picked a good location where he could eyeball him without being noticed.

At home and restless, he puttered and putzed, something he hadn't done since the night he'd found Laura murdered. She was never far from his mind; indelibly sewn into the story of his life. He vowed to live long enough to bring her killer to justice. After that, who knew?

*

SAM GOT TO HIS lookout spot long before Mike Dalton was due to clock out from work. He was dressed in layers: shirt, sweater, and a car coat with pockets deep enough to conceal the Ruger .22-caliber pistol. He wore inexpensive, low-magnification reading glasses and a plain baseball cap he'd purchased at a novelty store, more to create an undistinguishable persona as opposed to a disguise.

He entertained himself watching the ongoing parade of humanity. Sutton Place was near enough to the United Nations headquarters that representatives of virtually every world culture were on the streets, many resplendent in the clothing of their home countries, others dressed conservatively in tailored suits, trying resolutely to blend in. There was no other neighborhood on the planet quite like it.

When Dalton passed by at a brisk clip earlier in the day than usual, Sam fell in behind, a half block back, the latest copy of the *Herald Tribune* with Nick's piece about the unsolved diamond heist tucked under his arm. Three blocks from Duffy's, he picked up the pace and from the other side of the street passed Dalton without being recognized. Inside the pub, he made a quick phone call to Marilyn, and claimed Mike's favorite back-of-the-bar booth, facing the entrance. He put the *Tribune* on the tabletop, turned face up and opened to the page with Reddy's column.

Sam favored his right hand but was ambidextrous. Most people didn't know it, including Dalton and Osborne. He placed the pistol within easy reach, next to his left leg, and covered it loosely with the car coat.

It was early. The after-work crowd had yet to gather and the noise level had not become deafening. Dalton almost balked when he saw Sam, but he approached with a forced smile and a hearty greeting. Still smiling, he unbuttoned his jacket as he sat across the table.

Sam knew Mike carried his service revolver strapped to his belt above his right hip. Osborne, on the other hand, wore a shoulder holster under his jacket on the left side.

Sam smiled in return and slapped his hand down on the newspaper. "Did you read this?" he asked in feigned disbelief. "I can't believe Reddy is writing this crap. He thinks no crime should go unpunished. Always blame it on the cops."

Dalton visibly relaxed. "Beats me. He's just mudslinging, I guess." He gave a quick look over his shoulder.

Sam could tell he was uncomfortable sitting with his back to the door. "Last time I was here, Jack Osborne arrested me for murder. That was not a good day for me."

"I tried to keep you out of Rikers, but it didn't work out."

"But I appreciated your effort. Jack called me and said you wanted to meet. What's this all about?"

"Nothing much. I wanted to update you."

Sam looked past Mike. "Here comes Jack now. Maybe he has a better explanation." Dalton started to rise. "Don't get up. I've got a hand gun under the table pointed at your belly, and I will use it, if necessary. In fact, I'd like to."

Dalton's expression turned nasty. Sam cocked the hammer. Mike stayed put.

"I watched Jerry execute Johnnie Turner, so we three have a lot to talk about."

Osborne looked peeved, although he tried to hide it behind a fake cough as he sat down next to Dalton.

"Tell him," Sam ordered.

"He knows you iced Turner."

"No, tell him about the *gun*," Sam corrected. "We'll get to the execution later."

"He's got a pistol pointed at us under the table," Mike said dutifully.

"Thank you. I also know about Snyder and O'Reilly," Sam added.

"It took me a while to figure out why Johnnie had to die, until it hit me that you thought if I got to him first he'd spill the beans about your criminal enterprise."

Osborne sneered. "What enterprise? This is pure bullshit."

"Which part? Whacking Turner, or your robberies? I know about Snyder and O'Reilly, and I also know about Snyder's Hoboken stash house and your little Sutton Place hideaway. That's a very valuable piece of property." He switched his attention to Dalton. "Do you have any secret real estate holdings you'd like to share?"

Mike smirked. "Fuck you."

"That's not very polite," Sam retorted.

Osborne shifted position.

"Stay put," Sam warned. "One more thing puzzled me. Three of you go in and pull the jobs, Osborne stays back and heads up the sham investigation, so who is the wheelman? I'm guessing it had to be Johnnie Turner, otherwise why kill him? I'd ruined his promotion to Central Robbery by discovering he'd padded his conviction rate by planting evidence on suspects, and you were worried he might have squealed if I got to him first."

"He didn't like you for that," Jack said. "I was hoping he'd kill you, but couldn't risk waiting for him to do it."

"You got it all figured, do you?" Dalton's right had moved slightly toward his holstered pistol.

"Do you really want to start a shoot-out here?" Sam queried. "Which one of you ordered the Hoboken hit on me? Or was it O'Reilly?"

"I did," Mike said, relaxing his hand. "Jerry just wanted you out of the city. He figured if you believed the Carlucci family was gunning for you, you'd keep your distance and stop nosing around."

"So he deliberately misled me. Who was the dead kid in the panel truck?"

"An expendable," Osborne said.

"You are some piece of work." The bar was beginning to fill up. Sam doubted they would be stupid enough to kill him in front of so many witnesses. He switched back to Dalton. "Why didn't you and Snyder take Turner out at Susan Cogan's apartment?"

"We considered taking all of you out, including Hanrahan," Mike said. "But a bloodbath would have been too risky."

"You should've done it," Osborne bellyached.

"I used to think you were the brains behind the scheme," Sam replied, eyeing Osborne. "Until I realized Mike was calling all the shots and playing me for a sucker."

He smiled at Dalton. "It was your idea from the start, wasn't it, Mike? You thought it up, brought in three trusty best friends from your old precinct, and ran the operation. Hell, you even introduced O'Reilly to your sister, made him part of the family."

Dalton smiled and showed his teeth. "You should write paperback novels. You've got the knack for it."

"Thanks for the compliment." Sam caught a look outside of police cars arriving. "After the crash in Hoboken, why did you tell me to lie low?"

"We weren't sure what you knew and decided to find out before we made another move. We also needed to know if Carlucci was involved, because we didn't want a turf war."

"And I thought we were friends," Sam said, feigning hurt feelings. "I've got to compliment you for not unloading your ill-gotten gains all at once. Stashing it in Hoboken and fencing it little by little was smart. It was like making an occasional bank withdrawal, right?"

Osborne scowled. "This has gone on long enough. You've got nothing to pin on us, and you're not going to survive the night."

"Is that why I keep having this persistent feeling that you're still going to try to kill me?"

"Well, at least you've got that right," he snarled. "So listen up: We're gonna walk you out of here like we did before, and then you're gonna vanish. Don't make it hard on yourself."

"Too late, fellas, we've got company. I hope you're ready to tell your story all over again to some very eager listeners."

Six plainclothes cops, guns drawn, with Commissioner Key and Marilyn Feinstein bringing up the rear, stormed into Duffy's and swarmed the booth.

"Let me see your gun," Dalton said.

Sam looked at the nearest cop, who nodded approval. "You know, it's a shame, Mike. I thought you were one of the good guys." He put the Ruger on the table and the cop scooped it up. "You, on the other hand, Osborne, are scum. Who was the officer from the Garment District precinct you sent to kill me?"

"That you'll never know," he grunted, as an officer pulled him upright. "Watch your back, shyster," he cautioned with a sneer. "And get a bigger gun. You'll need it."

"Thanks for the friendly advice." Sam waved merrily goodbye as Dalton and Osborne were marched out the door.

CHAPTER 26

THE COPS EMPTIED DUFFY'S OF THE PATRONS AND STAFF, AND uniformed officers outside directed arriving customers away from the pub. Dalton and Osborne were on their way downtown to the Great White Castle for interrogation. Sam sat at the bar with Marilyn and Stephen Key, both of them looking at him with frustration. For the first time, he noticed the photographs of fierce-looking Irish nationalists lining the wall above the shelves of whiskey bottles.

"Why didn't you wait until the preliminary investigation had been wrapped up?" Marilyn asked.

"Because the department leaks confidential information like a sieve," he answered. "If I'd waited, the whole crew would be sunning on a beach somewhere in South America, while New York's finest were busy chasing dead-end leads."

"No, you did it because you just had to go to Hoboken and pay a visit to Eddie Snyder's aunt in spite of knowing better," Marilyn corrected rather sternly.

Her tone reminded Sam of his third-grade teacher. He smiled in agreement. "You're right, I blew it, but I'm glad I did. It got the ball rolling. Have you picked up Snyder and O'Reilly?"

"Snyder, yes; O'Reilly, no," Stephen answered.

Key went on to say that warrants were being prepared to search all of the suspects' known properties and a teletype advisory had been issued advising all regional police departments to be on the lookout for O'Reilly.

"We need you back with us," he proposed.

Sam smiled. "Can't do it, Commissioner. I still need to clear up a few leftover items. Besides, I can't be a prosecutor and a witness both,

especially if you're intending to charge Osborne for murdering Johnnie Turner."

"What are you going to do?" Marilyn inquired.

"I'll find something. May I have my handgun back?"

"No," Key replied. "Just be glad you're not being charged for possession of an unregistered firearm."

"No matter." Sam got up from the stool. "But I do have a favor
to ask. When Osborne's properties are searched, ask the detectives
to keep an eye out for a gold Swiss watch inscribed with my father's
name, Asher Monroe, on the back of the case. It has sentimental value,
and I'd like it returned if possible. Osborne took it to make it look like
an armed robbery when he killed Turner."

"How did Turner get your watch?" Key asked.

"He stole it from me at Rikers along with my cash." Sam looked at
the open front door. Outside, a seething pub owner paced back and
forth behind the police line. "Better let Duffy reopen for business," he
suggested. "Otherwise, he'll bust a gut. Let me know when you pick
up O'Reilly."

He left with a silent sigh of relief, turned uptown, and joined the
throngs heading home, stopping at their neighborhood markets to shop
for dinner, or peeling off into a bar to relax with an after-work drink.

Postwar Manhattan was changing as old buildings were torn down
to make room for towering new skyscrapers. Yorkville had yet to be rav-
aged by the developers, and the neighborhood still had a human scale.
The gathering dusk was gold and orange, with wide brushstrokes of
cirrus clouds streaming across it, traveling oceanward. For a few brief
moments, nature claimed the spotlight, and Sam smiled in delight.

A note tacked to his apartment door was not from DJ, but rather
from Delores Stedman, her secretary. Adella had left a message at DJ's
that she'd interviewed with the publisher's daughter-in-law and been
offered the housekeeping job on the spot. She'd start on Monday. The
news lit him up with pleasure.

CHAPTER 27

SAM SPENT THE NEXT THREE DAYS IN THE IMMEDIATE VICIN-
ity of the Garment District precinct house trying to ID the cop who
had been sent by Osborne to the Hell's Kitchen diner with orders to
kill him. At the time, he hadn't been close enough to ID the man, but
there weren't many cops under six feet tall with a slender build that
populated the precinct. Or, for that matter, in any precinct in the city.
The department liked their officers to be big and burly.

Sam narrowed his suspects to three and tailed them one by one
when they got off duty. He quickly dismissed a rookie who still lived
with his family in Flatbush. He vacillated about the other two, a plainclothes officer and a Casper Milquetoast–type desk sergeant, until the
plainclothes cop showed his true colors by leaving a nearby parking
garage driving a band-new Chrysler Imperial that cost at least four
times his annual salary. No honest cop could afford it.

At the first light of morning, Sam waited at the garage for the plainclothes officer to arrive for his shift. As the cop left the garage, Sam
dropped him to the ground with a quick leg kick and put him in an
armlock when he struggled to rise. He yanked him into a nearby alley
and slammed him against the side of a building.

"Were you looking for me?" Sam asked as he disarmed the officer,
took his handcuffs, and poked him in the gut with the weapon before
stepping back. "By the way, Jack Osborne sends his regards from
Rikers."

The cop, Colin McFerran, had a narrow face, with a short, flat nose,
and ears that were set high against his head. "I didn't do anything to
you," he snapped.

"Because you didn't get the chance," Sam corrected. "Turn around."

He cuffed McFerran with his hands behind his back. "How much did Osborne pay you to kill me?"

"I don't know anything about that."

"Is the contract still open?"

"Look pal, take off the cuffs, give me my weapon back, walk away, and we can forget all about this. What do you say?"

Sam laughed. "It's not that simple. Here's my counteroffer: you go downtown with me and get immunity from prosecution if you tell the DA everything you know about the Irish Cop Robbers, including who hired you to kill me."

After discovering that Eddie Snyder's mother had been Irish, Reddy had coined the catchphrase for his articles. Sam liked it. A rumor was flying that Nick would win the Pulitzer for exposing the cop cartel. Sam liked that also.

"I'm not gonna do that."

"Otherwise, you'll be charged with attempted murder and your car will be seized as ill-gotten gains," Sam continued. He had no authority to promise McFerran anything, but hoped he was caught too off guard to realize it.

McFerran mulled it over, but before he could answer, Sam decided to play a wild-card hunch. "Never mind. For a reduced sentence, somebody will probably finger you as the lookout for the heists. Which one will it be? I wonder. Eddie Snyder, I bet."

McFerran looked ready to bolt.

"If you run, I'll shoot you," Sam said. "Then immunity won't matter."

McFerran swallowed hard. "Full immunity?"

Sam smiled sympathetically. "Why not?"

McFerran nodded.

"Let's go." Sam marched him to a streetside pay phone, called Marilyn, and within minutes a radio car arrived with two of Stephen Key's task force members. They drove them downtown, siren wailing, where Marilyn waited at headquarters. As the detectives hustled McFerran away, Marilyn inquired if Sam was finished clearing up his few leftover things.

"Almost," he answered as they walked to a secluded corner near the public entrance. "Unless he confesses, the case against McFerran is weak, but I really think he should go to prison for a couple of years for attempting to kill me."

"I'll see what I can do."

"What's happening with the investigation?"

"Hoboken was a bonanza," Marilyn said. "You were right about parceling out stolen goods to fence gradually. Remaining merchandise from all of the robberies was stored there."

"With Eddie's sweet elderly auntie guarding the remaining stash," Sam cracked. "Wouldn't that make a great *New Yorker* cartoon?"

Marilyn laughed. Smaller amounts of valuables and cash had been found at other locations, except at Sergeant O'Reilly's. He, his wife, and their daughters had left everything behind and simply disappeared. Every law enforcement agency was looking for them. Still, with three of the four robbers charged and locked up, the DA and Stephen Key were proclaiming success in the war against corrupt and crooked cops.

"Will they remain in jail?" Sam asked.

"Yes, the judge has ruled they're flight risks."

"And my father's watch?" Sam inquired.

"It hasn't been found."

"Osborne probably dumped it in the river along with Turner's wallet. It might be helpful for Key to know that O'Reilly is married to Dalton's sister."

Marilyn's eyes widened. "That is interesting. I'll pass it along."

"Got to go," Sam said.

Marilyn held out her hand. "Gimme."

"What?"

"McFerran's service revolver."

Sam handed it over.

"We're going to need you to give statements," Marilyn said.

"Sure, anytime, just not right now."

"Tomorrow?"

Sam nodded. "Early. I'd like to get it over with."

"The commissioner sends his thanks."

"Tell him to put it in writing. I can use the reference."

"You can always come back to your old job."

"You know the DA wouldn't dare let me return until all the cases are adjudicated, and that could take months. Besides, I'm not sure I want the job."

"What if you were appointed to the commissioner's staff?"

"Come on, Marilyn, every ambulance chaser in the city knows enough law to argue my participation would strongly support a tainted investigation argument. Are you willing to risk the cases getting thrown out on appeal?"

"You're right," Marilyn agreed grudgingly. "Then what do you want?"

"What was promised to me before: the murder charge against me dropped with prejudice, along with a public statement by the DA to that effect. I want this over and done with, and my reputation back intact."

"You're giving up on finding Laura Neilson's killer?"

"I didn't say that."

"A statement that you've been cleared of the murder charge will be released to the press today," Marilyn promised.

"Thank you."

"No. Thank you," Marilyn replied.

Sam left, bone-weary and depressed. He sucked it up. First he needed a job. George Lemond said he'd take him back. Okay, one down. Next, he needed to repay Abe Silverstein. That would take some time. He'd chip away at the debt as quickly as he could. Finally, finding Laura's killer. That started back up right now. Well, maybe not today. Tomorrow would have to do.

CHAPTER 28

TWO DAYS AFTER ASKING GEORGE FOR HIS OLD JOB, SAM started work, welcomed back warmly by salespeople and coworkers. Even prissy Miriam Brewer, the jewelry department manager, was cordial. Any lingering suspicions of his guilt had been wiped away by the announcement of his innocence published in all the daily newspapers. The *Mirror* and several others made it front-page news. Of course, the sidebar story headline read: "Who Killed Laura Neilson?"

Sam had asked to work the late shifts when the store was open for evening shoppers, and George had obliged. That freed up some daylight hours, which he used to concentrate on re-interviewing his suspect list. In some instances, his newfound notoriety had unexpectedly made the task easier. For several of the men, being Laura Neilson's former lover now had cachet, and they willingly agreed to talk to Sam. One man, who lived out of state and had an ironclad alibi, even reached out through Nick Reddy to be interviewed. Sam spent an hour with him by telephone on the slim chance he knew something worth chasing down. Nothing.

Days dragged as he continued to find no cracks in anyone's stories. Several people flatly turned down his request to be re-interviewed, including the construction supervisor, two of the married men with families, and Kurt Bell, who said he was too busy and had already told Sam all he knew. In the spirit of letting sleeping dogs lie, Sam didn't bother with Richard Carlin or the rest of the Tony Carlucci family.

After one last careful look at everything, Sam was convinced something more than Laura's promiscuity must have precipitated her murder. She'd died lying naked on her penthouse balcony, almost garroted by the silver chain with Sam's dog tag and antique Korean coin she'd stolen from him. It had been an angry murder that reeked of sex. Or did it? Initially, he hadn't thought to check what the autopsy had revealed, but when he did, he learned there had been no findings of sexual intercourse. He knew better than to believe that made it conclusive.

When Sam had arrived the night of the murder, Carl DeAngelo, the doorman, mentioned Laura had called down to say he might show up. Had she invited someone else to be there when he arrived? Carl hadn't seen anyone else come or go. While sneaking a smoke in the basement stairwell, had he missed someone arriving? Someone with access to the front entrance that was always locked after midnight?

When he'd gone to Carl's house with more questions, it was too late. A house fire had killed him along with his sister and her family. To Sam, his death seemed far too coincidental, but the fire department arson investigators had deemed it accidental. That didn't mean much in a city that had a multitude of civil servants with itchy palms, including firemen.

As indictments were handed down, the Irish Cop Robbers story continued to be front-page news, while the continued failure to apprehend O'Reilly and his family was barely more than a footnote to the story. In his column, Nick Reddy had started referring to O'Reilly as the Irish Houdini, the only magician who could make a family completely vanish. He also mulled over who were the better criminals, the Irish mob, or the Italian Mafia. He decided it was a toss-up. Angry responses from both Irish and Italian readers appeared daily in the letters to the editor.

It irked Sam that not more had been done to track O'Reilly down. With permission from Marilyn to review the intelligence and background reports on Osborne, Dalton, Snyder, and O'Reilly, he dug in and started building profiles for each man. Also, as a precaution, he started to alter his route to and from work. Who knew what lurked behind Jerome Aloysius O'Reilly's friendly Irish cop demeanor?

He'd been beaten up twice by one bad cop and targeted for assassination by another. He couldn't risk underestimating O'Reilly's capacity for violence.

He used his first two paychecks to catch up on his rent and pay

Abe a little bit more back on his loan. He wrote another note to DJ, which got no response. At the end of his second month back at work, he received an invitation to attend a private reception at the Murray Hill club where he'd met previously with Nick Reddy, Stephen Key, and Marilyn Feinstein. He considered turning it down on general principle, with the excuse that he had to work. But George, who had also been invited, said he damn well better go, but wouldn't say why.

He called Nick Reddy, who told him he was getting a citizen award for bringing the Irish Cop Robbers to justice and that he better be there and look good for the occasion. Sam didn't argue.

He arrived on the night of the ceremony to a horde of reporters and photographers outside the building. Escorted into a large meeting room filled with dignitaries, including the police chief, the DA, Commissioner Key, Feinstein, and Lemond. DJ was also there, dressed to kill, in the company of a man he did not know. He was probably in his late forties and looked like he had money and plenty of it.

DJ introduced Sam to him, but the name failed to register, as the memory of being unceremoniously dumped by Laura at Stamm's Bar and Grill stampeded through his mind.

Jesus, not again, he thought, smiling tightly, shaking the man's hand, and quickly moving on to avoid saying something stupid he'd later regret.

The award, a nicely framed certificate praising his contribution to the Police Commissioner's Office, came with a cash prize provided by a subscription of the Murray Hill club members. It would immediately clear Sam of all his debts and leave a nice chunk of cash in his pocket. He might even splurge and replace his father's watch.

Nick Reddy said some nice words and Stephen Key added to them. It lifted his spirits, although his attention wandered to DJ, who seemed to be enjoying the company of her companion, which put a damper on Sam's evening.

He had a conversation with a lawyer, who gave him his business card, asked about his future plans, and invited Sam to interview with his firm. Sam promised to call, although privately he wasn't very enthusiastic about it. An eight-to-five desk job held little appeal.

Sam stepped away from a group of Wall Street bankers and their wives as Walt Seaver approached, looking out of place with his unruly hair and a suit badly in need of pressing. Walt had picked up some work from DJ while she'd been away, but didn't know where "away" had been. Walt did know the man with her was Elliot Perkins, whom he'd also just met earlier in the evening. He had no idea of what Perkins's status in her life was.

Walt's invitation to the event had come directly from DJ by telephone late in the day. Ergo, the unpressed suit. Sam was confounded; what was DJ's involvement with the event? Walt didn't know that either.

Sam thanked Walt for all he'd done. If it hadn't been for his research, Dalton and his buddies might never have been caught.

Walt smiled and shrugged. "No big deal."

"What's next for you?"

"I've a few cases to conclude, but then it's back to finishing my dissertation. Getting my butt kicked by Johnnie Turner has refreshed my interest in returning to the peaceful world of academia. It may prove to be too tame for me, but I'll have a Ph.D. to tack after my name."

Sam laughed. "Okay, Professor, if you learn anything about Elliot Perkins, give me a call."

"Will do," Walt said. "I want to know exactly who he is too."

The evening wound down. Sam caught up with DJ and Perkins before they could slip away. He cheerfully proposed taking her to lunch soon so he could thank her properly for all her help.

"You should have been recognized tonight as well," Sam added.

The expression on Perkins's face was decidedly impatient. "We must go," he said to DJ.

"That's kind of you to say, but lunch isn't necessary," DJ replied over her shoulder. "Goodbye, Sam."

That ruined it. Reluctant to turn down Key's polite offer of a ride home, he sat with Stephen in the backset of the limo forcing himself to make small talk during the short drive to Yorkville. The sky was a bleak, half-lit dirty gray, and the headlights of approaching traffic were blurred by stirred-up soot in the polluted yellow air. Along the avenue, the metal security shutters, which protected storefront after storefront, were ugly reminders of the lawlessness that frequently gripped the city in a vise at night. Sam wanted to escape both the limo and the city. He could do neither.

Curbside at Sam's building, Key rolled down the rear window and handed him the framed certificate he'd left on the backseat. When the limo turned the corner, he tossed it in the trash bin. It was a night he hoped to soon forget, but doubted he ever would.

CHAPTER 29

WINTER CAME EARLY IN THE MORNING WITH A FREEZING ICE storm that slowed the city to a crawl. Sam started the day off in the warmth of his apartment with a pot of coffee and the summary profiles he'd compiled on the Irish Cop Robbers. It was clear that among the four, O'Reilly was the odd man.

A bachelor, Osborne had used his cut to make smart real estate investments while quietly enjoying the good life without drawing undue attention to himself.

Divorced, with no children, Snyder had started a martial arts studio, where he posed as a part-time salaried instructor. He kept a low profile, but often used his annual leave from the U.S. Marshals Service to return to the Orient to study with various masters of the art of self-defense. There was a question about his sexuality due to some sightings at a Greenwich Village underground gay nightclub.

Dalton, married but separated and with two adult children, was a philanderer and gambling addict, who kept his marriage legally intact by underwriting his wife's extravagant living expenses at her home in Boca Raton, Florida, where she resided full-time. Over the years, he'd paid a pretty penny to keep her at arm's length and happily married in the eyes of the church, while he chased skirts in the city.

O'Reilly was a different breed. A devoted family man, he had three daughters, the youngest of which, a high school teenager, was a polio survivor who had spent two years in an iron lung at considerable expense to the family. The two other girls were college students enrolled in prestigious New England universities, until they dropped out at the same time of O'Reilly's disappearance. One had been a senior majoring in music and the younger one was a junior in premed.

In Hoboken, there had been nothing ostentatious or extravagant about the family's middle-class lifestyle that might have triggered suspicion. O'Reilly had used his cut from the heists to provide for the family and give his daughters advantages they otherwise would not have had. Now, as Sam saw it, he was using it to try to keep the family intact. In order for the plan to work, his wife had to be in on it, and perhaps even his girls. For them to successfully disappear, it had to be kept secret from everybody. Dalton professed no knowledge of O'Reilly's whereabouts. Nor did Dalton's wife in Boca Raton. Same for Osborne and Snyder.

How did O'Reilly do it? Recently, Ireland had passed a nationality and citizenship act that allowed Americans with one or more grandparents born in the old country to apply for dual citizenship. If O'Reilly's parents were native Irish, he and his daughters would be eligible, and his wife by marriage as well.

Sam called the Irish Embassy and was put through to the proper official. The records showed that all five had been granted dual citizenship and issued Irish passports. Sam called an international carrier at Idlewild. Only New York, Boston, and Chicago had flights to Ireland, all landing at Shannon Airport on the western coast of the country.

He called the ticketing agents for all the airlines with flights to Shannon. Four female passengers named O'Reilly and traveling with Irish passports had departed Boston for Shannon two days after the cops had picked up O'Reilly's three partners in crime.

Where was Jerome Aloysius O'Reilly now? Sam wondered. He guessed the man was on his way to join his family by some alternate route, with enough of his share of stolen treasure to provide a comfortable life for them in the old country.

Did Ireland have an extradition treaty with the United States? Did Irish laws exist to protect citizens from being arrested by the police for a crime committed in another country? He called the Irish Embassy again. There was no extradition treaty between the two countries. The official didn't know if the Guarda had the power to seize someone at the request of a foreign country. He'd check and get back to Sam.

Clearly, O'Reilly had planned the escape well in advance of when it might have been needed. After his wife and daughters flew off to Ireland, he'd probably traveled overland from Boston to Canada and found a roundabout way to join them.

Sam dialed Marilyn and briefed her on his findings. Out the front room window, the ice storm had turned into wet, heavy snowflakes and York Avenue was peacefully empty of moving traffic. Shopkeepers were out shoveling sidewalks, and neighborhood kids were having a noisy snowball fight. Nature could occasionally make the city appear serene, although it was always an illusion.

After his report, Marilyn asked a few questions for clarification, thanked him effusively for the information, and offered to buy him lunch sometime soon. He agreed to meet her on his next day off.

"You're not going to catch O'Reilly easily," he predicted.

"You sound almost pleased about it," she replied.

"No, conflicted," Sam said. "I do respect a man who takes care of his family."

He hung up, put his paperwork away, rinsed out his coffee cup, and bundled up for a run to the corner deli to buy takeout for lunch, shop the mom-and-pop market for dinner provisions, and visit the liquor store for some wine and a bottle of scotch.

Now that O'Reilly was accounted-for in Sam's mind, he had one more monkey off his back and cause to celebrate. On the way out, he'd invite Abe over as company for dinner.

But there was still Laura, always Laura. She'd remain in the forefront of his thoughts until her murderer was caught.

CHAPTER 30

EVERY APPROACH SAM TOOK TO SOLVE LAURA'S MURDER resulted in a dead end. He'd put it away for a time, hoping to return to it with a fresh perspective, only to be repeatedly stymied. Winter had embraced the city with a vengeance, and a sanitation worker wage dispute had filled the sidewalks with stinky garbage, which thankfully froze overnight as the temperature plummeted. Sam did little with his time other than work, carry on with the normal activities of daily life, and plug away at his evidence files.

By courier, DJ had sent him all of the photographs they'd amassed from Laura's darkroom, plus the snapshots from Sofia Huizinga's Brownie camera, and Laura's childhood scrapbook. He moved a chest of drawers away from one wall and plastered the wall with the photographs, examining them in detail. He spent hours paging through the scrapbook trying to see beyond her sketches and quotations for anything revealing or unusual.

When an unexpected reward check from an insurance company for the recovery of merchandise from one of the heists arrived, Sam decided winter was the perfect time to paint his apartment. He sent half of the money to Walt Seaver, who called with his thanks and to report that Elliot Perkins, DJ's escort at the Murray Hill award ceremony, was a ranking naval JAG officer who had been in the city on official business. According to Delores, he was not DJ's love interest, but rather a friend from her tour of active duty in the Navy.

Sam was relieved to hear it but had no idea how to proceed. Or even if he should bother trying at all. He started a letter to DJ explaining the reasons for his past behavior and expressing his feelings of affection for her. He kept putting it aside, only to pick it up again and again. As he added to it, the letter grew in size, his thoughts on the page careening all over the place, from childhood memories, to Korea, Laura, his parents, and the men he'd served with in the Army. He stopped when the nightmares of combat woke him up in a cold sweat, wondering if his head was screwed on straight. He thought of trashing the letter but put it away again.

Was he as irresponsibly impulsive as DJ had criticized? He never used to be. He worked a connection in the coroner's office to get permission to use the NYU Medical School library. He read up on shell shock and battle fatigue that shrinks were now calling a stress reaction to combat. Not everybody was onboard with the freshly labeled diagnosis, but Sam agreed with the majority of experts who had reviewed the new research findings. Having a thousand screaming Chinese soldiers charging down a frozen Korean mountain wanting to kill you would stress out any ordinary human being.

Technically, he was fit as a fiddle, just suffering the aftereffects of living through hell. At least he hadn't done it to himself. It didn't make the night sweats or the vivid nightmares go away. But since he wasn't officially deranged, he gave himself a clean bill of health.

With extra money in his pocket, he bought what he needed in order to paint the apartment, and during his off hours started on it one room at a time. He painted the walls a soft cream color and put a light oak stain on the woodwork, the doors, and the trim. When he finished, the apartment looked like a place where he'd want to be, and he began to look forward to returning home after work. Some new furniture would be nice, but that could wait until he found a better-paying job, which he was in no hurry to do.

Abe approved of the new look and wanted to reimburse Sam for the cost. Sam told him no dice. Abe had already been too generous. Sam counteroffered a special home-cooked meatball-and-spaghetti dinner to celebrate. Abe didn't argue. It had become one of his favorite meals.

At dinner, Abe mentioned an apartment in the building was about to become available. Sam jumped on the news and suggested that Abe consider renting it to Adella and her two teenage children. She'd had Sam over for meals several times to thank him for helping her find a job that she loved, and he knew how much she disliked her living conditions. Anybody would. The building was rat- and cockroach-infested, the plumbing was defective, and the landlord wanted everybody out so he could tear the dump down.

Sam gave Abe a complete rundown on the family.

"Puerto Ricans in Yorkville?" Abe asked pointedly.

A predominantly white, German-American neighborhood, Yorkville had been an insulated community for years, filled with residents, many of whom in their lifetime hadn't ventured north of Eighty-Sixth or south of Seventy-Second.

Before the war, the community had shown strong support for Hitler and Nazism. So much so that the movie houses throughout the city showed newsreels of men dressed in Nazi military-style uniforms marching up York Avenue, goose-stepping, carrying swastika flags, singing nationalistic songs of the Fatherland. There were newsclips of fiery speeches by prominent community and religious leaders at standing-room-only rallies defending the new Germany and praising the Führer as the savior of his country. After the invasion of Poland, many German-American patriotic organizations held demonstrations demanding the U.S. government remain neutral. They'd congregate afterward at Stamm's for a tankard and talk.

It took the Japanese attack on Pearl Harbor and a presidential declaration of war to stifle their voices, which never completely went away.

"Puerto Ricans in Yorkville?" Sam echoed. "It might upset a lot of people, but why not?"

Abe quietly sipped his Chianti and mulled it over.

Abe was a German-born Jew, an American citizen, and a U.S. Army veteran by choice. He'd been way over the draft age when he'd volunteered. Sam knew he'd been ridiculed and harassed by diehard Nazi supporters in the prewar years. Certain merchants had refused to serve him, and some people, including old women, would spit at his feet and curse when he passed them on the sidewalk.

After the war, the prejudice didn't disappear, it simply sank slightly below the surface. Only white Aryans remained acceptable. Racism never dies.

"What do you think?" Sam prodded. Except for Alfonso, the half-German, half-Cuban bartender at Stamm's, Latinos were truly foreigners in Yorkville.

"Can she stand up for herself?"

"Yes, she can."

"If you vouch for her, I'd like to meet her," he said with a wily smile.

"I'll set it up, but you'll probably have to suffer through another dinner."

"I guess I can bear your cooking again," Abe said straight-faced. "Speaking of which, what's for dessert?"

"Apple strudel from the bakery, to satisfy your German palate."

"My favorite is Northern Italian pastry."

"Really?"

"Truly," Abe replied.

They talked long into the night. Abe wanted to repaint every apartment in the building as people moved out. And if nobody wanted to move, he'd paint the units anyway. Make them look as nice as Sam's place. Even have new appliances installed. Of course, he'd have to up the rent a bit for the new tenants.

"If you help me paint the vacancy, I'll give you a month's free rent, plus put a new stove and refrigerator in your unit."

"You've got a deal, Mr. Silverstein." They capped the night by finishing the bottle of Chianti.

*

IT TOOK SOME TIME for Sam to arrange Abe's meeting with Adella, but when he did, he did it in style by hosting a party for Abe, Adella, Veronica, Pedro, and Adella's part-time boyfriend, Enrique. His apartment wasn't large enough to accommodate everyone at a sit-down meal, so finger food would have to do. He loaded up on what he needed at the market, the deli, and the liquor store, put trays of food out within easy reach, and set up a beverage table in the kitchen so guests could chat, drink, and nibble.

It was a huge success, primarily because Enrique, an engineer on a cargo ship that transported manufactured goods and commodities to and from the United States and South America, had a wicked sense of humor. He told hilarious stories of his adventures throughout the southern hemisphere.

The evening with Adella and her family sealed the deal with Abe. He took them on a tour of the recently vacated, newly renovated apartment. Adella loved it from the moment she stepped through the door. Her children would have more privacy, the kitchen put the one in Spanish Harlem to shame, and the rent would only be a few dollars more. In addition, the commute to Pedro and Veronica's high school would be shorter and less dangerous, and Adella's travel to and from work would be shaved in half. Everyone was happy.

As time allowed over the next few weeks, Sam helped them make the move. They did it in stages until it became necessary to rent a truck to cart the larger pieces of furniture. On a Sunday, with Pedro's help, they got the job done.

Once everything was in order and arranged to Adella's satisfaction, she threw a housewarming party that included Nick Reddy on the guest list. Invited by Sam at Adella's request, Nick had to be brow-beaten into attending. Only Enrique, who was halfway between a Brazilian port and New York City, was absent. The food was spicy, the drinks plentiful, and the mood jolly. Adella had also invited the other building tenants, and many came, bearing food and drink. Abe declared it to be the best tenant party ever. It had also been the first, he admitted.

Late in the evening, Reddy waylaid Sam to tell him Stephen Key had retained DJ as special assistant on the police corruption task force. Under contract, her job during the trial phases of the criminal cases would be to coordinate all evidence-sharing between NYPD, Key's office, the district attorney, and other law enforcement agencies. The appointment would be announced at the commissioner's press brief-ing in the morning. During her absence, Walt Seaver would run her PI business. The plan had been in the works for ten days.

"Good for her," Sam said. "Steve's got himself a gem. She'll do a great job."

He reeled at the thought that DJ had slipped farther away from him. She was on a path that would launch her way out of his league. He wished her luck, but it made him melancholy. He smiled through it and thanked Nick for the heads-up.

Soon after the announcement of her appointment, Reddy did a profile piece on her in the *Tribune* that spotlighted her service in naval intelligence, her credentials as a successful private investigator, and her pedigree as a member of an old-line New York City family. It received a lot of positive public attention, and soon she was being quoted in newspapers and interviewed on local evening newscasts.

As DJ's popularity soared, Key cashed in on it by elevating her position to spokesperson for the task force. She took to it like a duck to water. Almost daily, Sam read about her in the papers, or saw her on the nightly news. He couldn't get away from her, nor did he want to. But it made her so much harder to forget.

He tried dating a nice-looking salesgirl from work, who was going to college part-time and looking for someone to rescue her from the emotional dungeon of living in a Bronx walk-up with her unhappily married parents and two younger brothers, both jerks. She was hoping for a ring on her finger.

Why she would want that, Sam couldn't figure. There were better ways to escape. He took a pass.

With Adella's move into the building, he began to feel less lonely. Adella and her kids quickly pulled him into their family. It was an exuberant and vibrant world, brand-new to him, and he loved it.

It developed into frequent back-and-forth visits, impromptu potluck dinners, and an occasional shared cup of coffee and a catch-up conversation on the weekend. When Enrique's ship was in port, Pedro and Veronica virtually camped out with Sam, who gave them free rein of the apartment.

With the first signs of spring came the realization that his attempt to find Laura's killer had hit a brick wall. He boxed up everything and stuck it on a top shelf in the closet, but he couldn't contain the feeling of defeat that went with it. And it haunted him, as did his failure with

DJ. He gave up on the letter he'd started to her and wrote a short and sweet note about his feelings for her and his regrets for letting her down. He mailed it, not expecting a reply, but hoping for one.

One weekend evening, after a dinner at Sam's apartment with Adella and the kids, Adella mentioned that Albert Guzman, the senior doorman at Laura's building, was retiring and she'd been invited to a celebration on his behalf. She asked Sam to go with her and he readily agreed. The next weekend they joined Albert, his family, friends, and work colleagues at a Puerto Rican restaurant in the South Bronx that had closed for the night to accommodate his retirement party. Housed in what had once been a delicatessen, it had a long, narrow dining room that was packed with people.

Sam recognized several longtime housekeepers who worked in the building, a former nanny who'd moved on as a live-in with another family, and Albert's fellow doormen. He spotted a maintenance worker and the building superintendent, Dennis Finch, who was shoe-horned between the door to the kitchen and a jukebox blaring bomba tracks. He looked out of place and uncomfortable.

Sam didn't see any building tenants, nor did he expect to. Adella confirmed it before breaking away to gossip with a woman she knew from her old neighborhood. Sam worked his way past a couple trying to dance without knocking into the other guests, and rescued Finch, who followed him outside away from the noise.

"Have you been to one of these before?" Finch asked.

"Never," Sam replied.

"Me neither, and I didn't expect to be invited. Sometimes being the boss doesn't make you popular with everyone. I read you're off the hook for, you know . . ."

"Yeah, so far anyway. Has anyone moved into Laura's penthouse?"

"No, it got pulled from the market once they decided to make the building a co-op," Dennis answered.

Sam wanted to know more. Dennis told him the word was that Laura hadn't left a will, so the property had returned to the control of her family, who'd decided to bring in a new management team.

"Residents have been given ninety days to either buy their shares in the corporation or move. It's a rush job by new management. The Millers can't afford the purchase price, so they're leaving at the end of the month. So am I."

"Laid off?"

"That's a nice word for it," Finch said drolly. "They want their own people running things, and I get that. I'll be fine. A friend who owns an electrical contracting business will take me on until I land something else."

"You're licensed?"

"Yep, and I may stick with it. Better pay, better hours, less grief."

"Sounds good. When they cleaned out Laura's apartment, did they empty her basement darkroom?"

Dennis looked surprised. "You know about that?"

"I do. Did they?"

"Not as far as I know. It's still padlocked, and nobody has asked me about it."

"Mind if I stop by and take a look inside?" Sam had the padlock combination from Laura's diary. "No one other than you has to know."

"If you can get inside without anyone knowing, it's no skin off my back."

"Let me buy you a drink," Sam said.

"It's an open bar," Finch noted.

"Then let me buy you two drinks," Sam countered.

At the front of the restaurant away from the chatter, they talked some more. Finch was eager to be moving on to a new job. Laura's murder had cast a pall over everybody and everything. He'd be happy to help Sam out. You could only get fired from a job once, right?

Sam asked Dennis if he knew anyone in the building—workers or residents—who might have had a grudge against Laura or been in a spat or disagreement with her.

"I wouldn't put it like that," he replied with a laugh. "She had a strong personality, if you know what I mean, but not in a bad way."

"I do know what you mean," Sam replied.

Adella emerged from the back dining room, ready to leave. Sam thanked Dennis for his willingness to help him out and said he'd see him in the morning. On their way to the subway, Adella asked what they'd been talking about.

"He's letting me take another look around the building in the morning."

"I heard he's being let go," Adella said.

"He has another job lined up."

"Good for him."

"You don't sound very enthusiastic on his behalf."

"He's just another Anglo who thinks all Puerto Rican women are fast and easy."

Sam laughed. "Little does he know."

Adella squeezed Sam's arm. "There are exceptions."

*

EARLY THE NEXT MORNING, when Dennis was conveniently away from his cubbyhole basement office, Sam searched the untouched darkroom and found nothing until he moved the stand-alone bookcase and discovered that an envelope had fallen behind it. In it were various receipts for the western road trip Laura had taken. There were hotel receipts, bills for excursion trips to Indian pueblos, expired day passes to state parks and national monuments, and miscellaneous invoices for oil changes, tire repair, and gasoline purchases. Many were dated, and a number of the hotel room charges were for two occupants. With the new paper trail and what he already had in the files at home, he'd re-create the journey and pinpoint who'd gone with her. Did that person have something to do with why she was murdered?

At Sam's request, Dennis had left a note on his desk with a list of all the tenants who were moving out before the co-op deal went through. It was a short list and he recognized some of the names, but none that looked promising as sources of new information. He'd come back after his evening shift, when residents were more likely to be at home, and ask to talk to them then. He'd promised Dennis he would keep it brief. The doorman would let him in.

He felt encouraged. With new leads to sink his teeth into, he was eager to push on and find Laura's killer.

CHAPTER 31

SAM'S INTERVIEWS WITH THE TENANTS LIVING IN THE BUILD-
ing went as expected. A costume designer for a Broadway musical had been on the road touring with a show the night of the murder, a young married couple had been home with a newborn baby and the wife's mother visiting from out of town, and an independent filmmaker had been in a studio recording a soundtrack for a television commercial with a well-known jazz musician.

Although he'd spoken to her previously, Sam knocked at Julia Anderson's door and rang the bell. There was no answer. As he turned to leave, the door across the hallway opened, and Jay Miller stepped out. He'd aged considerably since Sam had last seen him, but he still looked alert and sprightly.

"Hello, Sam," he said with a smile. "I didn't expect to see you here."

"I'm persona non grata," Sam replied, putting a finger to his lips.

Jay laughed. "I won't tell on you. If you're looking for Julia Anderson, she's hardly ever here."

"Isn't she still teaching at the university?"

"I don't know. When we do see her, we barely exchange greetings. She's in and out in a hurry. Otherwise, we don't hear a sound from her apartment."

"She has no visitors?"

"When she first moved in, Laura would stop by to see her."

"Frequently?" Sam asked.

Jay shrugged. "I wouldn't say that. I did see them arguing in the hall-way once, when I looked to see what the commotion was all about."

"What was it about?"

Jay shook his head. "Sorry, Sam, my old ears don't work the way they used to. All I could tell was that Julia seemed terribly upset. Laura spotted me, apologized for the racket, and they went inside."

"This happened only once?"

"Another time, Janet heard them shouting at each other while I was taking a nap."

"Did she hear or see anything?"

Jay shook his head. "No, she just took a peek out the door."

"When was that?"

"Both times it was soon after Julia moved in."

"When did you stop seeing her regularly in the building?"

"A week or two after Laura was murdered." Jay's eyes got moist. "We miss her a lot. She was like family to us, if you know what I mean."

"I do," Sam replied. "Can you tell me anything else about Julia?"

"Just that Dennis told us that she's moving out tomorrow."

"Tomorrow? Where to?"

"I don't know. The new doorman should be able to tell you the name of the moving company. They have to get permission to enter the premises in advance."

"Thanks. You're moving also, I understand."

"Yes, we've found a nice one-bedroom nearby. We're going to be just fine. Find Laura's killer, Sam. It would put our minds at ease."

"I will," Sam promised.

He gave Jay a hug, said good night, and on his way out got the name and phone number of the moving company Anderson had hired. Two thoughts ran through his mind as he walked to the bus stop: Where was Julia Anderson going, and why? He also wondered why anyone with a moral compass would force an elderly couple to move out of an apartment they'd lived in for decades, and still be able to sleep soundly at night.

*

UP EARLY, SAM CALLED the moving company and learned the crew would arrive at Anderson's apartment at nine a.m. to box and load the van. The delivery destination was Albuquerque, New Mexico. The contents of the apartment would be placed in storage until the end of June.

He arrived at the building in time to greet the movers, expecting to find Anderson waiting for them as well. Instead, Dennis Finch was there to let the men in, explaining that she'd called to say she couldn't make it, but that the crew knew exactly what to do.

"If I was sticking around, she's one I wouldn't miss," he added.

"Why is that?"

"Too snobbish."

"That's it?"

"Some people you click with, others you don't."

To thank him for his help, Sam asked Dennis if he'd like to get together for drinks before his last day on the job. He suggested a date, time, and place, to which Dennis agreed.

Sam took a quick look inside the two-bedroom apartment. There were a number of various-sized sealed and labeled packing boxes scattered around the floor. The furniture was new-looking and modern in design. The wall art was framed posters of recent museum and gallery openings. A note on the kitchen countertop instructed the movers to either dispose of the posters or leave them behind. The place could have passed for a mid-priced midtown Manhattan hotel suite.

Sam asked the crew chief if he had a local phone number and address for Anderson. He checked his order sheet and gave him Anderson's university telephone number. The address on file was a storage facility in Albuquerque. Sam called from Finch's office and was told by the department secretary that it was spring break and Anderson was away until classes resumed. She did not know where Dr. Anderson might be.

He remembered Dennis had told him that Anderson's ex-husband had cosigned her lease. In Finch's tenant card file, he found a listing for Roger Anderson with a Chicago address and telephone number. He called it but there was no answer. He'd try again later from home.

He took a bus to Morningside Heights. Students and staff still roamed the university campus, but in far fewer numbers because of spring break. Anderson's office was locked, but a young man in a nearby office was behind a desk pecking away on a typewriter. Sam asked if he knew where Professor Anderson might be. The young man's expression turned livid.

"I don't even want to hear her name," he sputtered.

"Why is that?"

"She was on my dissertation committee, but she's resigned as of the end of this semester. Now I'm stuck scrambling to find a replacement."

"Do you know why she resigned?"

"Job offer at some southwestern college."

"In New Mexico?" Sam offered.

"Yeah, that's it. She gave up a tenure-track position here to go teach there. Don't ask me why."

"Why?"

He looked Sam up and down. "You don't work at the university, do you?"

"No, I'm a private investigator trying to locate her ex-husband." Sam held out his ID. "He cosigned a loan for her that's now past due."

"Ex-husband? That's a laugh."

"How is that funny?"

"She's a lesbo."

"Really?"

"One hundred percent."

"Know where I can find her?"

He shook his head.

"If you needed to speak to her right away, would the department secretary give you a phone number?"

He smiled and reached for the telephone. "Sure."

Feeling quite chipper, Sam left with Kurt Bell's phone number in his pocket. Finally, he was getting somewhere.

*

KURT BELL'S MADISON AVENUE office looked the same, except the advertising mockup on the easel now encouraged consumers to enjoy the man-sized satisfaction of Chesterfield cigarettes. He asked Sam what he could do for him.

"I need to speak to Julia Anderson," Sam answered. "Before she moves to New Mexico."

Bell raised an eyebrow. "Where?"

"Albuquerque, to be exact," Sam replied. "To start a new teaching job."

"I didn't know that."

"Do you know where she's staying now? She's not living in her apartment."

"After Laura's murder, she couldn't stand to stay there. I mean, she was totally irrational about it. She thought that what happened to Laura might happen to her. That kind of thing. She's commuting to the city from New Jersey. She's staying at an old farmhouse in Stillwater. It's an RFD address. She doesn't have a phone, as far as I know."

"I'll find her. Was Julia's maiden name in college Babcock?"

"Yes. How did you know that?"

"Did she like girls more than boys?"

"Sexually?"

"That's what I meant."

"If she did, I never caught on to it."

"Do you have an empty office and a phone I can use? It's a long-distance call but I'll keep it short."

"Use mine," Bell said. "I've got a meeting."

"Thanks."

After Bell left, Sam dialed Roger Anderson's number again. This time he picked up. He explained the reason for his call and asked Anderson if he'd known his ex-wife as Jeannie Babcock prior to their marriage.

"Yes, indeed," Anderson answered, seemingly unfazed by the news of Laura Neilson's murder. "She married me for my name, and that was quite all right with me. Both of us benefited from appearing to be a happily married couple. She's brilliant, you know. Living proof you can survive a horrible childhood and flourish."

"Did she know Laura Neilson before she moved to New York?"

"She was the love of Julia's young life. Laura is why she left Chicago.

I warned her not to chase old adolescent dreams, but she would hear none of it."

Sam's question about Julia's sexuality made Anderson chortle. "I'd say that she likes men and women equally, if they're up to snuff, so to speak."

Anderson professed to be unaware of any road trip with Laura that she might have taken. He had been in London as a visiting lecturer at a university at the time.

"Do you know where she might be?"

"She's not in Manhattan?"

"Apparently Laura's murder has unsettled her, and she refuses to live in her apartment. Any ideas of where she'd go?"

"She often talked about a happy time in New Jersey when she was young."

"At the Kittatinny Valley Farms?"

"No, that doesn't ring a bell. She lived with a foster family in an old eighteenth-century farmhouse at the top of a hill. It had a pond and a strawberry patch, and the school she attended at the bottom of the hill consisted of three classrooms, with a hitching post and an outdoor privy. She bought it as her vacation retreat long before we married, although I never went there with her. She described it as very quaint and charming. It shouldn't be too hard to find."

"You've been very helpful."

"Give her my regards," Roger replied.

Sam hung up and used Bell's phone book to locate the nearest car rental office. As he pulled into traffic heading for the Holland Tunnel, he remembered Laura had once asked him if he'd ever considered a threesome. He'd not taken her seriously and the subject was never brought up again. He was beginning to believe that he never knew her at all.

CHAPTER 32

DEEP INTO THE MORNING, SAM TOOK AN UNSUCCESSFUL TOUR of antiquated northern New Jersey schoolhouses, until he came upon the one Roger Anderson had described. With a hitching post and separate privy, it dominated a quiet intersection where two faded stop signs controlled occasional cross traffic. According to the sign above the entrance it was the Fredon School, not Stillwater. A poster on the door proclaimed an upcoming evening PTA meeting and community square dance party with parents and children invited. It was quiet, serene, and locked up tight; school was clearly not in session.

At the top of the hill, the farmhouse sat along a tree-lined country lane. It was one-story, long and low to the ground, and had a gambrel roof with flared eaves and a massive stone chimney that dominated the coursed stone building. Narrow windows and a divided front door further testified to the age of the house, although it looked well cared-for. Old-growth trees, about to bud, shaded the structure. A substantial barn and large pond were adjacent, and a patch of wild strawberries, still dormant in the early spring, wandered up the side of the lane.

No one was home and there were no vehicles inside the unlocked barn. Sam parked the car at the front of the barn facing the lane and waited. Several hours passed before Julia Anderson arrived and cautiously pulled up next to him. He rolled down the window as she approached with a quizzical look on her face that quickly changed to surprise.

"Mr. Monroe," she said.

"Julia Anderson," Sam replied. "Or is it Jeannie Babcock?"

Her surprise turned to apprehension. "I don't know what you mean."

"Sofia Huizinga told me you didn't like your given name. You remember Sofia, don't you? She lives nearby and is doing quite well."

"What is it you want with me, Mr. Monroe?"

Sam got out of the car. "Your story."

"Story?"

"Starting when you were a foster child placed with Sofia's parents. There's an old photograph of you standing next to the Kittatinny Valley Farms mailbox."

Julia Anderson took in a deep breath. "I had nothing to do with Laura's murder."

"Not directly," Sam countered. "Neither of us did. In my case, I often think I should have helped her more. I don't know how, or if she would have even accepted it, but I should have tried."

Some of Julia's hard edge dissolved. "She was not an easy person to see through."

"Will you tell me your story?" Sam asked again. "I think you already know mine."

"How did you find me?"

"Roger sends his regards."

She smiled. "Then you probably know something about me most people don't."

"He was very discreet in his comments."

She turned toward the house. "Come inside. Laura loved you more than anyone else, and I hated you for it."

She said it softly, as if she were trying to dispose of her animosity without it being noticed.

"Love can scar you when you least expect it," Sam replied.

Julia's hand froze as she reached for the door. "'There's more to him than meets the eye.'" She stood aside to let Sam enter. "Those were Laura's words about you. I hated hearing it. I'll put the coffee on, and we'll talk."

*

THE LARGE FRONT ROOM served as both a living area and a kitchen, with a fireplace against a wall wide enough to take a five-foot log.

A non-load-bearing interior wall had been removed to open up the space, and on the opposite side of the room there was a woodstove for cooking and a sink beneath a window with a pump-handled spigot for water from a well.

The furniture consisted of several upholstered easy chairs, side tables with reading lamps, and a kitchen table centered between the woodstove and the sink.

Julia made coffee in an electric percolator, and as they sat at the kitchen table waiting for it to brew, Sam asked about the house. She'd been raised in it by an elderly couple who had surrendered her when they became too frail to care for her. Those had been the best years of her childhood. She was an only child; her father had been killed in a highway construction accident, and when she was ten her mother ran away to Georgia with a man who'd molested her. Years later, when the farmhouse came on the market, she bought it.

He asked her about staying at the Kittatinny Valley Farms, but she didn't want to start there; rather, she spoke of more recent times, specifically the road trip she'd taken with Laura. As she described it, Sam didn't think Julia had been chasing the memory of young love as Roger had suggested, but rather that Laura had been more like a lifelong obsession.

After accepting the university faculty appointment in the city, Julia had sought Laura out, reminded her of what had happened with Allen Quick at the quarry, and asked her help to find an apartment. After Julia had settled in, it had been her idea that they take a road trip together, hoping it would rekindle their youthful friendship. It had been more than that, she admitted, but Sam didn't push for an elaboration.

"She halfheartedly agreed to do it," Julia continued. "Partially to appease me, and partially—although I didn't know it at the time—to purge her feelings about you. They didn't surface until after our trip while I was still trying to make her love me."

"She bent over backward to please you," Sam commented. "Why?"

"You're asking if I was holding something over on her."

Sam kept silent.

Julia sipped her coffee and eyed Sam speculatively. "You knew about the road trip, before you talked to Roger, didn't you?"

"Yes, but I didn't know it was you. There was a broken pair of prescription glasses and a Marshall Field's eyeglass case that had been left in her car. And the framed photograph of sandhills in your office matched up with some other snapshots we found, but I was still trying to put a name to Laura's companion. By the time I spoke to Roger, he simply provided the confirmation I needed. She wasn't interested in reuniting romantically with you, was she?"

"Not at all." Julia smiled thinly. "Makes me a perfect murder suspect, doesn't it?"

"It does, according to some. But it applies to me as well, with much more substantial evidence stacked against me. But I'm not her killer and neither are you."

"Who is?"

"I don't know."

Julia leaned back. "So why are you conducting this exercise with me?"

"Humor me. I've earned the right to it." Sam refilled his cup. It eased his parched throat. "Tell me about Allen Quick."

Julia stiffened. "What do you know about that? It was an accident. He was a show-off and a bully. We watched him dive into the quarry, hit his head, and die."

"The sheriff at the time didn't think it was accidental."

"It was never proven otherwise."

"True enough. Let's say you and Laura were at the quarry alone when Allen arrived and found the two of you in flagrante delicto, which would be an embarrassing situation for Laura's parents, to say the least."

"That's preposterous."

"One that, were it made into a rumor by the local high school hero, would not be well received in the community."

Julia toyed with her cup and stared at it intently.

"Or," Sam continued, "on the other hand, let's say that he attempted to sexually assault Laura again. That would be a much more reasonable cause to push him off the ledge or hit him in the head with a rock, don't you think?"

"I did it," Julia confessed. "I killed Allen Quick."

"I don't think Laura would have let you do that. She did it, and you were a potential witness against her for a capital crime that doesn't have an expiration date. I'm thinking the road trip and an apartment in a highly desirable East Side building were two examples of her generosity. There are probably more. I've wondered if you ever paid rent."

Julia colored and clamped her jaw shut.

"Also, why would she allow you to perpetuate a myth that you were a recent acquaintance, and not a childhood friend? Doing it to hide a youthful sexual indiscretion makes no sense. You were part of her past and she wanted to keep it that way as much as possible."

"And why would that be?"

"Under the pretense of a romantic rendezvous, Allen Quick viciously raped her. When her parents learned that she was pregnant, they sent her away to avoid a scandal, but she miscarried and almost died. Also, they paid a generous settlement to the Quick family to compensate them for Allen's supposedly accidental death. In a sense, it was hush money. Later, Laura's psychiatrist, who knew her and her family well, advised her to escape from everything, which is exactly what she did as soon as she could. Until you reappeared in her life, that is."

Julia put her head in her hands and sobbed. "I didn't know." Her head came up, her eyes wide open in dismay. "I was part of her nightmare. She could never love me."

Sam fell silent until Julia recovered. "You didn't kill Allen Quick, did you?"

Julia shook her head. "No, he tried to grab Laura and pull her away, and she clubbed him with a rock. She didn't mean to kill him."

"Maybe, or maybe not," Sam proposed.

"Is that what you think?"

"If it had been you he'd raped . . . ?" Sam questioned.

"I'd want him dead."

"What happened after Laura clubbed him?"

"We pulled him to the ledge and rolled his body into the quarry."

Sam reached for the coffeepot and poured Julia another cup. "Was he still breathing?"

"We just wanted him to sink into the water, but he kept floating and floating, face down. And then there were these little spasms, until they stopped."

It was a painful memory that tortured her into silence. She composed herself with a deep breath and sipped more coffee.

Sam changed direction. "The night Laura was killed, where were you?"

"Oh, God." Julia almost dropped the cup. Carefully, she put it down. "I knew she was planning to call you, but she wanted to see Kurt first to tell him it was over, that she was finished with him. She was discarding him and me, and anyone in the way of what she wanted. Once she knew that you hadn't taken up with another woman, she was unstoppable. I was so angry, I screamed at her."

"That night?"

"Yes, before Kurt arrived."

"Then what did you do?"

"I sat and fumed in my apartment alone."

"All night?"

Julia shook her head. "No, I went back to try to reason with her. But angry voices coming from inside her penthouse stopped me."

"Who did you hear?"

"Laura, of course, but the man's voice wasn't Kurt's."

"Not Kurt's?"

"No, and not yours either. I didn't recognize it but kept thinking it had to be someone from the building, because it sounded familiar. After her body was found, I couldn't stand the idea of staying there."

"Was there anyone in the building you suspected Laura might have taken as a casual lover?"

"I don't know." Julia thought about it a bit more. "She was demanding when it came to having her needs met immediately. I so wanted to be that person for her."

"It must have been painful to see her that way with someone other than you."

Julia stiffened in her chair. "You do think I killed her."

"I think you have important information to give to the authorities, which could help in the investigation," Sam replied.

"So that you can clear yourself?"

"Was the voice you heard when you were outside Laura's door mine?"

Julia shook her head. "I already said it wasn't."

"I'm going to drive you to the city to meet with Deputy District Attorney Marilyn Feinstein, where you will tell her this story."

"Why should I do that?"

"Because you're a material witness to Laura's murder and she deserves your help finding her killer."

Julia nodded her concurrence. Sam dialed the operator. Put through to Marilyn, he explained what was about to happen, gave her an ETA, and asked her to stand by.

"Let's go," he said.

"What do I tell this woman?"

"The facts that you've just told to me," Sam replied. Had he just witnessed an award-winning performance, or was Julia telling the truth? He'd leave it up to Marilyn and her team of investigators to decide.

"Will you bring me back here?" she asked as Sam ushered her to his rental car.

"Somebody will. What do you plan to do with the farmhouse?" he asked.

"Sell it," she snapped. "After I move to New Mexico, I'll never come back here again."

They rode to the city in silence, with Julia staring out the window, preoccupied and morose. Sam appreciated the lull, his thoughts tumbling over what he'd just learned. He needed time to break it all down and puzzle it out.

*

MARILYN WAS WAITING WHEN Sam and Julia arrived. As an investigator led Julia away, he fended off Marilyn's questions. He wasn't going to get snared in an interrogation. She could call him if she needed clarification. At a sidewalk pay phone, he talked to Nick Reddy at the *Herald Tribune* and Gideon Hollander, the publisher of the Newton *Town Crier*, and gave them the news of an emerging material witness in the Laura Neilson murder case. He had no reason to protect Julia Anderson from public scrutiny, and no allegiance to the DA, Marilyn Feinstein, Stephen Watts Key, or New York City's finest. He was finished with all of them.

He turned in the rental car, walked home, sat at the kitchen table, and wrote down everything from the last time he'd seen DJ right up to the present moment. It helped to clarify what he needed to do next. But more importantly, DJ had the right to know how much help she'd given him in so many ways. He signed it with *Love, respect, and admiration*, and mailed it at the postal box on the corner.

It was night in the city, and spring had lured New Yorkers outside in droves. Among them was a killer. Sam didn't know how many more nights would pass before he could catch him.

CHAPTER 33

THE WEEKEND ARRIVED AND ADELLA GOT ROPED INTO SUBSTI-tuting for a sick nanny during her employer's planned romantic get-away with her husband. Sam got tapped as honorary uncle-in-charge of Pedro and Veronica during her absence. It was no bother at all. With full access to two apartments instead of one, they could spread out and ignore each other, a rare treat for most city kids accustomed to cramped quarters. Sam called George Lemond at work, said he'd be a little late for his Saturday swing shift, left Adella's kids to fend for themselves, and took a taxi to Queens.

On the ride, he paged through Reddy's *Tribune* story proclaiming in bold type the emergence of a material witness in the Laura Neilson murder case, which had further exonerated former ADA and Korean War hero Sam Monroe.

The charred shell of the house where Carl DeAngelo, his sister, and her family had died was still cordoned off and posted against trespass. Sam transgressed anyway. He was at the back of the structure, peering through an opening that had once been a rear entrance, when the neighbor he'd talked to previously wandered over. This time he wasn't wearing fuzzy bunny slippers.

"What a mess, hey?" the man said. "It'll be weeks before they can demolish it. Bureaucratic red tape and all that crap." He sized Sam up. "You're that lawyer they thought killed that society woman. I never caught your name. Maybe it's because you didn't tell me."

"You're right, I didn't," Sam replied with a smile, holding out his hand. "Sam Monroe."

"Glad to meet you. I'm Ted Stanley. Why are you back here?"

"For another look, that's all. The fire investigation bureau report concluded the blaze was accidental."

Stanley snorted. "That bozo from the department was here for maybe all of fifteen minutes. He didn't talk to anybody in the neighborhood. He poked around and left. Later it came out in the papers that Carl had fallen asleep with a lit cigarette in his basement bedroom, which caused the fire. Bunch of hooey."

"Why do you say that?"

"Carl's sister had a rule you couldn't smoke in her house. Her kids had serious allergies and she hated the smell of tobacco. If Carl needed a smoke, he had to take it outside. The stairs to the basement are next to the back door, so it was easy for him to step out if he needed a couple of puffs before turning in. He kept an old coffee can for his butts over by the trash can. It's still there."

The one-pound coffee tin next to a small evergreen shrub was half-filled with soggy cigarette butts.

"I bet he could come and go without disturbing the rest of the family," Sam noted, thinking anyone else could do the same as well.

"That was what Carl liked best about the arrangement, besides not paying too much rent," Ted replied.

"Did you tell the fire marshal this?"

"Like I said, he didn't ask nobody nothing."

"Do you ever remember Carl talking about some of his pals from work visiting him here at home?"

"No, but there were occasional gatherings and parties, so maybe they would have been invited. You think it was set deliberately?"

"I'm no arson expert, but what you told me makes it look suspicious," Sam replied. "Five people died. I think you should call the Bureau of Fire Investigation and ask them to reopen the case. You don't want some pyromaniac roaming around the neighborhood killing people, do you?"

Ted Stanley shook his head. "No way. I'll call."

"Good deal. Thanks for your time."

Ted smiled. "No problem, and thanks for reminding me I should do something besides bellyache."

Sam walked a few blocks to a drugstore and asked for directions to the nearest fire station. It was within shouting distance. While he had hope Ted Stanley would make that call, he decided to give it a nudge in case his resolve to do the right thing dissolved. He sat with the supervisor on duty and ran down his suspicions. It didn't take much to get the lieutenant interested. As well as innocent victims, arsonists also kill firemen.

He took a bus back to Manhattan and called Marilyn at home. She didn't know whether to thank him for bringing in Julia Anderson or scold him for leaking the story about her to Nick Reddy. He heard her out and only asked one question: Were any fingerprints lifted from the chain with his dog tag and Korean coin that was used to murder Laura Neilson?

"Only a partial, and they haven't been able to make a match," Marilyn answered. "It wasn't yours, you lucky devil. What have you got?"

"I'm not sure. You may want to disturb the chief fire marshal's weekend plans and ask him to have somebody take a second look at a recent house fire in Queens." He gave her the name and phone number for the lieutenant on duty at the fire station. "He can fill you in. I suggest you don't wait too long to do it."

"Come on, give," Marilyn pleaded. "Where are you going with this?"

"To work," Sam said. "My job awaits. And if I don't hurry, I'll be late."

*

ON HIS WAY TO WORK, Sam made a stop at the Spanish Harlem barbershop and stood behind the right rear fender of the car parked outside. Within a few minutes, the skinny guy with the teardrop tattoo under his right eye came out and glared at him.

"I told you not to come back," he snapped.

"I apologize. But I'm hoping that you value return customer business."

"What happened to the Ruger?"

"It fell into the wrong hands before I had a chance to use it. Don't worry, it won't come back to bite you."

The man glared at him. "You've got some huevos, coming back here. What is it you need?"

"A sap, small enough to easily conceal."

"A billy club?"

"No, smaller, to hide under the sleeve of a jacket. And I need it now."

"Come inside. I'll make some calls."

It took twenty minutes for a delivery to be made. While he waited, Sam got a trim. He paid premium for the special order and the haircut, handed over a generous tip, and promised once again never to return. The tattooed barber/arms merchant waved him off like he was loco.

Once again, he survived Spanish Harlem. He got to work an hour late with George shaking his head in admonishment. He promised to be on time tomorrow when the store would hold a private, by-invitation-only runway fashion show. It was to be the store's highlight event for the upcoming summer season.

SAM WAS UP EARLY hoping to find Abe Silverstein at his apartment. Instead, Abe was at his workbench in the appliance repair shop. He looked up and smiled when Sam walked in the store. "I have a question for you," he said.

"Shoot."

"If you wanted to surreptitiously record a conversation, how would you do it?"

"If *I* wanted to?" Abe said, amused.

"Okay, okay, you got me. It has to be concealed."

Abe had spent the war years as a technical sergeant in the Army, stationed at Governors Island. He was too old for combat, but his skills as an appliance repairman had made him invaluable in keeping military radio and communications equipment operational.

"You'll need a compact wire recorder with a record and playback function, preferably battery-operated. The only problem is that the battery pack would be as big as the recorder and hard to conceal. But I could probably jerry-rig a smaller power source to it."

"Where do I go to buy this device?" Sam asked.

"You're in luck, I picked one up at military surplus. They're obsolete now that magnetic tape recording is standard, so nobody wants one.

But if you don't need high-fidelity sound, it will do the job once I tune it up."

"Perfect. Would you do that for me?"

"Sure. Where do you plan to use it?"

"I'll have to get back to you on that."

"When do you need it?"

"Very soon, I hope," Sam replied.

"You're lucky, last week was slow. Give me a day."

"You're a champ."

Abe stood. "Don't be schmaltzy. Go and leave me alone."

"A true champ," Sam elaborated.

Abe thumbed his nose at Sam as he headed back to the storeroom. "You better hope I can find the damn thing."

*

SAM MADE IT TO work on time. The Best & Company department store, on Fifth Avenue between East Fifty-First and East Fifty-Second Streets, was north of St. Patrick's Cathedral. Built at the conclusion of World War II, it rose twelve stories with a penthouse, was fully air-conditioned, and contained six acres of floor space. The first floor tempted shoppers with display cases filled with fine jewelry, French fragrances, leather goods, watches, high-end home goods, and expensive imported accessories. Large display windows fronting Fifth Avenue enticed shoppers passing by with the latest trends in men's and ladies' fashion, plus a window devoted to kids, a thriving postwar market.

The penthouse would host the private fashion show, and guests would be admitted through the East Fifty-Second Street entrance. A single elevator would be reserved for those customers and stop only on that floor.

Sam was given a clipboard with the names of all the invited guests. Throughout the show, he would be stationed at the entrance door to verify invitations, admit any late arrivals, and record all early departures. A doorman standing on the sidewalk would welcome arriving guests. Inside, another store detective would escort the guests to the elevator.

He was halfway through the list when DJ and her mother appeared.

She wore her hair pulled back in a French twist and looked stunning in a handsome spring dress with heels that showed off her shapely legs.

She handed him two invitations. "I haven't had time to read the manuscript you sent me, Sam." Her smile was polite but not warm. Mrs. Ryan nodded coolly.

He handed her back the invitations. "It's hardly book-length, but it's a story you're familiar with."

"Nick Reddy claims you're the next Dick Tracy. Or did he say Spencer Tracy?"

"On either count, he exaggerates." The line behind DJ was building. "Nice to see you, DJ. Enjoy the show, Mrs. Ryan."

DJ smiled politely. "Goodbye, Sam."

Sam kept smiling. When work was done later tonight, he had somewhere to be and someone to see, and he couldn't let his emotions muck it up. But, God, he missed her.

*

AT SAM'S REQUEST, Alonzo had reserved a corner booth for him away from the dining room. It was a slow night at Stamm's: a middle-aged couple nursed drinks in a booth close to the door; Abe was perched on a stool watching Alonzo mix drinks for a table of late-night diners; and a noisy, mixed foursome were discussing a first-run film they'd watched at an Eighty-Sixth Street movie house.

Dennis Finch came through the entrance, spied Sam, and joined him. "I didn't know Micks like you lived in Yorkville," he said as he removed his windbreaker. He had the build of a defensive lineman—all muscle.

"When I moved here, I didn't know any better," Sam shot back.

Finch laughed. "I figured you weren't from the city."

"I missed out on that cultural experience. How about you? New England, maybe?"

"Providence, Rhode Island," Dennis answered. "Came here when I finished high school and never left. I'm going back."

"I thought you had a job offer."

Finch shook his head. "Turned it down. I need a change of scenery."

Alonzo came over and they ordered drinks, scotch for Sam, a bottle of pilsner for Finch.

"That might be a smart thing for you to do," Sam commented.

"Why do you say that?"

"Because sooner or later the cops are going to figure out that you killed Laura Neilson."

Dennis leaned back and glared at Sam. "I should knock your block off for saying that."

"Come on, I'm on your side. We're talking about a woman we both knew well. She was all lust and passion—totally irresistible. Demanding when it came to having her needs met, but more than willing to reciprocate. And you were handy when she was feeling lustful, weren't you?"

"You've got nothing on me," Finch said.

Before Alonzo could approach with the drinks, Sam waved him off. "Carl knew you were in the building that night from outside the penthouse door, heard you arguing with Laura. Was she giving you the boot as well? Or had you just dropped by hoping for a quickie?"

Finch snorted. "That's all hearsay. I don't know what that cunt saw in you."

"Me neither. Did you ever stop to think none of us meant a damn thing to her?"

Dennis laughed. "It was nothing personal, right?"

"Right. Do you know why she was that way? As a teenager she was raped, and when the opportunity came, she killed her rapist and got away with it. From that point on, men were despicable, but they also had something she physically needed."

"I thought you were a lawyer. Where did you learn all this psychological mumbo-jumbo?"

"Think about it. You, me, all of us—it didn't matter. Take a number. Numbers, that's what we were. All the stick-it-in-your-face sexual escapades were a prelude to finding the right guy to come along and kill her."

"Put her out of her misery, right?"

"But, Jesus, Dennis, as strong as you are, you almost took her head off when you strangled her."

Finch's shoulders sloped. "What she said about me made me lose it."

"She tore into you, did she? Said things you didn't want to hear. What guy wouldn't lose it? But afterward, you still had a problem. Carl knew about your after-hours visits to the penthouse. But did you really have to kill him along with four other innocent people?"

"That was an accident. I didn't think the fire would spread that fast."

"It shouldn't be too hard to pin her murder on a retired fireman with a motive, who knew all the best ways to commit arson. The fire marshal bureau is reopening the case."

Dennis yawned. "I'm getting tired of playing this little game. You've got all these theories but no proof of anything. Tell the cops what you want, I'll deny it."

"The partial fingerprint on the chain you used to kill her is going to trip you up. Might as well go with me to the cops now and confess."

Finch glared hard at Sam and reached for his windbreaker. "Stuff it, Monroe."

Sam waited until Dennis was out the door before he turned off the wire recorder that Abe had mounted under the table.

Alonzo walked over with the scotch. "How did it go?"

Sam drained it. "Not an outright confession, but good enough for an arrest. A skilled interrogator will be able to take it from there."

He asked Abe, who'd remained anchored on his stool, to retrieve the recorder and call Marilyn Feinstein to come and get it. He had already alerted Marilyn and given Abe her home phone number.

"Where are you going?" Abe asked.

"I won't be long," Sam said. "Save a seat for me."

A starry sky dimpled the night. Sam was a block away when Finch stepped out of the shadows and grabbed for his neck. Sam whacked him on the head with his sap and hit him again for good measure after he landed face down in the alley. He dragged Finch by the collar down the sidewalk to the corner, where some teenagers were hanging out in front of a mom-and-pop market jiving and smoking cigarettes. "Somebody call the cops," he said.

One of the kids looked down at Finch, who was unconscious and bleeding freely from a head wound. "Shit, man, what did you hit him with?"

"The truth," Sam said. "Call the cops. I don't have all night."

＊

THE NINETEENTH PRECINCT ON East Sixty-Seventh Street, a four-story, stately neoclassical beauty with a slightly overhanging parapet, an arched entrance with double panel doors, and paired windows that marched up the façade of the building, invited citizens to enter.

Although Sam didn't enjoy the handcuffs, it was almost a privilege to be hustled into such a historic building. Marilyn met him inside with a report that Finch was in Bellevue under police observation, recovering from his injuries.

"The recording isn't quite what I was hoping for," she added.

"I thought you might say that," Sam replied. "But look at it this way: Until now you had no murder suspect in custody with sufficient probable cause to file charges. Now you do."

"I don't mean to sound ungrateful." She paused a beat. "The ER doctor at Bellevue said Finch had been beaten rather severely."

"I would have killed him if I thought I could get away with it. Am I being detained and charged for assault and battery?"

"You know you're not. I'll need your full statement and then you're free to go."

"Let's get started."

Although it was congenial, the interrogation took several hours to complete. As it wound up, Marilyn asked Sam not to leak the story to Nick Reddy. "We want to announce Finch's arrest as a win for all of us—you, the district attorney, the commissioner's office, and the police department."

"Right," Sam said as he walked with Marilyn to the exit.

"The DA wants to bring you back. You'd be on special assignment to avoid any fruit-of-the-poisonous-tree attacks by the defense during the trials."

"Doing exactly what?"

"We'll work that out," Marilyn said. "Think about it."

"I will." Sam said good night and turned north for the short walk back to Yorkville. He liked Feinstein, respected Key, admired many of the people he'd worked with at the DA's office, and knew there were good cops trying to do the right thing. But he wasn't cut out for government bureaucracy. He had a state of New York PI card, a valid handgun permit, and a law license. It was time to consider hanging out his own shingle. He'd keep the store job until he could find an office to rent and get his practice up and running.

It was night in the city, and for once he felt like maybe he belonged. When he got home, he'd call Reddy with the latest scoop. *Sorry, Marilyn, but a guy starting out on his own needs all the free publicity he can get.*

CHAPTER 34

THE FASHION SHOW HAD FEATURED THE NEW GIVENCHY READY-to-wear collection. Watching Audrey Hepburn movies, DJ had fallen in love with the fashion designer's dresses the actress had worn in her films. Although Givenchy ready-to-wear wasn't high fashion. It was contemporary, stylish, and more agreeable to her budget. DJ had picked out a black silk three-quarter-sleeve shirtdress with white piping at the collar which broke right below her knees. It fit her perfectly. The pumps she'd chosen gave her a little lift that made her feel willowy and elegant, and she'd topped it off with a Chanel quilted leather clutch and natural pearl stud earrings her mother had given her on her eighteenth birthday.

She'd never considered herself a beauty, but today she looked good enough to turn some heads.

The package on the coffee table, containing the letters and notes Sam had written her, was addressed and ready to be sent back to him. It had sat untouched for a week. Next to it was the three-day-old *Herald Tribune* opinion piece Reddy had written about Sam's successful capture of Laura's killer. In it, Sam had praised DJ for helping him solve the case. "It wouldn't have happened without DJ Ryan," he'd said. "She's the best PI in the city."

He was impulsive at times, but above all he was a man who had fulfilled his vow to the memory of a woman he had loved. What was more honorable than that? And he was genuinely gracious to others as well.

DJ took one last look in the mirror. Sam was the best, most honest lover she'd ever had. It was time to stop acting like a dummy.

On the avenue, she hailed a cab and directed it to the department store's Fifty-First Street entrance. It was forty minutes before closing time. Inside, she wandered around from counter to counter until Sam appeared, scanning the floor for potential shoplifters. He spotted her but kept his distance. At the jewelry counter, she asked to see a sterling silver cuff bracelet and quickly palmed it when the sales clerk turned away.

Sam stopped her at the exit. "What are you doing?"

"Can't you figure it out?" DJ replied.

"With you, nothing is easy."

"Thank you for the compliment."

"You have to put it back."

"Only if you take me back," DJ retorted. "Otherwise detain me and call the police. This is a limited, onetime offer."

Sam smiled. "Come to think of it, I am in the market for a business partner."

"Take me back and I'll throw in my thriving private investigator practice. We'll be the Ryan and Monroe Agency, discreet legal inquiries for discriminating clients."

"That's very catchy."

"Isn't it? I just thought it up. I'm sure Delores will agree to stay on. She likes you, although I can't understand why. And we can use Walt Seaver when the caseload grows, which I'm sure it will."

"What happened to his dissertation?"

"It was boring him endlessly. Do we have a deal?"

"Only if you'll marry me."

"I thought you'd never ask. Kiss me and I'll give you back the bracelet."

"Bracelet first, then a kiss," Sam countered.

"As you wish." It was a delicious, juicy kiss. "When do you get off?" she asked.

"At the top of the hour."

"Meet me at Stamm's. I made reservations for two."

"That place is always busy this time of night. How did you manage that?"

"I was owed a favor," DJ replied as she pulled away. "Do you know where it is?"

"I think so."

"Don't be late."

"You're very cheeky," Sam said.

"I know. Don't you love it?" She was out the door before Sam could reply.

He watched her walk away—classy, graceful, and lovely to look at. His smile turned into a grin. The Ryan and Monroe Agency sounded like the perfect fit for a new beginning. And what better place than Stamm's to celebrate the start of a lifelong collaboration with the woman he loved?